The Adventures of
Ethel King,
The Female Nick Carter

also translated and introduced by Nina Cooper:

Emile Gaboriau: *Monsieur Lecoq*
Antonin Reschal: *The Adventures of Miss Boston, The First Female Detective*
Pierre Yrondy: *The Adventures of Thérèse Arnaud of the French Secret Service*

The Adventures of
Ethel King,
The Female Nick Carter

by
Jean Petithuguenin

Translated and introduced by
Nina Cooper

A Black Coat Press Book

Edited by
Paul WESSELS

With the generous contribution of
Daniel AULIAC
Francis SAINT-MARTIN

Visit our website at www.blackcoatpress.com

ISBN 978-1-61227-233-7. First Printing. January 2014. Published by Black
Coat Press, an imprint of Hollywood Comics.com, LLC, P.O. Box 17270, Enci-
no, CA 91416.
Printed in the
United States of America.

TABLE OF CONTENTS

ETHEL KING
LE NICK CA...
FÉMI...
171

Un Banqueroutier.

«Je prends la mer dans quelques heures, Miss King. Quant à vous, vous aurez la plus belle fin qui se puisse rêver!»

Introduction

There were only two women sleuths in French popular literature before the mid-20th century. The first, *Miss Boston, La Seule Détective Femme du Monde Entier*, was created by Antonin Reschal (1874-1935) and appeared in fascicules in 1908-1909.[1] Jean Petithuguenin (1878-1939) wrote the second, *Ethel King, le Nick Carter Féminin*, shortly thereafter (1911-1914). The heroine of both works was named Ethel and both works purported to be presented from memoires or notes left by the female detective. Alwin Eichler, the major publisher of popular literature in France until 1913, was the editor for Petithuguenin, and published works originating in Paris (9-11-13, rue Briand, Paris XIV), in Dresden (Rosenstr, 107), and apparently in the United States (22 First Street, New York), as well as in Milan (Via Annuciata, 2). The Saturday publication date of some of the fascicules, in addition to the Wednesday publication date, may indicate the date the fascicules reached foreign ports, as the transatlantic crossing at the time was 3-5, days. Each cover had a multi-colored, garish picture on the front of some scene in which Ethel appeared and a sentence taken from the text, such as: "I hope that you've kept a piece of cake for me; by the way, I've just killed your husband." The installments published in Paris ceased at the beginning of WWI; they continued in Germany, not written by Petithuguenin, but by various authors.

---

[1] Available from Black Coat press under the title *The Adventures of Miss Boston, The First Female Detective*, ISBN 9781612271132.

Until the last few years, much of Petithuguenin's work was lost in time or attributed as anonymous, even though the Bibliothèque Nationale in Paris has a large collection of his works on microfilm. A survey was made by the Bibliothèque Nationale in 2002 to fill in the gaps of those works already catalogued in their files.[2] The survey is exhaustive and covers editors, titles, dates and other information. One set, which includes Stoerte-Becker (1910), is included within a group of anonymous authors by Eichler. All of these are now known to be by Petithuguenin. This survey lists, as of 1913, 100 fascicules of Ethel King, 32 of which were conserved in one volume with their covers. It also records publicity for Ethel King and other publications by Eichler on the back of the covers and indicates that the fascicules were published every Wednesday. However, there are full page advertisements at the end of some fascicules which say they were published every Saturday in Paris at 41 Rue Dauphine, New York at 22 First Street, and Milan at Via Annunciata, 2. Sections of the ad are separated by the name of Edith King in bold capital letters. The advertisements continue the detective's mythical life, maintaining that she was a real person and still alive at the time of the fascicules' publication:

THE FEMALE NICK CARTER
A GREAT FEMALE DETECTIVE!

It seems impossible that a woman could be capable of consecrating herself to a profession tied to such terrible dangers and which requires self-control, audacity, extreme resolution joined to shrewdness, and cleverness. Nevertheless a woman detective lives and works today in the United States of America, a woman who has been well-known for years for her preeminent abilities in the career she has chosen, and who has brought about numerous successes, one more marvelous than the next.

She is not an imaginary character; she actually exists and, since her very first case that she brilliant-

---

[2] "L'Édition en fascicules de romans français entre 1870 et 1914 et leurs conservation par la BNF." Available at: http://www.enssib.fr/bibliotheque-numerique/document-21200

ly conducted in Philadelphia, her native city, her fame has grown from day to day.

The advertisements go on to say that copies may be picked up directly from all book and newspaper sellers, or received through the mail with an additional 13 centimes in stamps sent to A. Eichler at the Rue Dauphine address, and that foreign stamps will not be accepted.

Each fascicule also contains several pages advertising other Eichler publications as varied as *Les Recettes de ma Tante* [My Aunt's Recipes] and *Nouvelle Médecine pour Tous* [New Medicine for All].

In the 1987 edition of *Le Guide du Polar*, Michel Lebrun lists Petithuguenin under Other Authors:

Jean Petithuguenin (?-1939). This professor at the Faculty of Sciences was the official translator of the *Nick Carter* series, the author of the second series of Stoerte-Becker, *Le Roi de la Mer* (50 issues, 1912-1913), and very probably the author of a curious series: *Ethel King, la femme Nick Carter* (100 bi-weekly issues, ed. Eichler, 1912-1914).

"At the beginning of the 1930s he published some mystery novels (*Le roi de l'abîme, Ned Pic, detective*) with the occult collaboration of his nephew.

"Daughter of a detective, Ethel King took up her father's career in order to avenge his death as well as that of her fiancé, both brought down the same day by an assassin's bullet."

Petithuguenin, a professor at the Faculté des Sciences at The University of Paris, was also a linguist. He translated English, German and Norwegian into French. He translated at least one novel (*L'Eveil de la Glèbe*, 1917) by Knut Hamsun, winner of the Nobel Peace Prize in Literature for 1920. He also translated at least one novel by the German writer, Robert Kraft, *Atalanta, La Femme Enigmatique* (1912-1913). In the early 1900s, he both wrote and translated popular literature such as *Ethel King*, and his translations of the American detective Nick Carter series belong to this early period. Eichler, his first early editor and the major publisher in France of translated popular literature, such as the *Buffalo Bill* series, in 1913. His principal editor in the 1920s and 1930s was Jules Tallandier. *Ethel King* was continued in German in Dresden by other authors.

A list of selected works include: *Le Roi de la Mer* [The King of the Sea] (Livre Moderne, 1913); *Houdini, le Maître du Mystère* [Houdini, Master of Mystery] (Ferenczi, 1921); *Le Roi de l'Abîme* [The King of the

Abyss] (3 vols., Baudinière, 1928-29); *Une Mission Internationale sur la Lune* [An International Mission To The Moon] (serial. 1926; rev. 1933); *Faust* (Tallandier, 1927); *L'Amante Réincarnée* [The Reincarnated Lover] (1931); *Une Âme en Perdition* [A Lost Soul] (Rouff, 1931); *Le Secret des Incas* [The Secret of the Incas] (1931); *Le Grand Courant* [The Great Current] (1931) and *Le Visiteur Invisible* [The Invisible Visitor] (Ferenczi, 1932).

Petithuguenin also penned historical romances based on Napoleon and Josephine and a biography of Queen Victoria. He was also involved in translating and adapting film novelizations, working with companies such as Film Aubert, Société des Films Kanminsky, Productions Svenska-British, Edition Artistic-film, Fox-Film, Editions film Albert Lauzin, Argus Films, Sascha Film, etc. Such projects covered included *Sa dette* [Her debt] (Ferenczi, 1921), *Le Fantôme du Ranch* [The Phantom of the Ranch] (Ferenczi, 1922), *A l'aube* [At Dawn], based on Edith Cavell's novel (Inter-Films, 1929) and *La Danse rouge* [The Red Dance] (Tallandier, 1929).

Petithuguenin's heroine, like Antonin Reschal's and Pierre Yrondy's, is an extraordinary woman, a woman before her time in the early 20th century. Although she practices a masculine profession, she, like Miss Ethel Boston and Thérèse Arnaud, as each of their authors insists, is very feminine. She is well known and moves comfortably in high society, dresses elegantly, is seductive, charming, and intelligent. These characteristics hide her more masculine traits: incisiveness, daring, physical fitness, litheness, strength, and accuracy with a revolver.

Endowed with these virtues, talents, and abilities, Miss Ethel King investigates and solves cases involving murders, kidnappings, forgeries, extortions and evil by many names. She brings the guilty to justice, earns a more than satisfactory living and leads a comfortable life in Garden Street, Philadelphia.

Nina Cooper

Bibliography of Ethel King

** : included in this volume.

1 Le Diamant vert [The Greeen Diamond] **
2 Le Maléfice [The Evil Spell] **
3 Jack l'éventreur, Tueur de femmes [Jack the Ripper, The Woman-Killer] **
4 Le Signe du Diable [The Sign of the Devil] **
5 Une Salomé moderne [A Modern Salome] **
6 Une Association de malfaiteurs [A Criminal Association] **
7 Les Roses blanches ensanglantées [The Bloody White Roses] **
8 Une Journée parmi les monstres femelles [A Day Amongst the Female Monsters] **
9 Rivalité tragique [Tragic Rivalry] **
10 Ruby, le Meunier nègre [Ruby, the Black Miller] **
11 Un Ennemi de l'humanité [A Foe of Humanity]
12 Les Cadavres de la Delaware River [The Corpses in Delaware River]
13 Un Mystérieux Boarding-house [A Mysterious Boarding House]
14 Mariage de bandits [A Bandits' Wedding]
15 Un Dangereux prétendant [A Dangerous Suitor]
16 Livrée aux lions [Thrown to the Lions]
17 La Vengeance d'un malfaiteur [A Villain's Revenge]
18 Un Cœur de tigre [Heart of a Tiger]
19 Frères ennemis [Enemy Brothers]
20 Chez le millionnaire Armfield [At Millionaire Armfield's]
21 Une Carrière hantée [The Haunted Quarry]
22 Le Fantôme de Chesterland [The Ghost of Chesterland]
23 Un Drame dans la maison de fous [A Drama at the Lunatics' Asylum]
24 L'Assassinat de la loge 5 [Murder in Loge 5]
25 Un Drame dans le rapide [A Drama in the Express Train]
26 Meurtrière de son mari [She Murdered Her Husband]
27 Le Crime du comédien [The Comedian's Crime]
28 Enfermée comme folle [Locked up as a Madwoman]
29 La Terreur du club [Terror at the Club]
30 Les Moines de Saint-Pierre [The Monks of St.Peter's]
31 Un Banqueroutier [The Bankrupt Banker]

32 La Croix de la mort [The Cross of Death]
33 Une Chapelle hantée [The Haunted Chapel]
34 Le Club des revolvers [The Gun Club]
35 Jane Davies, la Faiseuse d'anges [Jane Davies, Angel-Maker]
36 La Bible volée [The Stolen Bible]
37 Des Maures infâmes [The Infamous Moors]
38 La Valse mortelle [Deadly Waltz]
39 Une Tragédie dans un cloître [A Tragedy at the Cloister]
40 Famille de malfaiteurs [A Family of Villains]
41 McLann, le Voleur de chevaux [McLann, The Horse Thief]
42 Un Malade bizarre [A Bizarre Patient]
43 Les Conséquences d'un faux serment [The Consequences of Perjury]
44 Une Femme bestiale [A Bestial Woman]
45 Le Lac solitaire [The Lonely Lake]
46 Chez McStuffing [At McStuffing's]
47 Un Coup de réclame [A Publicity Campaign]
48 Les Cigares empoisonnés [The Poisoned Cigars]
49 La Femme aux bombes [The Bomb-Making Woman]
50 L'Or fatal [Deadly Gold]
51 Une Contagion de suicides [A Contagion of Suicides]
52 Vengeance d'étudiant [The Student's Revenge]
53 Triomphé trop tôt [Triumphed Too Soon]
54 Le Spectre d'Israel [Israel's Ghost]
55 Un Voleur de tableaux [The Paintings Thief]
56 Nouvel An tragique [Tragic New Year]
57 Un Calomniateur sans scrupules [A Merciless Slanderer]
58 Un Magasin mis au pillage [The Looted Store]
59 Vol d'héritage [Stolen Inheritance]
60 Sur la voie [On the Road]
61 Les Bandits de La Havane [The Bandits of Havana]
62 Un Sinistre présent [A Sinister Gift]
63 L'Enigme du phare [The Mystery of the Lighthouse]
64 Un Drame à l'agence matrimoniale [A Drama at the Matrimonial Agency]
65 Une Aventurière [A Female Adventuress]
66 Sous le masque de la loyauté [Under the Mask of Loyalty]
67 Miss Ribson, la Statue vivante [Miss Ribson, The living Statue]
68 L'Assassin du jardin zoologique [The Murderer at the Zoo]
69 Les Pirates de Westend [The Pirates of Westend]

No. 3 Chaque fascicule contient un récit complet. 10 Cts.

ETHEL KING

LE NICK CARTER FÉMININ

Jack l'Eventreur, le Tueur de Femmes.

«Bonjour, Mr. Henry Alton... ou plutôt Mr. Bloody Fox», dit le détective d'un ton ironique en braquant son revolver sur le criminel étendu à terre.

1. THE GREEN DIAMOND

Introduction: A Visit to Ethel King

During my penultimate trip to America, whilst having lunch with Nick Carter the famous detective of whom I have the honor to be a friend, I talked to him about Ethel King. I had learned of her name and of the great deeds associated with it through her fame, as have all those who, by profession, or by taste, are interested in the career of great detectives.

"Why don't you go see her?" he said to me. "I'll give you a note of introduction to her. She would certainly be pleased to make her files available to you and to tell you a thousand interesting stories about herself and her adventures. Although she works in a masculine profession, and one which requires precisely the most masculine virtues, she's a charming woman. You won't regret having met her."

I caught, as they say, the ball on the bounce, and eagerly took advantage of this unexpected opportunity. So it was that two days later I rang the doorbell of a pleasant cottage, 77 Garden Street, the "street of gardens," one of the nicest in Philadelphia.

I waited a long minute and then rang a second time. I was beginning to lose patience when I noticed a young man who was watching me from a half-opened window on the second floor.

I don't stand on ceremony very much, and as I don't like to wait, I called out to the unknown person loudly.

"Sir," I said to him, "I'd like to see Miss Ethel King. I come with an introduction from Mr. Nick Carter of New York."

I didn't get an answer, but the window closed and half a minute later I heard a shambling footstep in the hallway. The door opened and I found myself facing a middle-aged maid, tall and proportionately large, with big feet, strong hands, a mulish forehead and unwelcoming expression.

She looked me up and down with an irritating insistence.

"What do you want, sir?"

"Give this letter to your mistress," I answered, annoyed, "and ask her if I may see her."

She had me go into a small sitting room where I again waited some minutes. I know a lot of detectives in a lot of countries, and I'm not unaware that they are obliged to take great precautions to be on guard against the undertakings of criminals. But I am, I admit, rather sensitive and when I'm the one who's the object of such formalities, I tolerate it badly.

So, when I was finally introduced into the detectives' office, I couldn't help remarking in a partly acid tone:

"I see that your door is well defended, Miss. No one can get in to see you without getting thoroughly checked out."

Ethel King smiled and my bad humor disappeared immediately.

"In fact, sir, I'm forced to defend my door," she answered. "That precaution is indispensable in my line of work. If I hadn't observed it right up to the present day, I wouldn't have the pleasure of greeting you; I would have been sleeping under six feet of earth a long time ago. But believe me, it's as much a burden to me as it is to my visitors."

I was already conquered, because, believe me, Ethel King possesses extraordinary charm. But if you were to examine her photograph, you would find her forehead too high, her nose too long, and her lips too thin.

Still, a halo of thought floats around that wide forehead; the nostrils of that aquiline nose vibrate, controlled by the thousand sentiments which agitate a noble soul; all kinds of smiles move across those lips, turn by turn ironic, menacing, tender, seductive, or simply pleasant, but never indifferent. And what about the eyes! Ethel King's eyes! The entire universe seems to be reflected in her deep pupils. You couldn't tell if they were blue or brown, their shade varies so much according to the mood and the impressions of their owner. Her expression is bright, open and loyal, and, even so, enigmatic. Even when she's looking at you kindly, you have the feeling that you're undergoing a serious test, as if none of your most secret thoughts must escape her; but if you have some misdeed on your conscience, then you tremble and have the fearful conviction that Ethel King can guess your ignominy under all the masks that you've decked yourself with to hide it from her. All that makes up something more than beauty; it's the imprint of genius that gives those traits, not recognized by photography, a sublime grace that you cannot tire of contemplating.

Seated across from Ethel King, I looked at her without trying to hide my admiration, which didn't seem to bother her, but rather amused her.

"You've already met my two bodyguards," she said to me. "The young man that you saw at the window is Charley Lux, a cousin, made an orphan very young, who was brought up by my father, and later by me, and for who I'm like a big sister. He's brave, intelligent, and strong. He has taken up the same profession as I have and acts as my assistant. His help, and most of all, his protection, are invaluable to me. The woman who met you at the door, that's Mrs. Sara Cramp, my housekeeper or my companion—treating her as a maid would annoy her. You've seen that she's solidly built; she has a good fist and a man doesn't scare her; she's proved it more than once."

I listened to these details with interest. However, since I was in the presence of Ethel King, a question was burning my lips. At the risk of offending the one I was questioning, I couldn't resist any longer the desire to ask it.

"Excuse me, Miss," I began, hesitatingly, "but could you explain to me by what bizarre chain of circumstances a woman like you, attractive, charming—oh! I'm not a man to reel off insipid compliments to you; don't insult me by believing it—I'm telling the truth: a woman like you, gifted to please, created in fact for love, by what strange destiny has she come to adopt an essentially masculine profession which requires her to renounce the prerogatives of her sex?"

Ethel King didn't answer immediately. Her look, fixed on me, wandered however very far from my person. I understood it. For her, the present was effaced and the sad world of memories appeared before her eyes. She was completely woman then in the dreamy and gentle expression on her face. A wrinkle of bitterness formed at the corner of her mouth and she finally answered.

"It's a sad story and I don't like to talk about it, even though I keep the memory of the past like a cult. I can tell you that I am, like Nick Carter, the child of a detective. My father, who perhaps didn't have the reputation that he deserved in Philadelphia in his lifetime, had as his assistant, a high-minded young man. Herbert, that was the first name of that young man, asked for my hand when I was old enough to be married, and I gladly became engaged to him because I loved him. I had lost my mother at an early age. Brought up by my father, I had taken a taste for the profession he followed. He often let me go along on the operations against criminals that he undertook with my fiancé. That was how I served my apprenticeship in my profession. I expected that, once I was married, the duties of a wife wouldn't keep me from contributing to Herbert's success as a detective. The beautiful dream of my youth had in store for me, alas, a terrible awakening."

The detective was silent a few moments as if to hold back the emotion overcoming her, then she continued:

"Don't expect a story full of exciting ups and downs. The drama was brief...striking like lightning. One day, when my father and fiancé had gone out in a car, a criminal who had sworn a mortal hatred against them threw a bomb. The unfortunate men were literally torn to shreds. I didn't even have the sad consolation of looking at their dear features and kissing them after having closed their eyes. The murderer, I must say, was himself a victim of his attack. He was killed by a piece of shrapnel."

After another silence, which I didn't dare interrupt, Ethel King added:

"Do you understand now why I have consecrated my life to fighting crime? In your country, perhaps, a young girl, tested as I have been, would have entered a convent, but it isn't in my character to abandon myself to passive despair. My disposition is too combative. I'm devoured by too great a need for activity to shut myself away in a cloister, or, as a nurse in a hospital."

She made a gesture as if to chase away the sad thoughts and smiled at me with her limpid eyes, where I thought I still saw sadness trembling, ever alive.

"You may," she told me, "go through my notes. They're all open to you. They are most often simple notes, but if I may believe Nick Carter," she added, motioning to my letter of introduction, "you have enough imagination to supply details for that lack."

I bowed at the praise.

"And, sir, I'm very ready to supply you with information you may ask me for. You perhaps intend to write an article about me for a French newspaper?"

"Better than that, Miss. With your consent, I would like to publish the story of the 'sensational cases' which you have been involved in. My editor, I'm sure, would jump at the proposition."

Ethel King nodded.

"The idea doesn't displease me," she said, smiling. "Since, as you say, I've renounced the prerogatives of my sex, it's just that I at least take advantage of that renunciation. I'm not, I admit it to you, insensitive to fame...Let's admit that's a weakness, but who doesn't have one? Publish then my notes, or rather the stories you will compose using them.

However, I add one condition: that you respect the anonymity of the persons who, directly, or indirectly, found themselves involved in my police activities."

"Nothing is easier, Miss. I'll change the names and, when necessary, the places. Aside from that conventional alteration of reality, I will set myself, if you don't see any reason I shouldn't, to re-creating the facts and their consequences as exactly as possible. That is to say that I won't always methodically follow the 'professional' order of your files. I'm going to present the public with dramas in which you are the main character. In order to give them life, I will re-establish, when necessary, scenes where you were not present, but which it may be logically concluded that they are circumstances you related. I will be scrupulously careful of the truth, nevertheless. Conjecture, but never invention, will be a part of 'our' stories. To sum it up, I want to do the work of an historian who doesn't limit himself to coldly compiling texts."

"I applaud your intentions, sir, and I will do everything in my power to help you carry them out."

With these words, Ethel King stood up and showed me the numerous file cabinets where her dossiers were arranged in meticulous order. Her supple movements, her stances, revealed the harmonious vigor of a being used to all bodily exercises. That woman, to judge by the ease with which she, while chatting, moved about the heavy volumes placed on her desk, had the strength of an athlete.

"Here are my files, sir. Go through them at your convenience," she continued. "My house is open to you. Come back whenever you like, and as often as it pleases you. I must excuse myself and leave you. An urgent matter requires my attention."

This is how I have come to present to readers this publication which will, I hope, make them appreciate at her just value, Ethel King, the great detective. I went to the great detective's house almost every day for five months, going through and copying her notes. Since then, aided by what I learned, I've spent almost two years composing the stories of the "sensational cases" of Ethel King and bringing them out. If I have succeeded in interesting the public, I won't regret the trouble I went to.

The Legend of the Green Diamond

Sara Cramp knocked discreetly at the office door and handed her mistress a calling card.

Ethel King read:

John Light
Private Detective

"John Light, I know that name. Have him come in, Sara."

A few minutes later the visitor bowed before Ethel King.

"Please sit down, Mr. Light," she said, motioning the detective to a chair. "Your name is not unknown to me. What brings you here?"

"A serious motive, Miss King. I've come to propose a business affair to you, a very interesting case."

The young woman considered, not without surprise, the man speaking; a man about 30 years of age with an open and attractive face.

"You will allow me to express my astonishment, Mr. Light," she observed. "We are in some ways competitors."

"That doesn't keep me from having esteem and respect for you, Miss King. Besides, your fame places you too far above me for my modest person to overshadow you."

"Celebrity aside, Mr. Light, it would be doing me an injury to attribute to me a feeling of mean jealousy…But let's get to the point. My time is valuable…and yours also, undoubtedly."

"Here it is, Miss King. I'm charged by a third party to watch over the security of a young girl. This girl must not be aware of my intervention, which makes my mission very delicate, you understand. A man cannot, without inconvenience, get himself easily admitted into the personal life of a young girl, nor as a consequence ward off the dangers she's threatened with."

"In general, no, I agree…But if the girl you're protecting is ignorant of your mission and perhaps of your existence? By whom were you hired, Mr. Light?"

"By Mr. Isaac Loewenmaul, a jeweler. I'm going to explain the situation to you as succinctly as possible; however, afterwards, if you consent to lend me your valuable collaboration, I would ask you to go with me to visit Mr. Loewenmaul."

"Six months ago my client acquired a seven-carat diamond known as the Green Diamond, even more famous for the perfection of its cut and its unusual coloration than for its weight. In addition, that stone, of a very beautiful shade, is tinted in green by metallic oxides picked up in its formation. This jewel, if its weight, its beauty and its rarity are considered, is of inestimable value. But it is considerably depreciated by a bizarre legend that has grown up around it. In fact, they claim that it brings bad luck to those who acquire it. The curse spares only those who buy and sell as jewelers, who buy it to resell with the intention of making money, and are actually only trustees. Except for these businessmen, everyone who has owned the green diamond has been the victim of some kind of catastrophe within a week after they have gained possession of the stone. One was murdered; another burned to death; another was ruined or changed, struck by blindness or deafness; another committed suicide.

"If what they recount is true, this would naturally be seen only as a series of bad luck, or of the man who committed suicide, of autosuggestion. For a century and a half the diamond has belonged successively to ten persons having no tie of relationship to each other, excepting, naturally, the list of jewelers. Of this number four died a violent death; five were victims of various accidents and quickly got rid of the diamond. Only one, that was a woman, remained unscathed and kept the stone for 50 years, but she was almost killed three days after acquiring the diamond by the collapse of a ceiling. She was only saved by the heroic intervention of her brother, who saved her life by sacrificing his own for her. The fatality that has successively struck the owners of the green diamond has made the jewel almost unsellable. Thus, in the last 150 years, the stone has passed almost 100 of them to jewelers from whom, from time to time, a strong character has taken it, to his great loss. Now, Mr. Isaac Loewenmaul is about to sell the stone to Miss Eva Newborn, whom you undoubtedly know by name. The sale is supposed to be settled today. Miss Newborn is buying the jewel for $200,000 on the condition that nothing happen to her during the next week, beginning today. She reserves the right to return the stone and to take back her money if a misfortune strikes her or reaches a person associated with her. The jeweler, persuaded that it's a matter of chance or a suggestion, has commissioned me to watch out for Miss Newborn so that nothing happens to her during the fixed time."

"Well, Mr. Light," the female detective said, "I have a feeling you won't have any trouble earning your honorarium. Eva Newborn is reputed to be an active young girl, not given to superstition. I don't see what my role would be…"

"Pardon me, Miss King. I have two reasons for coming to you. First of all, however firm Miss Newborn's character may be, the danger of autosuggestion remains; let me tell you that in fact the stakes for the young girl have been particularly increased by another legendary virtue of the diamond, not more ill-fated than this one. The green diamond confers on is owner the gift of unmasking lies and impostures."

"Mr. Light, you are, I believe, about to tell me the prologue of a story from *A Thousand and One Nights*. But you have given me only one of your reasons. Let's hear the second."

"Miss King, when I took up the profession of detective, I was still a bachelor. I have since married a charming woman whom I love dearly, and who has just given me a child. Maud—that's her name—is urging me to give up my profession. Each time I undertake a new case, she goes through all the frights of worry. I had finally promised her to find another profession, when Isaac Loewenmaul contacted me. The jeweler, for whom it was important to conclude his sale, didn't hold back. He offered me $20,000 if I successfully completed my mission. My word, that tempted me! With half of that sum I could buy a farm in Virginia and live there happily with my wife and child. Maud has one weakness. She is superstitious. When I spoke to her about the green diamond, she raised her arms to heaven and begged me not to take up that case. After trying for a long time to quiet her fears, I mentioned your name. My wife, Miss King, worships you as a kind of superior being. She thinks your presence would be enough to conjure the worst spells, to turn away an imminent catastrophe."

"There she attributes to me a power I don't have," exclaimed Ethel King, laughing.

"Let's say instead, Miss, that she sees a supernatural power in what is the purely natural effect of your genius."

"You flatter me, Mr. Light."

"No, Miss...To sum it up, Maud and I have agreed that if you agree to collaborate on this case, I will accept it; if not, I'll ask Mr. Loewenmaul to find someone else. I'm offering you half of the fee, Miss King, $10,000. By agreeing, you will make both me and my wife happy."

"That last consideration is enough to make me decide, Mr. Light. I accept."

A gleam of joy lit the eyes of the visitor.

"Thanks! Oh! Thanks, Miss King...My gratitude..."

Smiling, Ethel interrupted him.

"Let's not waste our time, Mr. Light. Do you have a plan?"

"Yes, Miss. It just so happens that Miss Newborn is looking for a female companion. Couldn't you get that position?"

"Eva Newborn knows me. I've met her two or three time in society. But I'll disguise myself…So, oh, yes, I can apply for that position with the best chances of getting it. I'll arrange for the highest recommendations. My friend, Mr. Golding, the Chief of Police, won't refuse to give me a good letter of introduction, eulogistic as fits the situation."

"Good…Good, Miss King, marvelous! I'll tell Maud the good news. In an hour, if that's convenient for you, I'll pick you up to take you to see Loewenmaul, who will tell us about his last meeting with Miss Eva Newborn. We can start our operations tomorrow morning."

"It's agreed, Mr. Light. I'll expect you in an hour."

Eva Newborn

"That's good, Miss Briar; I'll engage you at $100 a month. That letter of Mr. Golding, the Chief of Police, helped me make up my mind. I had almost settled on someone already, but I didn't find that person very likeable and her references were not nearly as good as yours."

Ethel King, who, for the situation, had taken the pseudonym Ethel Briar, bowed silently as if she was very pleased with the praise of the young millionaire.

"Could you start immediately, Miss Briar?" Miss Newborn asked.

"Whenever you like, Miss. But as I haven't been in Philadelphia very long and I have some business to take care of, I'll ask your permission to be absent for an hour or two each day during the first week."

"Please yourself. If you would like to keep your liberty two or three days more…"

"No, no, Miss Newborn. That would slow me down in getting settled here."

"Frankly, I prefer this, Miss Briar," declared the girl, giving the visitor a pretty smile from her sweet mouth and her clear eyes. A ray of sunlight glinted in her soft tawny hair.

"Since things are arranged," she continued, "I'm going to have my maid show you to your apartment. Take off your hat and jacket and come join me here. You'll spend the morning and lunch with me. Then you are free to spend the afternoon to have your baggage delivered and get moved in here. Is that all right with you?"

"Completely, Miss. I'll be down in five minutes."

A quarter of an hour later, the rich orphan and Ethel King were the best friends in the world. Miss Newborn had at first examined her new ladies' companion closely. She wondered where she had seen that head before. But, since the detective had hidden her brown hair under a blonde wig, modified the color of her eyebrows, whitened her complexion, brightened the rose of her cheeks with make-up, and changed the shape of her nose by putting little tubes of invisible celluloid into her nostrils, the girl didn't recognize Ethel King.

"I like you a lot, Miss Briar," she said after a minute. "If it's all right with you, since we're destined to live in constant intimacy, we can leave all formality aside and call each other by our first name, can't we, Ethel?"

"Gladly, Eva."

Miss Newton clapped her hands like a child.

"Oh! How happy I am. I feel I'm going to like you a great deal!" she exclaimed.

She thought a moment and then gave Ethel King a questioning look.

"What are we going to do while we're waiting for lunch?" she asked. "Let's see. I have a great number of letters to write…You could help me with that…Just think, I have to announce my engagement to my friends…and to my acquaintances. What a chore! No, we won't do that this morning; it's too boring. Tomorrow will be time to think about that."

The girl made a mocking gesture to show how little she thought of social obligations.

"Don't you find absurd, Ethel, that custom of keeping other people up on the 'great events' in one's life?"

"No, Eva," the detective replied gently. "Don't we live a little for our friends?"

"For our friends, the real ones, agreed! But there are so few of them," Miss Newborn said, making a face of disdain. "Do you believe that my 'good friends' will spare me their criticism when they learn of my official engagement to Mr. Jack Hawfinch? I can hear them now: 'What a choice, my dear! What nest did that bird fall out of? A man hardly off the boat from England. No one even knows his family!' "

Ethel King, amused, smiled.

"Speaking of that, Ethel, you don't yet know that I'm engaged, or almost," the girl continued.

She made a bow with comic gravity to add:

"Well, Miss Briar, I officially announce to you that I have given my hand to Mr. Jack Hawfinch, a man of independent means, born an Englishman and a recently naturalized American."

Ethel King, joining in the game, bowed ceremoniously and answered:

"Allow me to congratulate you, Miss Newborn."

The orphan burst out laughing.

"Good, good, that's exactly right. That's the way all my friends will congratulate me. But then what, I ask you? What they'll say when my back is turned, is basically true. They don't know my fiancé. Can they know if I'll be happy with him? How can they congratulate me on what is perhaps foolish. I would prefer that they had the courage to give me their opinion to my face. But there isn't one who would dare to, not one."

The girl stopped for a moment, looked at her companion with a strange expression and observed:

"You must find me silly, Ethel…or badly brought up."

"Neither one nor the other, Eva, but I'm afraid that you're a little confused."

Miss Newborn looked at Ethel King with astonishment.

"Well! You're certainly frank, you are!"

"I force myself to be so," the great detective answered, without taking offense at that somewhat brutal reply.

"You're astonishing," the girl exclaimed. "You're poor, since you've tied down your freedom to earn your livelihood, and you dare to tell truths straightforwardly to the woman on whom your situation at this moment depends?"

"Poverty is a harsh test, Eva. It kills a great number of souls, but those who survive are better tempered by it than by wealth."

"You're decidedly the companion that I need, Ethel. I see Mr. Golding didn't exaggerate in being lavish with his praise."

The girl sat down beside Ethel and took her hand confidentially. Her playfulness had given way to gentle gravity.

"If you knew, Ethel, how hard it is to learn the truth when you're as rich as I am. Nobody tells it to you. Everybody around you lies or dissimulates. Everybody. Even my fiancé, I've noticed."

"He does that, Eva? He lies to you, and you love him?"

The orphan shook her head sadly.

"They're all alike, Ethel! He at least doesn't need my fortune to live. If he makes love to me, it isn't in self-interest…like the others."

"Ah! He's rich?"

"He once showed me proof of income which guaranteed him $80,000 revenue."

The comments Miss Newborn had just made about her fiancé greatly intrigued Ethel King and made her suspicious of Jack Hawfinch.

"Don't you find it strange, Eva, that the man who wants to marry you, has in this way spread out proof of his fortune for you to see?"

"Oh! Yes I did. Jack showed me his proofs one day when he had them on him by chance. They were English papers and, as I had never seen any, Jack asked me if I wanted to look at them…Since then I've thought that Jack had acted out a little comedy for me."

"It seems so!"

"Yes. He wanted to prove to me that he was rich and that he wasn't courting me for my fortune. Can I blame him? No, but that was really one of the principal reasons that decided me to look at him favorably."

These words were followed by a silence during which Ethel King carefully observed Miss Newborn, who finally said:

"What pleases me more in Jack is that he's alone in the world, an orphan like me, free from all ties. He talked to me little of his past and I guess he must have had some terrible trials in his life. He only loves me better because of them. At least he doesn't have behind him a procession of relatives, each one more churlish than the others, or abominably mealy-mouthed, who have to be pleased before the husband is pleased."

Ethel King was struck by the tone of fatigue in which the girl confided in her. Such melancholy wasn't in Eva's character. How could she have given in to it if she had really loved Jack Hawfinch? She gave the impression of having resolved to make a marriage of reason because she despaired of ever finding a sincere lover.

Miss Newborn suddenly got up and ran to a secretary with that kind of child-like grace which was a characteristic of her beauty. She took a jewel case from a drawer and showed it, the cover open, to Ethel King, who immediately recognized the famous green diamond.

"So, Ethel, look at what I bought yesterday."

The detective manifested admiration which, moreover, wasn't feigned.

"I'll have it mounted on a headband," the young girl said. "It's a unique piece…incomparable. They also claim that it's a talisman."

"A talisman?" Ethel King repeated, pretending to be surprised.

"Yes, it lets its owner unmask lies and impostures," Miss Newton explained.

And she added in a slower and graver voice, as if speaking to herself rather than to her companion:

"For example, if my fiancé is lying to me, this green diamond will let me find it out."

The detective didn't appear to understand the implication of those last words.

"Is that its only virtue, Eva?"

The young millionaire began to laugh. A casual observer might have believed that her gaiety had suddenly returned, but Ethel King had too much good judgment and understanding not to discern a disturbing nervousness in that burst of laughter.

"They say—it's naturally a legend—they say the green diamond brings bad luck. Its owner doesn't possess it a week without being the victim of a horrible catastrophe, unless another person sacrifices himself to break the charm."

Two Men

In the afternoon, Ethel King went by her pretty cottage on Garden Street to confer with John Light. She had set up a meeting at her house with him and Charley Lux.

They saw immediately by her expression that the case was more serious than they had at first supposed. Ethel repeated to her cousin and to Light the conversation she had had with Eva and added:

"Miss Newborn is 22 years old, but she's a child. She's absolutely left to herself, without a protector, without an advisor. She gives the impression of having foolishly gotten engaged to a man she doesn't know well and with whom she is not truly in love. I hope to meet this Jack Hawfinch soon and to have the opportunity to judge him. While waiting, I ask you to follow him, Mr. Light."

Ethel handed a paper to the detective and continued:

"Here's his address. I got it skillfully from Miss Newborn. This fellow is too mysterious for my taste. It's possible that Mr. Hawfinch is not what he wishes to appear. The young girl realizes that instinctively and I'm persuaded that the mistrust she has in regard to her fiancé isn't without some relationship with the purchase of the green diamond."

"And me, Ethel, what mission will you give me?" Charley asked his cousin.

"Stay here until you get further instructions. I'll telephone you if I need you. In case I risk being overheard by someone, when I speak to you on the telephone, I will only say some commonplace sentences or something having nothing to do with the case. But that doesn't matter. You'll go hang around Miss Newborn's town house, and I'll arrange to communicate my instructions to you, by throwing a bill out of a window, for example. My bedroom window is on the third floor, in the front. It's the last one on the right."

When Ethel King went back to her "mistress's" house at about 5 p.m. and joined Eva in the drawing room, she found her talking to a young man with a loyal, likeable, and remarkably intelligent face.

The detective breathed a sigh of relief. She was wrong to be upset. If this was the orphan's fiancé, she hadn't made a bad choice. But Eva had already begun the introductions.

"Mr. Edward Outburn, Chief Engineer of my steel works."

That was a disappointment for Ethel King. The man she had at first taken to be Eva's fiancé was the Director of the metallurgic establishments which made up the principal source of revenue of the young orphan. Miss Newborn's father had been the owner of ironworks. He had contributed truly remarkable progress to his industry. Before his death he had advised his daughter to trust the direction of the factories to Edward Outburn, a poor, young engineer, whose great abilities he had appreciated. Perhaps Newborn had even conceived more than esteem for Outburn and would have hoped to call him his son-in-law one day. If the industrialist had conceived that project, death had prevented his seeing it come to pass. When he died, Eva had just begun her 16th year. Since then, the young girl had lived in complete independence. Her guardian had taken care of managing her fortune until she was of age, but Eva's upbringing had remained the least of his worries.

Miss Newborn finished the sentences interrupted by Ethel King's arrival.

"That's good, Mr. Outburn, build the new constructions that you judge necessary. I rely entirely on you...How much do you need? $500,000?"

"I think $200,000 would be more than enough, Miss Newborn. That's still a great expense, but the changes I have in mind will almost double the production of the steel mills."

"Then do it. You'll have dinner with us, Mr. Outburn. We're having Mr. Hawfinch, who will be delighted to see you."

An expression of sadness suddenly spread over the young man's face. Then his expression froze. His look became hard.

"I thank you, Miss. I would accept with the greatest pleasure if business…"

Eva interrupted him, saying in a playful tone:

"Come, come. You accept, Mr. Outburn. There's no more business this evening."

"Excuse me, Miss, but…"

"There's no but. If you don't stay…I'll take your refusal for an offense, I warn you."

The young engineer gave the young girl a look of entreaty that she didn't seem to understand, and submitted, resigned.

That little scene, very significant in Ethel King's eyes, had scarcely finished when a maid came to announce Mr. Jack Hawfinch.

When her fiancé appeared at the door, Eva ran to the door with an eagerness that the detective didn't find very natural.

Jack Hawfinch was the perfect ladies' man, a gigolo with jade black hair parted impeccably in the middle, a part going right down to the neck, lifted symmetrically over the temples and slicked down with a great deal of pomade. His clean-shaven face was more tanned than his English origin would seem to indicate. He had regular features in the photographic fashion, melting almond eyes whose languor was compensated for by an insupportable haughtiness. He wore a perfectly cut riding coat, but the elegance of his attire was unfortunately spoiled by a scarlet tie with an enormous solitaire stick pin. His fingers were loaded with rings. A square monocle that he pinched, grimacing, between his eyebrow and his cheek, made up the character.

Hawfinch bowed before Miss Newborn and kissed her hand with an affected gallantry. He scarcely deigned to notice Ethel, even though Eva had introduced him to her. He held out his hand to Outburn, who shook it with manifest repugnance.

"Let me tell you what just happened to me, my dear," he said as soon as he was seated. "I'm still shocked and indignant."

He was speaking loudly and striking an affected pose.

"Really? What was that?" Miss Newborn asked.

"Can you imagine, my dear, that this afternoon, being at my club, I heard three worthless young men saying bad things about you. My blood boiled; I jumped into the middle of the trio. I gave a resounding slap to the most impertinent. I shook up the others. I demanded apologies."

The girl had frowned. She gestured with bad humor.

"You were wrong, Jack," she observed. "I worry very little about what two or three hare brains can say about me. Their gossip doesn't risk compromising me. It's not the same with your getting mixed up in it."

"I'm completely of Miss Newborn's opinion," Outburn declared.

Hawfinch glanced at the engineer, then turned toward the young girl and protested:

"I agree that I acted too quickly. But you are everything to me, Eva. My love places you so high you are in my eyes of an essence so superior to ordinary humanity…"

"Please, Jack, you must know that I don't like stuff and nonsense."

"After all, how could my intervention compromise you, since we're engaged?"

"We aren't officially so, Jack, remember that. But finish your story. I suppose there was a scandal at your club."

"Yes, I confess it. One of the rogues wisely slipped away, but the two others stayed and I had a violent altercation with them. Everyone came running at the noise, of course. I admit," Hawfinch added, lowering his head with a contrite air, overcome by anger, "I talked more than I should have. Facing these boors, I declared that I was your fiancé and I considered any reflection directed at you as a personal offense. As a beginning, although it's not the custom at the club, I challenged two of the disparagers to a duel."

Hearing this story, Eva turned alternately red and pale. Outburn moved about in his chair as if he were tempted to strike Hawfinch. Ethel King didn't take her eyes off the narrator, but her impassive expression did not betray her sentiments.

"You have acted in an unbelievably inconsiderate manner, Jack," Miss Newborn declared with irritation. "I haven't yet authorized you to say we're engaged. I'm angry, very angry! I want you to stifle this scandal immediately. I don't want the duels to take place."

"But, my dear, to draw back now, that would be to expose myself to ridicule, to shame!"

"Too bad for you, Jack. My reputation is well worth the sacrifice of your ego."

Hawfinch bowed. Ethel King thought she saw a mocking smile on his lips.

"Your wishes are commands for me, Eva. I'll take care of that business, whatever it may cost my pride."

Eva's Hesitations

After dinner, while the gentlemen were smoking their cigars, Eva led her lady companion into the winter garden, and, when she was very sure that Outburn and Hawfinch couldn't hear them, she asked:

"What do you think of my fiancé, Ethel?"

She lifted her eyes to the detective with a worried look, as if she wanted to read her most secret thoughts.

"I can't answer such a question," Ethel King answered gravely." My opinion wouldn't change anything about yours."

"Who knows?" the girl said sadly.

Ethel suddenly took a great gamble. She sat down on a bench, under a palm with large leaves and gently drew nearer to Eva, who still did not suspect the authority of the famous detective.

"Listen, Eva, I must speak to you very seriously. I'm older than you are. Life has been hard for me and I have a great deal more experience than you do. I can counsel you like a mother, or, if you prefer, like a big sister."

Miss Newborn seemed at first astonished, then confused. Without saying a word, she leaned her head on Ethel King's shoulder as if looking for the protection of which she had so long been deprived.

"I have the impression, Eva, that you aren't very sure of your own sentiments. Am I right?"

"Yes, that's right," the girl answered.

"Would you like me to help you read your heart?"

"Yes, Ethel."

"Then answer me frankly. Do you love Mr. Hawfinch?"

Miss Newton made a despairing gesture.

"I don't know at all. There are moments when it seems to me that I love him, and others…when he gets on my nerves."

"Then that means that you don't love him. You don't yet know true love. It doesn't leave any room for doubt. When you're in love you'll see that it's impossible to be in doubt."

At that moment a mocking voice made the two women tremble. Hawfinch came out from behind a massive tree fern, two steps from Ethel King. He had to have walked very softly, placing his feet on the borders of the flower beds, for the sound of his approach not to have alerted the experienced ear of the detective.

"Well, well! Ladies!" he said, snickering. "You are, it seems to me, about to take up a very interesting subject! A dissertation about love! May I not be allowed the honor of hearing it?"

Ethel King bit her lip. She understood that the gigolo had spied on at least the last part of her conversation with Miss Newborn. Eva, at first taken aback, rose, trembling.

"You were listening to us, Jack?"

The young man smiled and answered with biting sarcasm:

"No, Eva, I only surprised the end of your conversation, which wasn't, admit it, very favorable toward me."

The young girl raised her head proudly.

"And so?"

"I find your behavior more or less misplaced, Eva. You don't tell a stranger that your fiancé gets on your nerves."

"I say what I please, and, besides, I forbid you to give yourself the title of fiancé so long as I haven't officially authorized you to."

Hawfinch turned toward Ethel and looked at her with contemptuous coldness.

"I regret, Miss Briar," he said, "that your mistress has thought she should take such a bad counselor as a companion. If you've taken on yourself the task of disuniting lovers who were until now tenderly in love with each other, I don't compliment you for it."

Ethel King judged it preferable not to respond. At that moment, Outburn, who had stayed behind in the smoking room, entered the greenhouse and looked with surprise at the attitude and the angry expressions of the two women and Hawfinch, who spoke stiffly to Eva.

"This painful incident shows me, Eva, a number of things I didn't know. I want to have a clear understanding with you. After this, it is indispensable, you'll agree. Both of us are too overexcited this evening to finish our quarrel. I will come back tomorrow and ask you to see me in private."

He bowed and turned to leave. Despite the calmness he pretended, he was obviously very troubled. As he went away rapidly down the pathway, he caught his foot in the watering hose that the gardener had forgotten at the edge of one of the flower beds, and fell flat on his face.

Eva and Outburn instinctively went to help him get up. But Hawfinch was already standing. He stifled a curse, rapidly wiped himself off with his handkerchief, and reached the exit. While Eva and the engineer followed him into the sitting room, as if to show him out, Ethel King leaned over the edge of the flower bed at the spot where Hawfinch had fallen and picked up a red Moroccan billfold which had slipped out of the pocket of the gigolo's riding coat.

Her first thought as to give it to Eva for her to return it to its owner. But it occurred to her that the contents of the billfold could furnish interesting information about Hawfinch and that it would always be time to return the object the next day.

Unmasked!

It was afternoon the following day. Miss Newborn was sobbing, prostrate on a sofa, while Ethel King, seated in front of her was looking at her in compassion and trying to console her.

"My Heavens! When I think that I was going to give my hand to a forger! But how did you think about examining the contents of the billfold. After all, that was indiscreet of you."

"I admit it, Eva. Mr. Hawfinch had inspired me with distrust. I'm a physiognomist. I had an idea that I would find curious information in it about the person and perhaps the way to overcome him if he was an imposter. The circumstances have proved that I was right."

The girl sat up and smiled through her tears.

"It's the charm of the green diamond that's operating, Ethel. The legend claims it can uncover imposture. Let's just hope it doesn't bring me bad luck and that I won't be the victim of a catastrophe."

She gestured tiredly.

"After all," she said, "it doesn't matter to me. The existence prepared for me scarcely tempts me. My wealth will keep me from being truly loved."

Ethel took her hand.

"You're wrong, Eva. You can be loved. You're only a child, not experienced in discerning the feelings of those around you. You couldn't know it without that. There is a generous heart that beats only for you."

"Do you think so? Who are you talking about, Eva?"

"Mr. Edward Outburn."

"Bah! He's poor. It's my fortune that attracts him."

"No, Eva. Think about it. Has he ever declared his love to you?"

"No."

"Wouldn't he have done so if he had dreamed of becoming rich at your expense?"

"Perhaps."

The maid knocked at the door and announced:

"Mr. Hawfinch."

"Have Mr. Hawfinch wait a moment in the big drawing room. You can bring him in when I ring."

When the maid had left, Eva asked:

"Should I see him, Ethel?"

"I doubt that you are strong enough, Eva. But if you like, I will see him in your place and tell him how it is."

"No," Eva said resolutely. "I'll do it myself. Let me be alone, Ethel."

"Do you think it's wise to be alone with that man in the present circumstances?"

"What danger can I be in?"

"Remember that Hawfinch's plan seemed to have been to spread around gossip of your engagement with the aim of doing away with your last hesitations. He could now try to compromise you to force you into marrying him."

"Then?"

"Let me hide in a corner of the small drawing room. Let's say, behind the piano. I can intervene if necessary."

"But you will be horribly uncomfortable."

"Don't worry about that," Ethel said, smiling.

"And you're only a woman, after all. How can you protect me from a man?"

"I'll protect you, don't worry, Eva. Besides, my presence will probably be enough to ward off danger."

Miss Newborn couldn't keep from thinking that her lady companion was very extraordinary.

"What a strange girl you are, Ethel! You'd think you weren't afraid of anything."

A minute later, Ethel was hidden behind the piano and Eva rang to have Hawfinch come in.

The visitor came toward the young girl with the same casual and haughty air as the day before, as if nothing had happened. But Eva quickly drew back her hand, on which he was about to place his lips.

He sat down beside her on the sofa.

"Are we still angry, little Eva?"

"Mr. Hawfinch, I forbid you to call me familiarly by my first name from this moment. What's more, I have seen you only to tell you my intention of breaking off with you."

"Can that be!" the young man exclaimed, staggered. "Then what crime have I committed to merit such harshness? Is it because I took your defense with too much zeal?"

"That's one of your mistakes, Mr. Hawfinch. If you are incapable today of taking care of my reputation, you wouldn't be any more so if I were to become your wife. But there are more serious..."

"Ah!"

The girl suddenly changed her attitude and observed with very well acted indifference:

"But I remember, Mr. Hawfinch. Didn't you lose a red billfold yesterday, in the greenhouse?"

"Yes, I did precisely that, Eva...Pardon, Miss Newborn. I would like to ask you for it, if you found it."

"Yes, here it is...It was my gardener who picked it up this morning. To find out who it belonged to, I looked at the contents. There was something that astonished me, Mr. Hawfinch."

"I can guess what, but speak."

"I'm surprised that you constantly carry around in your pocket four income documents, each of £800 sterling. These papers represent a huge fortune, more than $500,000!"

"I had them on me by chance, as I did the day I showed them to you."

"Yes...You don't seem to be very worried, Mr. Hawfinch, for a man who has lost $500,000!"

"Actually...Miss Newborn, I only noticed the disappearance of my billfold this morning. I immediately thought that I lost it at your house when I fell yesterday evening. I wanted to come back here immediately to reclaim it, but then I thought it wouldn't be any more inconvenient to wait for the time of my visit. What's more, I admit to you, that subject didn't occupy my thoughts very much. The loss of your love made me indifferent to that, a relatively small part of my fortune."

"Are you very sure that there isn't another reason for that indifference?"

"What do you mean?"

"If, for example, these papers," Miss Newborn continued, taking one of the documents of income out of the billfold and spreading it out on her knees, "if these papers, I say, didn't have the value that you claim to give them."

Hawfinch remained speechless, dumbfounded.

"If these were forgeries," the young girl continued, becoming animated, "common forgeries, you fabricated to take advantage of my naiveté, to make me believe that you were rich and in that way to make me decide to marry you."

She contemptuously threw the documents and the billfold in the direction of the gigolo, who, confused, didn't know anything else to do but to alternately take out his monocle and put it back in.

"Leave, sir! You are unmasked! You're nothing but a vile imposter! If I don't turn you over to the police, it's only to avoid a scandal."

Hawfinch made a desperate gamble. He hid his face in his handkerchief and pretended to burst into sobs. Then he threw himself on his knees at the girl's feet.

"Eva, my dear Eva," he stammered in a broken voice. "Don't send me away! If you knew...Yes, it's true...I'm poor...I deceived you. I made a mistake to make you believe I was rich...But it was love that drove me to that act of folly...I swear it...I didn't think about your fortune."

"You're lying!"

"No, no, I'm not lying...Eva, don't send me away, I beg of you. I love you! You will make me go mad!"

"Leave me, sir."

Hawfinch had taken the young girl in his arms. He had closed her mouth with a kiss. Eva was struggling; pulling away, panting from the imposter's embrace. Her dress front was torn in the battle, showing her naked breast.

Hawfinch increased his pressure. Eva tried to avoid him.

"Turn me loose, sir! Do you want to dishonor me?"

At this moment Ethel came out from behind the piano and brandished a revolver at the scoundrel.

"Stop, you rogue!" she shouted. "Get out immediately and never set foot in this house again if you want to avoid getting acquainted with the Union's prisons."

Hawfinch stopped, disconcerted. He looked at Ethel King with astonishment, while Eva, swooning, leaning on a piece of furniture, was holding up with one hand to her bosom the torn shreds of her dress.

The imposter coldly picked up his cane and his hat, adjusted his monocle, without taking away a contemptuous look at Ethel.

"Ah! It's you I owe for all this, Miss Briar," he said with contained rage. "I suspected that. The trap was clever. My compliments! You'll be sorry for your stupid meddling, Miss Briar. I'll get revenge!"

With these words, he turned his back and left quickly, as stiff and as correct as when he entered.

"Thanks, Ethel," Eva stammered. "That man is a villain...and a coward."

Eva fainted in her companion's arms.

Epilogue

"You're saying, Mr. Light, that this man claiming to be Hawfinch is none other than a man named Hard?"

"Yes, Miss King, that individual was condemned by the New York courts to 20 years of hard labor for attempted murder. Held in Sing Sing Prison he found a way to escape...and he's continuing his criminal career with glamour, as you see."

"It's too bad I didn't know about that sooner! I had a great opportunity to arrest that prison escapee! But that's just been put off. We'll manage to pinch him. The essential thing is to have saved Miss Newborn. When I think that, without your intervention, the poor girl might have perhaps married that scoundrel!"

Ethel King tapped softly on her desk to show her willingness to act.

"Charley," she said, "go quickly and find Mr. Golding, bring him up to date on the case, under the seal of secrecy, tell him that Hard was in Philadelphia 12 hours ago and he may still be here."

As soon as her assistant had left, Ethel observed, smiling:

"Well, Mr. Light, our mission wasn't so simple after all. The green diamond almost gave us trouble."

"That's true, Miss King, and without you, the adventure would have finished badly. My idea of soliciting your collaboration was a good one."

"Say, rather, that your wife had a good idea," Ethel joked.

"Yes, Maud will be happy. I'm now sure of getting my farm."

"Wait, Mr. Light, wait. The green diamond has already proved one of its virtues in allowing us to unmask the imposter. Miss Newborn has had it only three days. The fatal period only expires in five days. A lot of things can happen in five days."

Ethel King began to laugh and John Light had a hearty laugh with her.

2. THE EVIL SPELL

An Intruder Finds Out Who He's Dealing With

"Yes, Mr. Light, our mission won't be finished for another five days, and in that lapse of time the green diamond can play a great many tricks on us."

While speaking, Ethel King was tapping her desk with the point of a pencil and her laughing eyes had suddenly taken on a worried expression. John Light, a private detective with whom she had collaborated in solving a case, was seated on the other side of the table. He seemed very satisfied.

"It's true, Miss King. Mr. Isaac Loewenmaul, the jeweler, hired us to watch over the safety of his client, Miss Eva Newborn, for a week, to protect her from the evil spell of the green diamond. But we've just saved Miss Newborn from the advances of an imposter, Hard, an escaped criminal, who took the name Jack Hawfinch and was found out. On the point of being engaged to him, the young girl found out, thanks to you Miss King, the true character of the man who wanted to marry her, and sent him away. What could we now fear for her?"

"For a detective, Mr. Light, you seem to me to be very little discerning. We have everything to fear, everything, from Hard."

"What! Do you think he would dare show himself again at Miss Newborn's?"

"He's a man full of hatred, vindictive, who doesn't stop at murder. And he swore to get revenge."

"Toward you, Miss King. But we know what those who try to get revenge toward you can expect: prison or hanging. What's more, Hard doesn't know that it was you he was dealing with. He met you under the name of Miss Ethel Briar, Eva Newborn's lady companion and hasn't seen you in the home of his ex-fiancée except metamorphosed by clever make-up. Ethel King is a brunette with an olive complexion. Ethel Briar is blonde, with very pale skin and rosy cheeks. Two tiny tubes of celluloid put into her nostrils make Ethel Briar's nose somewhat thicker than that of Ethel King."

"I'm not worried for myself, Mr. Light. I am for Eva. Hard threatened only me, but be assured that he holds a grudge against Miss Newborn and that he'll get revenge on her if he finds an opportunity. By a strange chance, the legend of the green diamond was partly confirmed by the event. That curious stone confers, they say, on its possessor the gift of seeing through imposture. Eva unmasked the false Hawfinch. It's up to us to prevent the fatal power that superstition attributes to the jewel to be manifested also."

"You don't seriously believe, Miss King, that possession of the green diamond could cause Miss Newborn to be at risk?"

"No, certainly not. I'm not the least superstitious in the world. But in the present circumstances, the simplest thing is to act exactly as if we were. Eva Newborn is menaced with peril; whether or not this is the effect of the green diamond doesn't matter. The fact remains."

"That means that we must follow to the letter the mission Mr. Isaac Loewenmaul hired us for. Even go beyond what we're obligated to do, if it's necessary. According to the terms of our contract, we must take care of Miss Newborn's security for a period of eight days, during which time, according to the legend, the evil curse of the diamond is in effect. Loewenmaul has contracted to take back the diamond if, before the expiration of the fatal period, any misfortune happens to the rich orphan. In order not to miss his sale, since he's a cautious man, he hired us, unknown to Miss Newborn. If nothing happens to the young girl, if she keeps the diamond, we will receive $20,000 from the jeweler."

"I pocket $10,000 and I quit the profession! I buy a farm in Virginia and I go there to end my days, happy with my wife and child."

"Yes, Mrs. Light didn't let you take the case except on that condition."

"My dear Maud is so afraid of a catastrophe! Besides, I have, I admit it, a lot less taste for the profession since I married. Ah! Maud will be very happy, Miss King, when she knows that we're a good way toward success!"

The detective was interrupted by the sound of a voice in the vestibule. Ethel King recognized the rough accent of Sara Cramp, her housekeeper, to which a strident and light tenor voice was responding.

"I'm telling you, you won't come through here," Sara was shouting. "Miss King is out. Come back tomorrow or write instead, giving your address. You'll be contacted if your business is important."

"I absolutely insist on seeing Miss King. I know she's here," the man protested. "I saw her come back in."

"And what if you did see her! Whether she is or is not at home, you can't come in; do you understand. The only thing you can do is leave."

There was a moment of silence; then Sara began again with indignation.

"Not through there, sir! That's the sitting room. Nor that way; that's the library. No, pardon, you can't go upstairs."

"Well! Just let me pass, old fool!"

There was the sound of a struggle. Ethel King went out noiselessly onto the landing and looked, without letting herself be seen, through the posts of the railing. Sara Cramp had seized a puny looking man by the ear. He was shorter than she by a head.

"Old fool? Old fool?" she was repeating, exasperated, while the groaning man struggled.

She opened the door and threw, none too gently, the intruder to the bottom of the flight of steps.

"That will teach you to be more polite some other time!" she proclaimed loudly. "Clear out, and promptly, or I'll set Pluto on your heels. Here, Pluto!"

She whistled, and a Great Dane with dreadful fangs bounded into the vestibule through the kitchen door. He was Ethel King's dog. Sara had just enough time to grab him by his collar. He growled and seemed about ready to jump on the imprudent visitor.

The man beat a retreat, blustering. He went across the little garden in front of the pretty villa of the famous detective and went through the gate of the wrought iron fence onto Garden Street.

Ethel King had observed that scene with surprise and amusement. She turned toward John Light.

"Since I don't have Charley at hand, Mr. Light, and you have nothing to do at the moment, would you do me a favor. Follow that man, try to find out his name and address, and what he wanted with me."

A few seconds later, Light fell in behind the importunate man's footsteps, while Ethel King congratulated Sara, still overexcited, for the courage she had shown in defending her door.

Light knew his job of following a suspected person without being noticed rather well. He followed the visitor he was shadowing, a young man dressed in cheap elegance, to the corner of a wide avenue.

The individual seemed very annoyed by the scarcely friendly reception Sara had given him. He was talking to himself, brandishing his cane, pushing his hat back, and stopping occasionally as if to argue with invisible antagonists. He hesitated a moment, as if to take a tramcar, then continued his way on foot through a labyrinth of small streets and paths. Light didn't lose sight of him. During that shadowing, the detective changed disguises twice with the help of false beards and wigs, exchanging his soft hat for a helmet, turning his reversible hat and coat inside out. A halt of a few seconds under a doorway or in a corner was enough to bring off these superficial metamorphoses.

The unknown man finally stopped in a deserted little street in front of a narrow, dilapidated two-story house. He looked to the right and left as if to be sure that he hadn't been followed. He didn't see anyone for the excellent reason that Light had crouched behind a flight of steps which hid him completely.

The man took a key out of his pocket, went into the house and closed the door behind him.

The detective hesitated a moment about what to do. He finally decided to go into the building to spy on the suspect. The appearance of the house inspired him with serious distrust. Without having any reason to confirm it, he vaguely suspected that the intruder who had been so mauled by Sara was an accomplice of Hard.

The ex-convict was an even more dangerous criminal because of his perspicacity and his audacity. Ethel King's energetic behavior might have helped him guess the identity of Miss Newborn's lady companion. If such was the case, the scoundrel was very capable of sending an accomplice to the house of the great detective to set a trap.

Imbued with that idea, Light inspected the house to find a way in. Finally, he went around to a parallel street and jumped the fence to get into a muddy courtyard. He wasn't running any great risk of being seen because he had noticed a shed which he could hide behind as soon as he entered.

The detective huddled up in his corner for some time to observe. All the shutters on that side of the house were closed. There was no one to be seen. Light became confident, left his shelter, went across the little courtyard and reached a door on the lower level that opened onto a basement. A minute later the detective was in a vaulted corridor which was totally dark. He turned on his pocket flashlight for a second to get oriented and noticed the stairs to the first floor in front of him. He mounted the stairs, listened at the door, and passed noiselessly into the vestibule.

What he did was extremely daring. If anyone had surprised him there, he would have been unable to explain his presence, and the inhabitants of the house would have had the right to treat him as a burglar. But Light had daring that bordered on rashness. He sometimes did things that were not prudent, that detectives more able and more experienced than he, would have avoided.

Half of the vestibule was filled by a stairwell. There were two closed doors in front of the detective. He listened to each of them in turn. Having heard the sound of voices behind the second one, he looked through the key hole. His lips tightened in a grimace of satisfaction. What he saw was certainly made to excite his interest.

Some men were seated around a table in a little sitting room with faded wallpaper and dilapidated furniture. Two of them had their shoulders turned to the door and Light couldn't make out their features. Another, seated to the right, was the one the detective had followed. There was a fourth one on the left and a fifth one facing him. That one Light had recognized at first glance as Hard, the Sing Sing escapee, the fake Jack Hawfinch with his gigolo head and hair well slicked down and symmetrically parted, his impeccable frock coat, his glaring red tie ornamented with a big solitaire, his fingers filled with rings and his monocle, that at the time he was letting hang down on his embroidered waist coat.

Hard struck the table and said forcefully:

"I don't want to let such a beautiful situation escape. What gave that foolish little Eva the idea to take on such a silly goose as a lady companion! It's too bad Jimmy wasn't able to see Ethel King at her house! Since he had seen Ethel Briar on one of her outings, he was able to give me an exact description. I know Ethel King! I've had the opportunity twice since I've been in Philadelphia to observe her, and you can well imagine that I profited by it. Ethel King is a dangerous person for fellows like us. That afternoon, when Ethel Briar stood in front of me, a revolver in her hand, her behavior for a woman somewhat surprised me. Then I looked

43

at her carefully. I at first wondered if it wasn't a man in disguise; then I saw she had a remarkable resemblance to Ethel King."

"So, in your opinion," said Jimmy, the puny looking little man that Light had followed, "in your opinion Eva Newborn has called in a detective to study you and protect her from you, if need be."

"Yes, I could see very well that she was hesitating. People found it strange that Eva Newborn, an orphan 50 times over a millionaire, was marrying some unknown person. Our engagement wasn't official, but everyone was already talking about it. Naturally, certain gossip, very little flattering to me, reached Eva's ears. It caused Eva to begin to distrust me. I can't explain that rupture any other way, because I had played my part well."

One of the men, whose shoulder was turned toward Hard, nodded and observed:

"Your plan was daring, Jack. But you would never have been able to marry Eva Newborn. Your identity would have had to be verified when the contract was signed."

"I had taken my precautions, Bob. My papers in the name of Jack Hawfinch are in order. However, I might not have gone all the way to the end. A week before the marriage I would have arranged to draw off two or three million from the little girl; then I would have disappeared as if by magic."

"That wasn't badly put together," Jimmy declared, "but the job is bungled. We have to find something else."

"Yes, we have to find something else…and I already have."

"Well, we're here to listen to it. Explain it to us."

"Understand, first of all, that I intend to get revenge on Eva and that Ethel, whether she's Briar or King. As for Eva, I could kidnap her and force her to become my mistress."

"That would be amusing but damn dangerous!"

Light, behind the door, shivered with horror.

"As for Ethel," Hawfinch continued, "I intend to open up her stomach to see what's inside. That will teach her to meddle in what doesn't concern her!"

"Scoundrel!" murmured the detective, gritting his teeth.

Hard's accomplices received the exposé of his criminal projects somewhat coldly. They remained silent a few moments as if they were thinking. Then one of them said:

"I don't like to work with you, Jack. You don't have enough self-control. In my opinion, to succeed in our profession, you have to be very calm, put aside all question of ego, never let yourself get wrapped up in passion…You think you're very wicked because you speak of getting revenge! And supposing that you succeed, how far does that get you? What does that bring you? The rope!"

"You have no blood in your veins, Ralph! Revenge is divine voluptuousness. Well! People like you who don't have a grain of the ideal in their heads, exasperate me! You never see anything in it but the practical side. I'm not like you. I have passion, enthusiasm, and the joy I get from them is immense. Danger itself doesn't displease me. And if I must die at the end of a rope, I'll die proudly."

"Whatever pleases you… But if you have only danger to offer us, you can keep it for yourself."

"You don't know me very well. Aside from that, you should know that I pay generously for the services of friends."

"That's true," Jimmy said.

"So there it is. I've decided to burglarize the townhouse of the little Newborn girl."

"When?"

"Tonight. It's 6 p.m. now. We still have time to make our arrangements. I know the house like the inside of my pocket and it will really be a superb job to pull off. I know that Eva has, right now, in her safe about $2,000,000 in cash and in jewels."

"Madness!" Ralph said. "Even so, it's tempting."

Hard stood up.

"Wait for me a minute," he said. "I've drawn a map of Eva Newborn's townhouse. I'm going upstairs to my bedroom to look for it."

Light had just enough time to go across the vestibule and hide in the cellar stairway. He had hardly closed the door silently than Hard left the sitting room.

The detective remained perplexed for a moment. He wondered if he wouldn't do well to listen to the remainder of the bandits' conversation. But he reflected that he knew enough and that by remaining in the house any longer he risked getting caught.

He therefore left as he had entered, ran to the first telephone office, and was connected with 77 Garden Street. Ethel King was no longer at home. It was Charley Lux who answered the telephone.

"Ethel is at Eva Newborn's, disguised as Ethel Briar," the young man said.

"Well, Charley, get in touch with her there immediately. Hard and four accomplices are getting ready to burglarize Miss Newborn's townhouse tonight. Your cousin's life and Eva Newborn's honor are threatened."

Light repeated to the young man what he had heard the bandits say and added:

"I'm going to alert the police and ask that they send me the necessary authorization and reinforcements to go ahead with the arrest of the scoundrels. We'll try to take the gang in their hideout."

A Murderous Encounter

"This is all they send me! Two men to arrest five determined criminals! Ah! Where's the Chief of Police? Wasn't Mr. Golding there?"

It was 7 p.m. and the twilight of a beautiful autumn day was turning into night. The street lamps lit the little street badly. John Light crossed his arms in indignation, reproaching the two plainclothes policemen they had sent him to go ahead with the arrest of Hard and his accomplices.

"No," said one of the agents, "the Chief wasn't there. It was Inspector McNiff who replaced him. He gave us our instructions, saying that he had no one else to send with us and that strong fellows like us shouldn't be afraid of a gang of cowards capable of murdering women, but not of standing up against armed men."

"Cowards? That's easy enough to say," John Light grumbled. "There are some in the game who aren't without courage, Hard most of all. This is a mistake, a serious mistake on the part of Inspector McNiff. It might even cost us our lives."

"That's what I told him, but he laughed in my face and asked me if, by chance, I hadn't drunk too much gin with my dinner."

"You see, John," the second policeman observed sententiously, "all you private detectives think alike. You imagine that all the forces of the regular police are at your service. I'm not saying that about you, but about others. You're a brave fellow for whom I have a great deal of respect. I'm speaking in general. Those who aren't in the regular police force would do better to let us take care of things by ourselves. If we had discovered Hard ourselves, we would have arranged to take him in quietly, without danger to anyone. We would have been careful to get in touch with our superiors before having everything stacked against us. As for you, you put your foot in it. You telephone the office of the great Manitou. You're given the order to go ahead and you have to obey willy-nilly. It's too bad if there's some breakage!"

"Should we give Hard time to disappear?"

"Bah! If he disappeared that would be only one more scoundrel at liberty. There are so many of them! That would be better than risking the skin of good people who have wives and children."

"Still, if we were paid like you! You have, perhaps, a $5000 or $6000 honorarium to take care of Hard. For that price, you might be willing to spend six months in the hospital. But us, with our measly $60 a month!"

Light, impatient, interrupted him.

"I wish you weren't right, George, but this isn't the time to talk about it. Come on! Let's go! Let's get into the house."

"Through which way?"

"Through the little courtyard. Let's go around."

"Well! If they surprise us, we've had it!" George grumbled, but even so he and his comrade followed the detective.

We owe it to the truth to admit that Light wasn't a policeman with a great deal of talent. He gave in too much to his impulses and didn't calculate the consequences of his actions enough. Masters like Ethel King, Nick Carter, or Pinkerton would never have thrown themselves, uselessly, in this way into the mouth of the wolf with hesitating companions. Light should have been content to guard the exits of the house and gather up the criminals in the streets, one by one, when they left their hideout, or shadow them while waiting for a favorable opportunity to arrest them, letting one or two of the suspects escape to be picked up later. But he thought he was doing the right thing in attacking the band in its stronghold.

The three representatives of the law entered the house in the same way John Light had done the first time. The night was absolutely black; the vestibule was completely dark.

Light, first of all, partially opened the door to the sitting room, then that of the room next door which was a dining room. There was no one on the first floor.

"Let's go up to the second floor," the detective whispered to his comrades.

The men, tip toeing, climbed the stairs together. That was yet another mistake. Instead of all three of them going up together, they should have left one of them on guard in the vestibule to guarantee a line of retreat.

They were scarcely halfway up when the entry door opened, then quickly closed. Almost immediately a band of light appeared on the second floor landing and a voice from above demanded:

"Is that you, Edgar?"

"Yes," another voice answered from below. "The errand took longer than I thought."

Saying these words, the man who had just entered turned on the light switch and bright light filled the vestibule. A second later, the second floor landing was lit in its turn. While the policemen, dazzled, were blinking their eyes, the voice from down below began to shout:

"Who are those people there? Jimmy! Bob! Come to me!"

It was John Light who first recovered his presence of mind.

"In the name of the law, I arrest you! Don't try to resist!" he roared.

He drew his revolver.

"Shoot! Shoot!" screamed Hard, whose accomplices were quickly joining him. "They're cops! No quarter! Come to us Edgar, shoot!"

A veritable fusillade broke out. The two policemen fell, riddled with bullets, without having time to defend themselves. John light fell in his turn and tumbled to the foot of the stairs. He was wounded in the stomach. He still had the strength to raise himself and find himself face to face with Edgar, who brandished his revolver at him. In his fall, the detective hadn't dropped his weapon. He fired point blank at the criminal, who fell dead immediately.

He ran to the entry door, but tried in vain to open it. The other criminals were already coming down the stairs yelling. Two shots greeted the policeman's flight, but didn't hit him. Light went like lightning through the dining room, which was beside the street, opened a window, jumped to the sidewalk, took a few steps and stopped in a corner to take a breath. He examined himself. His wound wasn't causing him to suffer, and he did not appear to be losing a lot of blood.

He waited a few minutes, leaning against the wall of a house. The criminals hadn't dared to leave the house to chase the detective into the street.

"Ah! the scoundrels," Light said, gritting his teeth. "I must warn Ethel King and the police."

He stood up straight and walked in the direction of the telephone office. At the end of a few steps, he was overcome by violent nausea, his head swam, and he had to sit down on some steps. The wounded man wiped his forehead, bathed in sweat.

"The rogue really hit me," he murmured. "Poor Maud!"

Light got up once more, climbed the steps with a last effort, rang the bell and remained clinging to the balustrade, holding himself erect with great effort. A maid came to answer the door and by the light of the street lamp looked with astonishment at the unknown man who, without saying anything, fixed his haggard eyes on her.

"What do you want, sir?" she finally asked.

The detective tried to gesture. His lips moved, then he articulated weakly:

"Warn Ethel…"

He didn't finish. His clenched hand let go of the balustrade and the unfortunate man collapsed across the doorway. He was dead.

A Test

"I've thought about what you told me this afternoon, Ethel. Edward Outburn sincerely loves me."

"I'm persuaded of it, Eva," Ethel King answered. "I closely observed the Chief Engineer of your steel mills when he came to lay out his plans to you. He's a loyal man with a superior mind who would be the spouse worthy of a woman like you. It's true he has no fortune, but isn't intelligence wealth? Managed by a man like him, your millions would double in ten years, while in the hands of a lazy wastrel like Hawfinch, they would be exhausted in a few years."

It was before dinner, almost 6 p.m., Eva Newborn, the young millionaire orphan was in her sumptuous townhouse with her new lady companion, Ethel Briar, whose real identity she still hadn't guessed.

She shook her pretty blonde head, smiled impishly, fixed her clear eyes on the detective and replied:

"Decidedly, Ethel, you're a valuable companion. I don't consider you any longer as just a companion, but as a friend. Thanks to you I avoided the terrible mistake of marrying a man unworthy of me, and you've finally managed to put a grain of wisdom in my poor little head, which doesn't have very much of it."

A butler knocked and announced:

49

"Mr. Outburn asks if Miss Newborn can see him."

"Certainly, have him come in."

The servant had scarcely left than the young girl, taking on a mysterious air, said to Ethel:

"Quickly! Hide over there, in that storage cabinet."

"Why?" Ethel asked, surprised.

"You'll see. Quickly! Hide. I don't want Mr. Outburn to know you're here. I'm going to try a test."

"A test?" Ethel asked. "Wouldn't that be somewhat silly?"

"Yes, it would, but a nice silliness. Hide!"

Ethel King obeyed. Eva fell down into an arm chair, dug her little fists into her eyes and rubbed them to make their pupils red, took out her handkerchief, and assumed a mournful expression.

A man, about 30 years old, elegant without affectation, with an open expression, attractive, remarkably intelligent, came in and went toward the young girl. He stopped, troubled, noticing Eva looked upset.

"Excuse me, Miss Newborn, I've perhaps come at a bad time. I can put off my visit until tomorrow morning."

"No, please, stay, sit down, Mr. Outburn. It will do me good to see a true friend."

"A true friend, as you've said, Miss Newborn," the engineer repeated in a shaking voice. "Your father, when he was dying, asked me to watch over your interests as if they were my own. I've done my best to fulfill that mission, for the part of your fortune you've given me to look after."

"Yes, Mr. Outburn. I know that."

"A woman cannot take revenge for certain insults, Miss Newborn. But I'm a man and I can take revenge for you. Use my arm."

"Thank you, Mr. Outburn. Are you referring to Mr. Hawfinch?"

"Yes, Miss," the engineer replied, almost under his breath. "Pardon me for perhaps reviving a painful wound. I see that you've been crying."

"Oh! That's not because of a man I from now on despise with all my being."

A look of joy passed over the engineer's face.

"I'm glad for you, Miss Newborn. That man was unworthy of you," Outburn exclaimed with feeling.

Eva made a gesture of despair.

"Unworthy of me, yes," she repeated, "but how can I find one worthy of me. If I knew one, alas! If I could read the depth of souls!"

Outburn didn't speak, but he was obviously prey to a violent emotion. Eva, who saw that between her half closed eyelids, without seeming to, suddenly asked him:

"Do you, yourself, know one, Mr. Outburn?"

The engineer blushed, turned pale, and stammered some unintelligible words.

"Me? What a question! No, Miss Newborn, no."

As if with effort, the young girl sat up in her armchair, and changing tones, said:

"But you didn't come to speak to me about my little heart problems, Mr. Outburn. You probably have some business to take care of with me."

"Indeed, Miss. I've come to ask you to sign the line of credit which we talked about yesterday."

"Good. Before taking care of that question, however, I have some serious revelations to make to you. My rupture with Mr. Hawfinch has terrible consequences for me."

The engineer opened his eyes wide.

"You'll be very surprised, Mr. Outburn. You'll consider me a little idiot, a little featherbrain. You'll scold me, and I won't complain because I deserve it."

"Explain, Miss Newborn. I don't understand."

"Oh! It's very simple, terribly simple. A week ago I had decided to marry Mr. Hawfinch. I signed a contract with him despite the advice and the entreaties of my lawyer, who found the document too much to my disadvantage. Let me inform you that Mr. Hawfinch is now in control of all my fortune, or almost all. He can take all I have, and, I add, he already has."

Outburn had become very pale.

"What? That's not possible! Come now, Miss Newborn, you're surely mistaken. Someone's fortune can't be taken like that. That would be the first time…"

"Well, I'm the first one. I've just had a long conference with my attorney. I'm defrauded, and there's nothing to do about it, absolutely nothing."

The engineer shook his head.

"I can't believe that…no, I can't believe it," he repeated.

"I have left only my ironworks and my steel mills. I'm still going to have to sell them for a mouthful of bread, because I don't have enough capital to keep them running."

"As for that, Miss, let me give you some advice. Don't sell your steel mills. This catastrophe is terrible, but, what the devil! You have to fight. If there's no way to take back from the thief what he's taken from you, keep at least what you have."

"But how can I do that, since I have no capital?"

"Have confidence in me, Miss. As an industrialist I have some value. I know some financiers who will risk capital on my signature. I'll borrow to keep your enterprises alive. I'll work hard to repay the money lenders in ten years. I'll buy back your factories for you, Miss Newborn, even if I have to work night and day without rest to do it."

The young girl, touched, stood up, and held out her hand to the engineer.

"Oh, thank you, thank you, Mr. Outburn. Yes, you are a true friend."

"More than a friend, Miss Newborn. I have never dared to tell you; your wealth placed you too far above me. But if you need someone to protect you, someone to lean on, take my arm. It's that of a loyal and courageous man who'll remake a fortune for you!"

Miss Newborn let herself go to the arms of the young man, who embraced her passionately, and then she wept in earnest.

"Forgive me, my friend. I used a trick. I lied to you. I'm not ruined...and I've just found the greatest of riches, a love that no other could replace."

State of Siege

It was after dinner. Ethel King, Eva Newborn, and Edward Outburn had come together in the small sitting room to have coffee. All three of them were standing and seemed very excited. Ethel was holding a note that a messenger boy had brought a quarter hour before.

"Indeed, Ethel, you surprise me more and more, Eva was saying. You receive a letter from one of your detective friends, who tells you that a gang of criminals intend to burglarize my house. Then you tell me that the leader of the gang is no other than Hawfinch, whose real name is Hard, an escaped convict. Since it was you who opened my eyes about Hawfinch's true nature, I'm beginning to wonder if you didn't already suspect yesterday the identity of this sad character. All that is already very startling: such clairvoyance, such an aptitude for protecting me from a criminal on the part of a simple lady's companion! But you absolutely staggered me when you advised me against calling the police. I was urgently asking them to send a squad of policemen immediately. You answered me: 'Don't do anything; there's no need. I'll take charge of defending you with my friends.' Your friends…so who are they? Detectives…? I'm thinking about it. You have a letter of recommendation from Mr. Golding, the Chief of Police. Come, now, Ethel, you're hiding something from me. Who are you exactly?"

"I no longer have any reason to hide it from you, Eva. I'm a detective. My real name is Ethel King. "

"Ethel King, yes! Now I understand!"

"Good! Let's not waste our time with explanations; the situation is too serious. My friends will try to arrest the criminals before they come here, but they may fail. Let's make arrangements to guard against any danger. First of all, Eva, I ask you to leave your house and go sleep at a hotel."

"Never, Ethel. Do you take me for a wet hen? I'm staying. I know how to shoot a revolver."

"Well, good. Let's not argue," Ethel continued. "Stay if you like. Do you have a weapon on you, Mr. Outburn?"

"No, but Eva can certainly lend me one."

"Yes, I have some revolvers to spare," she declared.

She rang for the footman, who appeared almost immediately.

"Bring us all the revolvers that you find in the house, with shells, Tom."

The footman bowed, very surprised at this caprice of his mistress, and left to obey.

"You have three male servants, Eva," Ethel King noted. "As soon as Tom returns, tell him to go find his comrades and bring them here. As for the women, order them to go up to their bedrooms and lock themselves in securely. I'm going to telephone Charley Lux, my assistant, to come lend us a strong hand. By automobile he will be here in ten minutes."

That conversation ended at 8 p.m. At 8:30 p.m., all the persons able to bear arms were on a war footing at Miss Newborn's townhouse. Each one had his post. Walter, the steward, was on watch in the entry hall. Tom, the footman, was standing on the second floor landing, to cut off the burglars from the upper floors and to help Walter, if he needed to. Freddy, the cook, was standing guard in the butler's pantry behind the courtyard door. He had cut off the inside electricity. The outside of the house was lit by the rather bright light of two street lamps. Charley was in reserve, under the staircase, at an equal distance from the entry door and the door to the basement which opened onto the vestibule. His mission was to fly immediately to the area under attack in case of an alert. The door to the service stairs, in the butler's pantry, was locked with a key and bolted from the outside.

As for Ethel, Eva, and Outburn, they were together in the small sitting room. The room opened, on one side, onto the dining room; on the other, onto the vestibule. The blinds to the windows, which opened onto the street, were closed and the drapes closed to prevent an audacious criminal firing from the outside, through the window panes, on the occupants in the room. The detective hadn't taken off her Ethel Briar disguise.

"So, the scoundrels want to kidnap me and murder you, Ethel! When I think that I let Hawfinch pay court to me, such a rogue, a murderer..."

With these words, Eva hid her face in her hands as if to hide her eyes from a horrible sight.

"Let him come, the wretch!" Outburn growled. "I'll take care of greeting him."

"I hope he won't come," Ethel observed, "and that Detective Light will go ahead with his arrest and that of his accomplices in the old house on Gowan Street. But we're ready for any eventuality."

Eva Newborn had sunk back into her armchair. She remained thoughtful, her look stubbornly fixed on a point in the ceiling. Suddenly she said in a serious voice that a strange emotion made tremble:

"It's bizarre, even so, Ethel. The green diamond. Everything said about it seems verified. I'm not superstitious, but I'm becoming so. The gem revealed Hawfinch as an imposter, and now, am I not menaced with a catastrophe?"

"Come now, Eva, it's not the time to let yourself go with such ideas. Are we not here to watch over you? Don't you have faithful protectors around you, Mr. Outburn, first of all?"

"There's no doubt about it, Eva. I would give my life for you with pleasure!" Outburn exclaimed.

The young girl turned pale. Her clear pupils, looking at the engineer, were troubled.

"Your life! No, no...Edgar. If you were to disappear now, I would follow you to the tomb. My God! Now I remember. The green diamond brings misfortune to the one who possesses it unless another person sacrifices himself for her. But I don't want anyone else to sacrifice himself for me...not you, Edgar...no, not you...Nor you, Ethel! Oh! My God! I'm so afraid."

Ethel took Miss Newborn's hand and in her soft and firm voice talked to her.

"Don't upset yourself this way, Eva. There are five men here: Mr. Outburn, your three servants, Charley Lux, who, despite his youth, is a solid fellow. Finally, me, and here you can count me as a man. We are therefore six, on our guard, entrenched, to face five criminals, that our resistance will certainly surprise. You can still leave the townhouse escorted by Mr. Outburn, but it's beginning to be a little late. If these scoundrels are watching the house, which is possible, they'll see you leave and you'll be more in danger outside than inside."

"You're right, Ethel...forgive me for that moment of weakness. I've gone through so many emotions today I'm a little nervous. That's over. I'll be brave. And as far as that's concerned, you can count me in with the besieged forces. We're seven to defend the place."

The Assault

"It's 9 p.m.," Ethel noted. "I don't think we have anything to fear before midnight. At 11 p.m., we'll turn off the electricity everywhere, so as not to show our positions to the enemy."

As she said these words, someone rang at the entry door. Ethel and her friends listened and heard Walter carrying on a conversation with a late visitor. Finally, the butler had had the man sit down in the vestibule, in a spot he knew was under the surveillance of Charley Lux, and passed through the dining room to enter the little sitting room to refer the matter to his mistress.

"Miss, there's a man here that looks like a cowboy. He's come, he said, from Winnemucca, Nevada. He claims he's your first cousin."

"I do have, in fact, a first cousin in the Far West. What's this man's name?"

"Robert Newborn."

Ethel King and Outburn listened in silence. They were very intrigued. Eva seemed perplexed.

"Yes, I certainly have a cousin with that name...But this isn't an hour to come calling on a young girl. Tell him to come back tomorrow morning."

"I told him that, Miss, but he insists. He says he was robbed of his billfold with $8,000 in it during his trip, and he doesn't even have enough to pay for a hotel."

As Eva was still hesitating, Ethel King advised:

"Have Walter give him some money, and tell him to come back to-morrow."

"But if he's really my cousin, that might offend him. People from the West are very sensitive."

"Do you know him well?"

"It's been a very long time since I've seen him. I was four years old! I would certainly not recognize him."

"This is difficult. Did the fake Hawfinch know you have a cousin with this name from the Far West?"

"Yes, I talked about him, Ethel. But we're perhaps wrong to be alarmed. That man is alone. He came openly to the main door. Another evening I would have received him without hesitating. If he had evil intentions, do you believe he would have come like this to the town-house, at 9:30 in the evening, while all the servants are still up?"

"Criminals are sometimes very brazen, Eva. Well, receive this visitor. There are three of us here; we're on our guard, and we have help within calling distance. We won't risk a great deal."

Eva made a sign of agreement.

"Agreed," she said. "Have the visitor come in, Walter."

A minute later, the steward showed in a tall man with sunburned, parchment-like skin, long hair, a drooping mustache, dressed in a worn and out of fashion grey coat, wearing heavy boots and holding in his hand a soft hat with wide brims.

The person bowed clumsily in front of Ethel King, without seeing Eva, who had risen to greet him.

"Forgive me for coming to your home at this hour, cousin," he said with the rough accent of the Nevada country man, "but I am…"

"You are mistaken, sir," Ethel said. "I'm not Miss Newborn."

"Oh! Pardon me!" the man said, turning toward the mistress of the house. "You were so little, Eva, the last time I came to Philadelphia. Indeed! You've become a fine girl. I would never have recognized you."

"That doesn't surprise me," the young millionaire replied, laughing. "What's more, I wouldn't have recognized you either, Bob."

The visitor sat down and the conversation began with commonplaces. Ethel King examined the man from the Far West and discovered nothing suspicious about him.

Freddy, who was on guard in the cook's pantry, was getting tired. He had been up since 6 a.m. and sleep was beginning to overcome him. Plunged into darkness as he was, he began to dose off and didn't watch the courtyard of the townhouse with all the necessary attention.

Toward 10 p.m., a big, perfectly silent limousine stopped in front of the wrought iron fence. Four men got out without making a sound; it was Hard, puny Jimmy, and two of their accomplices.

"Bob is in place," the fake Hawfinch murmured. "We can start our operations. That little fool Eva doesn't suspect anything. Let's go in fast. I'll break down the door to the pantry; we'll go through the house like a burst of wind. Jimmy will guard the retreat; Pete and Ralph will be in charge of putting down any attempt at resistance. I'll go up to the library with the sacks and I'll dynamite the safe. I'll throw the sacks down to the courtyard, as soon as I fill them. We'll pick them up when we leave. Bob will grab the little girl, and if he can't finish off the lady's companion, I'll take that pleasant task on myself. Do you understand? No misunderstanding? Does everybody know what he's to do?"

"Yes...Yes, Jack."

"Well...? Let's go!"

Hard took out an enormous ax that he passed through the wrought iron bars of the fence, then a somewhat hefty package that he threw over the obstacle. The four men jumped the fence which backed onto a deserted street and slipped silently to the door of the pantry. Hard lifted his ax and struck a formidable blow on the lock, which exploded as if struck by a cannon ball. The windows were shattered into bits. The criminals pushed open the door.

"Help!" Freddy yelled, awakening with a start.

A blow from a cudgel sent him rolling into a corner of the pantry, stretched out inert.

While Jimmy, his revolver in his hand, posted himself at the exit, the other three accomplices burst into the vestibule.

Charley got up at the noise. Seeing the three criminals enter, he let out a shout of alarm and fired on the first one. It was Hard. The criminal was carrying his packet of sacks under his arm, against his chest; the detective's bullet was lost in that kind of shield.

The fake Hawfinch, counting on his friends to get rid of Charley for him, went across the entry hall without stopping and mounted the stairs four at a time. However, Ethel King's assistant fired a second time and Pete fell dead, hit in the middle of the forehead.

Walter hadn't gotten his weapon out soon enough to prevent Ralph from jumping on him. The criminal grabbed him by the throat and the two men began to roll on each other, fighting in the entry hall. The tiles resonated under their feet.

"What's happening!" Ethel King, sitting up, suddenly shouted.

"What's that noise?" the man claiming to be Robert Newborn, exclaimed.

He suddenly leaned forward and let fly a blow of his fist to Outburn's chin, which knocked him over in his chair. His arm turned and struck Eva's head. The young girl gave a sigh and no longer budged.

The criminal remained in front of Ethel King alone, and thought he had easily got the best of her. He jumped on her, brandishing his knife. But, just as he was going to strike, the young woman seized his wrist with her left hand and held back his arm. At the same time she drew her revolver with her other hand.

Bob understood that if he hesitated he was lost. He quickly pulled himself away from his adversary's hold and jumped backward. The jerk backward was such that the detective was for a second thrown off balance. The criminal took advantage of that situation. He picked up the table in the little drawing room and threw it with all his strength at Ethel King, who was struck down and stretched out on her shoulder, dropping her revolver. Then he picked up Eva, still unconscious, and ran into the vestibule, going through the dining room.

Just then, Charley, who had heard the noise of the struggle, opened the door of the little drawing room, which led directly to the entry hall.

Ethel King and Outburn were getting up.

"Eva! Where is Eva?" the engineer shouted, panic-stricken.

And he ran through the dining room, looking for Bob, while Ethel and Charley got into the dining room just in time to see Walter knocked unconscious by a last blow of Ralph's fist, and Hard struggling with Tom at the top of the stairs.

Ethel King, who had picked up her revolver, struck Ralph's neck a formidable blow with its butt. The criminal fell with a howl of pain, like a felled ox.

Hard had gotten free from Tom's grasp. Understanding that the house was well guarded and that his burglary had failed, he disappeared into the pantry to escape. Outburn had just taken exactly the same path in pursuit of Eva's abductor.

In the courtyard, Jimmy was trying to force open the wrought iron gate of the fence with the help of a crowbar to let Bob get out with the young girl under his arm. Eva was beginning to regain consciousness and was struggling.

As Outburn was jumping on Bob, Hard, disarmed during his fight with Tom, stopped him by grabbing him by the scruff of the neck. Outburn turned around and seized his adversary by the throat, bellowing:

"Ah! You scoundrel, I've got you! I'll kill you, do you understand! I'll kill you!"

"Shoot her, Bob!" Hard again yelled to Eva's abductor.

Bob, exasperated by the failure of the burglary, threw Eva on the pavement and drew his knife to carry out the order of his chief.

Ethel King burst into the courtyard. Seeing the danger to Eva she fired without hesitation and Bob crumbled, killed by the shot.

Hard was moaning under Outburn's furious restraint.

Charley pointed his revolver at Jimmy.

"Get your hands in the air, you rogue, or you're dead!"

Jimmy, terrified at the death of his accomplice, obeyed and let himself be handcuffed without resistance, while Ethel King pulled Hard away from Outburn and handcuffed him also. The engineer picked up Miss Newborn and took her into the sitting room.

Ethel and Charley reviewed the situation.

Two of the burglars, Bob and Pete were dead. Ralph, Walter's adversary, was unconscious. When he regained consciousness, he found himself expertly tied up along with his two accomplices, Hard and Jimmy.

Those besieged had been less tested. Freddy, as punishment for his lack of vigilance, had a fractured skull, from which he wouldn't recover for two or three months. Walter had gotten off with a black eye, two cracked teeth, and some contusions of no seriousness. Tom had his left cheek and chin painfully scratched.

Ethel was experiencing a very painful left side. Eva was complaining of violent headaches and her fall onto the pavement had given her a backache. Outburn had a stiff neck. Only Charley had come off unharmed.

"What a hot alert!" Miss Newborn observed, with a smile in which tears still mingled. "But thank God! The curse of the green diamond didn't go into effect right to the end. I've been saved without anyone needing to sacrifice himself for me."

The steward appeared at the door.

"Miss, the upstairs maid is hysterical," he announced.

"Splash some water on her face, Tom," Ethel King advised. "Charley, go find the doctor. There's work for him here."

The front doorbell rang.

"Now what!" Outburn exclaimed.

Ethel advanced to the threshold of the vestibule door.

"They're policemen, Miss," announced Walter, who was holding a wet towel to his eye.

"Policemen? They've arrived just in time. Well, it's you Herdsman. Has Light sent you? Don't you recognize me? I'm Ethel King."

The policeman saluted and replied:

"He's the one...and he's not the one, Miss King. That depends on what you mean by that."

"You're speaking in riddles, Herdsman."

"Well, I have bad news to tell you."

"What! Has something happened to Light?"

"Unfortunately, Miss."

"Is he wounded?"

"Dead, with two of our comrades. They've been killed by Hard and his accomplices."

"Oh! My God. The poor devil"

"We've been to tell Mrs. Light. It was through her that we learned that you were working with him and that you were here. The poor woman is mad with despair."

Eva, who was listening, let out a cry of horror.

"What! Your friend, Light, you've told me about, was killed by the burglars, Ethel! Then he was the one who sacrificed himself for me. By giving his life, he warded off the curse of the green diamond!"

3. JACK THE RIPPER, THE WOMAN-KILLER

A Terrible Admirer

Garden Street in Philadelphia is comprised of a large number of small, vine-covered houses, most of which are single family dwellings. They are all set back from the street by small, pretty, well cared for gardens which awaken in the passerby the attractive image of family contentment, most often in harmony with the comfort and elegance of the interior.

One of these houses, No. 77 Garden Street, is that of Miss Ethel King, who is already famous throughout the Union as a detective, not only because she was the first woman to take up that career, where stress is seasoned with danger, but because she has had successes worthy of being compared with the most famous of detectives, such as Nick Carter and Pinkerton. Her household staff consists of a general custodian or housekeeper, Mrs. Sara Cramp, and a young man of 16 years, extraordinarily gifted with both intelligence and physical strength combined with unusual amounts of both the most subtle good sense and the most audacious courage. Charley Lux—that is the name of that adolescent—had several times rendered valuable service to the detective, who used him whenever it was a matter of a stakeout or of gathering information.

One gloomy November day, a little delivery boy appeared in Garden Street carrying a magnificent bouquet of roses and stopped at the gate of the garden in front of No. 77. He vigorously jangled the bell. The elderly Sara Cramp came quickly and asked what he wanted.

"I'm bringing Miss Ethel King this bouquet with this letter and many compliments," said the young messenger, "but I must put every things in the right hands."

"Of course," Sara grumbled, "that's certainly not for me! Come in, my boy. Miss is going to be delighted to receive such beautiful flowers."

For herself, Sara didn't seem at all delighted. She went across the little front garden with the delivery boy and took him into her mistress' study. Ethel King was seated at her desk, busy studying different handwritings, and seemed deeply absorbed in that work. At the entry of the delivery boy, a big dog rose from the bearskin rug on which he was lying at his mistress' feet and showed his teeth at the new arrival, who retreated frightened.

"Lie down, Pluto!" Miss Ethel King commanded, and the powerful animal immediately obeyed, without taking his eyes off the urchin. Ethel got up and went to him. She was a slim and lithe woman, but you could see she had well-toned muscles and her face, with strong, sharply outlined features, was lit by unusually lively gray eyes.

"Good evening," she said in response to the young man's greeting. "What have you brought me?"

"I bring you greetings," said the boy, while throwing worried looks in the direction of the dog. "Then I am to deliver this letter and this bouquet."

"From whom, my boy?"

"From an old and well-dressed gentleman who gave me this commission at Diamond Street."

"Did he tell you to bring him back an answer?"

"No, that was all I was told to do."

"What's your name, young man?"

"Edward Saunders."

"You're employed by the Central Office of the Messenger Boys, aren't you?"

Ethel King asked him all these questions in a pleasant tone, but the urchin seemed visibly uncomfortable under her sharp look.

"Yes," he answered timidly.

"How old are you, and where do you live?"

"I'm 15 years old and I live at No. 98, Oldham Square."

"Very well, I'm going to verify that."

She went to the telephone, was connected to the Central Office of the Messenger Boys and asked if the information given was correct. She received a satisfactory answer, and speaking again to the messenger boy:

"I see that you've told the truth," she said. "Now, describe for me the appearance of the man who gave you this errand."

"I didn't look at him closely. He wore a gray overcoat; he had raised the collar, and his hat was pulled down over his eyes. I don't think he had a beard."

"What was he like: thin, fat, tall, short?"

"Slight and skinny. His overcoat was a lot too big for him."

"His trousers? His shoes?"

"I didn't pay any attention to them."

"That's good. Now, listen to me, my boy. Here's $5. If you meet that man again on your rounds, and he asks you for a report on your commission, tell him that I was very happy and I put the bouquet in water. But don't tell him that I inquired about him. If you do that, your boss will be very unhappy and may fire you immediately. Do you understand me?"

"Yes, certainly, Miss King! And thank you very much! I'll follow your instructions exactly."

The young delivery boy bowed and left.

Ethel King, as soon as she was alone, leaned over so as to put her ear very near the bouquet she was holding cautiously. A smile, which didn't look particularly joyful, played across her lips and she murmured:

"I believe, in fact, that I've acquired an admirer of a nice sort. He seems to love me to the point of not being content to consider my happiness on earth, but wants to give me eternal felicity."

She put the bouquet carefully down on the table and opened the envelope which accompanied it. A little card with gold edges fell out of it. On that card she read the following lines, written in a heavy and firm masculine hand:

Very respected Miss Ethel King
Star of my sleepless nights.

Please allow a man who, lately, has nourished a feeling of adoration for you, to place at your feet his heart with these roses. May their perfume please you and give you a pleasant memory of the donor, who languishes with the desire to fold you in his arms.

Your very devoted,

Henry Alton.

"It's certainly strange, the ideas that sometimes spring up in the head of rogues. It's up to me to see that ardent declaration doesn't ignite a fire."

Sara Cramp came into the study at that moment. She glanced across at the splendid bouquet of roses and said in a grumpy tone:

"Well! That's how it's done! They begin by sending her bouquets, and from one thing to another, she'll quickly come to her wedding, if I'm not very mistaken. Look here, Miss King, you're troubling me! These roses have gotten to you, naturally! I can very well see it in your smiling expression. And then, do you really want to get married? Take me, for example. I had such a bad time with my late husband that when another came round who wanted to marry my savings account, I told him to look elsewhere, thanking him very kindly."

"Calm down, Sara," Miss King answered, laughing. "I'm not yet thinking of getting married. But most of all these roses need water, and please bring me a bucket full immediately."

"A bucket full!" exclaimed the housekeeper. "The roses don't need that much water. I'm going to put them in the big green vase. That will do very well."

"Hurry up, Sara, please! I need a bucket full and right now!"

The tone was a command and not to be argued with. Sara didn't try to discuss it any further. She left quickly and soon returned with a full bucket. She was accompanied by Charley Lux, the detective's faithful young assistant who had just returned from an errand. The elderly woman had rapidly told him the history of the bouquet. He greeted his mistress politely and didn't dare ask what she was going to do with all that water, despite the fact that he wanted to. That seemed to him extraordinary, but respect prevented his questioning Miss Ethel King.

Miss King placed the bucket on a chair; then she took a small, very sharp, pocket knife from her desk at the same time as the bouquet. She brought the bouquet close to the housekeeper's ear.

"Listen, Sara," she said to her. "Can't you hear that the person who sent me this bouquet has cleverly hidden a nice surprise in it?"

The housekeeper listened an instant and answered:

"Exactly! I hear something. It sounds like the tick-tock of a watch."

"And you, who know about these things, what could that be?"

The housekeeper shook her head.

"Maybe a pretty ladies' watch in gold, set with diamonds."

"Ah! That would be delightful," Ethel King retorted, "but I can scarcely believe it. It's hardly likely that a man who wants to send me into the next world, would make me a present like that."

Sara took two steps backward, and pale with fright, exclaimed:

"What do you mean, 'send you into the next world'?"

The detective turned to the young Lux.

"Look, Charley, can't you almost say what's in this bouquet?" she asked him. "Go on, try!"

Saying this, she slowly dipped the entire box of roses with the stems downward into the water and she began to carefully cut the strings which held the flowers together so that they were each separated, one from the others.

Charley thought a moment and suddenly a thought struck him. He exclaimed:

"That isn't a…bomb, is it Miss King?"

He had hardly said the word 'bomb' than Sara, letting out a loud scream, disappeared like lightning.

Ethel King nodded affirmatively to Charley, who couldn't keep from turning pale, but he bravely stayed still.

During this time, Ethel King had finished separating the stems of the roses. From the middle of them, she took out a somewhat elongated metallic object tied to a minuscule clock mechanism. She detached the clock movement from the metal object, which resembled a small pine cone. She put the whole thing on her desk in order to examine the mechanism and explain it to her student.

"You see, Charley," she told him, "the movement of the clock mechanism is constructed so that when it stops, it would let that little sort of hammer strike the top of the pine cone, which is just a percussion bomb. The impact would have set off the explosion, and we would have been blown to pieces. Judging by the state of the spring, I estimate we would have had about 30 minutes. But now that the two sections of the apparatus are separated, there's no longer any danger. Such is, my dear Charley, the hellish refinement used against me by a man who says he adores me."

Charley had almost stopped breathing. He had been in unspeakable agony while watching the ease with which his teacher fearlessly manipulated those terrible gears.

"I'm going to carry this same bomb and its mechanism to the police today," she added, wrapping them separately in paper. "Please call Sara."

Charley, completely reassured, rushed to the door, but he had to call a long time before the housekeeper, still trembling, risked putting her head through the half opened door.

"What am I to do?" she asked, still terrified.

Ethel King burst out in happy laughter and answered in a good natured voice:

"Just come in, Sara! There's nothing more for you to be afraid of. You can bring the pretty green crystal vase. The roses now have nothing but their sweet odor. We're going to put them in the window so that they can be seen from the outside."

Sara brought the vase and her mistress arranged the roses artistically so as to keep the look of the bouquet brought to her. She placed it on the window sill.

"Now, Charley, watch carefully!" she said. "I'll bet there's someone who's waiting to see the effect of the bouquet of explosive roses. If I'm not mistaken, it's the man who's hanging about there on the other side of the street."

In fact, in the place she pointed out, there was seen a poorly dressed individual with a hangdog expression who seemed to be drunk. He staggered a few steps from time to time, and after two or three zigzags, he braced himself against the wrought iron fence of the garden he was in front of.

"Watch how he's going to become worried as soon as the half hour has passed and nothing has happened," she continued.

There were still ten minutes left before the expected moment of the explosion. Staggering, the man came even closer to No. 77. He arrived directly across the street and leaned against an iron fence, his legs spread apart, his drunken eyes looking in every direction. Then he took a bottle out of his pocket and drank from it as if he was very drunk. From this moment he never stopped consulting his watch.

"Time has run out," said Ethel after a silence. "Now look at the man."

In fact, he looked worried. He stood up straight, looking anxiously at his watch. Then he stamped nervously. His drunkenness had disappeared, or at least he had forgotten about it.

"It would be cruel to leave this poor man any longer in suspense," said Ethel in a calm voice.

She put on her hat and left quickly. Crossing the street, she went straight to the man. He trembled slightly on seeing her, and suddenly remembered he was drunk. He leaned heavily on the garden grillwork and took his whiskey flask from his pocket. Ethel King stopped very near him and looked him in the face. She laughed softly.

"You're admiring the beautiful bouquet of roses over there on my window sill," she said, jeeringly. "They are, in fact, very beautiful and the bouquet pleased me very much. If by any chance you know the noble and generous gentleman who sent it to me, please be kind enough to give him all Ethel King's thanks. And tell him that I took the liberty of removing from this delightful bouquet a little clock with its accessory. I will take it today right to my good friend, Police Inspector Golding."

While she was talking, the man, laughing derisively, pretended to be looking in the distance in front of him. The fact was that he was torn between fear and rage. Nevertheless, he controlled himself and answered, stammering:

"What...what do you want with me? I...I don't understand. Leave me alone!"

And he stumbled off.

Ethel King went into the house where Charley and Sara had been watching her.

"Quick, Charley," she said, "follow that man and leave a trail behind you. I'll soon be on your tracks."

The young man immediately left the house, not by the front, but through a passage he knew at the back. He first went across several neighboring fences and reached the street by way of another private house rather far from his own. The man was still in sight, and he began to shadow him with an art he learned from Ethel King.

Shadowing

About ten minutes after Charley Lux's departure, the detective in her turn left just as secretly, but without going through the same acrobatic exercises as her young helper. The courtyard and the small garden which extended behind her house had a rather narrow, and almost always deserted, side alley. She left through there, pulling shut behind her the door whose well-oiled hinges made no noise.

She had dressed up in rags, which gave her the pitiful look of someone dying of hunger. No one would have recognized Miss Ethel King wearing those. At the end of the street, she discovered the first traces left by Charley. They were little pieces of chalk which the young man had thrown down in front of him from time to time and crushed with his foot so as to press a light white mark into the ground. Following that trail, the detective came to the center of the city. There the signs continued in a maze of streets and alleys where they were often difficult to make out. Finally they led her down a narrow and obscure path beside a house. In the middle, Ethel King, who was advancing with the utmost caution, thought she heard a slight noise and stopped to listen. In front of her, at the end of the passage, she saw a little courtyard littered with boxes and all kinds of rubbish where daylight hardly entered. It was one of those courtyards called, in slang, a sink hole.

Listening, she had just stopped when she heard a little, barely distinct, whistle. A human form in black immediately took shape in the door frame and in an instant Charley Lux was beside his teacher.

"Where is he?" she asked very low.

"He went down this passageway and entered the courtyard where I followed him. I didn't see anything. The house has several exits onto that courtyard, but I didn't risk going inside. There's also a shed full of packing cases and junk, like the courtyard."

"Go stand watch at the front of the house," whispered Ethel King. "If you hear a whistle or a loud noise, call the policeman at the corner. But I don't think that will be necessary. I'm just going to look around a little."

Charley then went back to the street and Ethel went calmly into the courtyard. She had a brazen and carefree attitude which matched her costume perfectly. She looked at the stacks of boxes, sized up the stacks of debris accumulated in that narrow space and discovered nothing.

In the shed, where it was darker and the air was thick and humid, she noticed other boxes, sacks piled up, and similar things, but the man they had shadowed was no more visible there than in the courtyard. She had already noted that in the enclosure of the courtyard there was no opening or break which a man might slip through. She didn't believe the person had taken refuge in the house. It was occupied by working people and everything there appeared very calm. She then returned to the shed and searched it very carefully a long time without result. She finally went back out, promising herself to return the next day with the police.

She met Charley in the street and told him to return to the house while she, in her tramp rags, went to the Central Police Bureau. The policeman on duty at the entry there wanted to turn away that tramp, but a few words were enough for the man to stand aside respectfully.

Inspector Golding, Chief of Police, heard his office door open and was more than a little astonished to see enter, alone and unconcerned, a ragged bum.

"What is this?" he exclaimed. "How did that person get in here? Is there nobody on duty at his post?"

"I don't have any bad intentions, inspector. I just want to murder you a little," said the intruder.

Golding jumped out of his chair, shouting: "This is a bit much. Now riff-raff come and slip in here and insult you to your face!"

The fake tramp broke out laughing and held out her hand to the astonished inspector.

"I'm really not flattered that you don't recognize your old friend Ethel King," said a clear and pleasant voice.

The Chief of Police, wide-eyed, asked:

"Ethel King? Ah! Yes, it really is Ethel King!"

He shook hands with her cordially and continued:

"You are truly remarkably disguised. I certainly would not have recognized you. When I see ability like yours used in our interest, I'm cheered by it and I'm very grateful. And I'm glad every time I see you, Miss King, because you always bring something new."

"Yes, well, here's something completely new," Ethel repeated, taking a small package from her pocket. She opened it to place the bomb and the clock mechanism on the inspector's table.

"You have here, Mr. Golding, a pretty little bomb sent to me at my house in a superb bouquet of roses."

She then told him what had happened.

"That's a scoundrel that should be arrested," exclaimed the inspector, indignant at such an attack. "Didn't you arrest the person watching outside your house?"

"That would have been a very big mistake. I was immediately convinced that this scoundrel wasn't the principal author, but simply a spy. If I had arrested him, it would probably have been impossible to make him say a word. And since he couldn't have been charged with any precise act, he would have had to be released."

The inspector had to recognize that she was right. He called a policeman, to whom he gave the bomb to explode in a courtyard with the necessary precautions set up to do just that. Then, turning to the detective:

"And now, what do you intend to do?" he asked.

"Pick up the criminal, and, if need be, ask you to put some men at my disposal."

"As many as you like. Do you really think you can catch this person?"

"I'm convinced of it, Mr. Golding. In any case, he'll try again. He'll want to make up for his failure today. And I may be able to take advantage of that to lay my hands on him."

As Ethel King was leaving the police building, a terrifying clap of thunder coming from one of the courtyards, told her the bomb had been exploded.

Ethel went back home very persuaded that there would shortly be a new attempt against her. She foresaw that the vexation the criminal must have felt at his failed first attempt would incite him to make another attempt very quickly, probably that same night.

She resolved, therefore, to take her precautions, to stay alert, taking turns with Charley Lux, while Pluto, her big dog stayed in her office. The dog was an excellent guard-dog. The least noise approaching him, even completely silently, of a man coming through the garden in front of the house, was enough to make him give the alarm. Charley's bedroom was at the back. He would be on careful watch from that direction and would let nothing suspicious pass by so that Ethel King, whose bedroom occupied the middle of the ground floor, could go to bed and sleep peacefully.

She was an extremely light sleeper and woke at the least noise. She knew too well what cunning and perverse beings she was dealing with not to be constantly on her guard. She fell asleep immediately and slept deeply for two hours. She then woke with a start and sat up on her bed. There was absolute silence around her. Moonlight coming through the window cast a large ray of light through the room right to a curtained doorway leading to the stairway.

Ethel King didn't hear anything, but she felt a foreign presence. She looked around her in vain. She saw nothing suspicious, but the suspicion didn't leave her mind. She got up, took a revolver in one hand and a little electric torch in the other. She went toward the front room, which was her office.

"Pluto," she called in a low voice.

The dog jumped off his bearskin rug and bounded toward her, wagging his tail. She stroked him with her hand, showing him the window and saying to him:

"Watch there!"

The dog understood what his mistress wanted and crouched under the window. She then returned to her bedroom and went back to bed. She hadn't gotten completely undressed because she knew she had to be ready that night for any situation. She was just closing her eyes to go to sleep when she felt the same vague feeling, which had worried her before, return stronger. She had often experienced that her premonitions did not deceive her and she was sure she was in imminent danger.

70

She mechanically picked up the revolver that she had before placed on the night stand. She then raised her head and looked around the room. The moon was still spreading a large band of light on the floor. The curtains on the door were especially inundated with light. Ethel could clearly see the designs as well as the folds of the fabric. The hanging didn't completely reach to the floor and the detective soon made out a sort of white spot in the interstice. What could that be? She stared at that spot so intensity that her eyes smarted, and suddenly she saw what it was. That vague white something was nothing other than the end of a naked foot.

At the first moment of that discovery, Ethel King thought her heart had stopped beating. It was a shock of surprise and not of fear. She was most of all startled that a man had succeeded in gaining entrance right up to her bedroom without being noticed. How easily she would have been his victim if she had been asleep! Fortunately he hadn't come when she had first fallen asleep. If he had, she would no longer be alive.

All of these thoughts went through her head like a flash of lightning. Then, a few seconds after that troubling discovery, she moved her hand softly to the electric button placed near her bed. She had never been calmer and more self-possessed. The bedroom was inundated with light. She ran to her office door, and called out:

"Pluto! Here!"

The powerful animal immediately rushed into the bedroom to the side of his mistress. Ethel was already near the door curtain. She pushed it aside with her left hand, raising a revolver ready to fire with her right.

She recognized the man standing in front of her as the counterfeit drunk who, earlier in the day, had been loitering about waiting for the effect of the bomb. He was struck with mortal fear; his ugly, puffy face was livid. And the fright caused by the dog, whose open mouth showed his fangs, was visibly still greater than his fear of the revolver pointed at him.

"We've already met," the detective began, with a jeering calm. "I wouldn't have believed that my modest little house could hold such charm for you."

The man didn't have anything to reply. He was pressing against the door, fixing frightened eyes on the ironic and haughty detective. But the dog was growling more and more and preparing to jump on the miserable man.

"Get back, Pluto," said Ethel.

The dog obeyed unwillingly, since he evidently understood that the individual hadn't come animated with good intentions.

The man didn't lack weapons. He held a revolver in his left hand and a very sharp knife in his right. But he had been so surprised that he hadn't been able to use either one. And when he wanted to raise his hands, Ethel King told him in a commanding tone:

"Don't move or I'll put a bullet in your head! And at one word from me, Pluto is ready to rip out your throat. Characters of your kind don't deserve anything better."

The man remained silent. It was evident that fear was choking him.

He didn't budge. Then the dry and menacing sound of a revolver being armed was heard.

"Let me go!" the man said in a hoarse and surly voice. "It'll be too bad for you if you decide to keep me here. But nothing will happen to you if you let me go."

"Do you know Ethel King?" she asked with a disdainful laugh. "No, you don't seem to know her very well. Obey right now! Pluto, attack!"

The man had just thrown himself with his full weight against the door, which opened, and he darted away to escape through the stairs and the basement. But he had hardly turned halfway around when he let out a stifled cry. The dog had jumped on the criminal, planting his fangs on the side of his neck and throwing him to the ground.

While the muffled, hoarse cries of the half strangled man followed one another, someone dashed into the bedroom, shouting:

"Great God! What's going on?"

It was Charley Lux, who was immediately reassured on seeing before him his mistress unhurt. The stranger, Pluto still holding him by the neck, already had his hands delicately tied together by the steel bracelets called handcuffs.

"I've caught a beautiful bird," Ethel declared. "You probably recognize him, Charley?"

Charley leaned over the prisoner's face and, very astonished, exclaimed: "Well, that's our friend I trailed a while ago. He's got himself nicely pinched."

"Now, Charley, go find two policemen to take charge of this fellow."

Charley didn't have to be told twice. While he was accomplishing his mission, Ethel, having called off her dog, ordered the dazed criminal, the blood flowing from two deep wounds in his neck, to get up. The scoundrel obeyed painfully and sat down on the chair the detective pushed toward him.

"You're a female devil, a dangerous and dreadful female devil," he growled, furious.

"Thank you. Coming from you, that's a flattering compliment," she answered. "Maybe now you'll tell me if the attempt made against me with the bouquet of roses and this new attempt against me are due to your own initiative—which I don't believe. In the opposite case, I could perhaps find out from you who charged you with this double mission."

The man glanced slyly at the woman who had vanquished him and said nothing.

"Well, since you aren't answering, I'll myself look for the instigator of these two excellent farces," Ethel King continued, without being upset. "He's probably still in the back courtyard of No. 14 Dark Street."

That was the name of the street where in the daytime she had fruitlessly looked for the man she now held prisoner. At that name the criminal trembled as if he couldn't believe his ears.

"You...you know that too?" he asked, grinding his teeth. "Bitch! Just wait a while. You'll be repaid for everything...and with interest."

"The good thing is that I know from now on how to go about it. You have very nicely completely betrayed yourself. But your last so pious and so charitable a wish will only be granted with great difficulty."

Charley Lux reappeared in the midst of all this with two policemen who took possession of the prisoner.

"Oh!" said one of the policemen. "It seems to me we've made a good catch. I already know this fellow from his description, which was distributed to us a long time ago."

Ethel advised them to pay close attention to their prisoner, so that he wouldn't slip through their hands. They left in the direction of Police Headquarters.

"We can now rest peacefully, my dear Charley," Ethel King then said. "I believe we won't be bothered any more tonight."

Jack the Ripper

The next morning the post brought Miss Ethel King a letter. The address seemed to be in familiar handwriting. It had the same thick up and down strokes she had already seen on the gilt-edged card sent to her with the bouquet of roses. This letter said the following:

73

My Ethel King, oh ardently loved woman!

Yesterday, giving way to the inclination of my heart, I wanted to procure you a free passage into the other world. But I have to admit, to my very deep sorrow, that I do not find in you a love equal to my own; otherwise you certainly would not have refused such a delightful diversion. However that may be, I assure you that, like every true lover, I will not let you go, and the time will come when you will please me by making the trip to Hell, a region where your faithful fiancé must have already been waiting for you some ten years. May you not have long to wait. And to better understand, read what follows.

I have only been in free America for some weeks, coming from Europe where dozens of your male colleagues in London, in Paris, in Berlin, in Monte Carlo and other places, have, for years, given themselves uselessly all the trouble in the world to catch me. I have consistently thumbed my nose at them and I have just crossed the ocean to observe somewhat how I will succeed in my occupation here. But now I learn from my brave and honored colleagues, that in this country where nothing is impossible, a woman, a certain Ethel King, instead of staying at home knitting stockings, has begun chasing criminals. That seems to me a bit much and that's what immediately inspired me with a violent attraction to you, because I love strength. And then I made a bet with several of my comrades and associates that I could send you very quickly out of this world. The business has already begun. You survived yesterday morning, but I won't stop constantly surrounding you with little loving attentions of the same kind until I succeed in making my beloved happy in spite of herself. I will begin work seriously on my task tonight and it can be questioned if you will still be in a state to read this letter when it reaches you.

Believe in my sincere devotion until you die,

Your Henry Alton.

At that letter, Ethel King laughed to herself and murmured:

"This again shows that the most unmitigated scoundrel hides a depth of stupidity, which, sooner or later, will cause his downfall. My opinion is that the famous Henry Alton, beginning tomorrow, will have occasion to think about his stupidity behind bars."

She had noted in the letter she had just read that Henry, after having bragged about his exploits in Europe, alerted her to the fact that he was,

74

that same night, beginning his work. He must therefore have done something, not just by an intermediary as in the attacks directed against her, but directly, by his own hands.

She got up and went to the telephone. She asked to speak to Chief Golding, although she knew that he wasn't usually in his office at such an early hour.

"Central Police Bureau, here!" someone answered her call.

"I am Ethel King. Is Mr. Golding there? I wish to speak to him."

"Yes, the Chief is here. One moment!"

Something extraordinary must have happened, or else Golding certainly would not have been at his post at such an early hour. Shortly thereafter, she heard his voice.

"Hello, Miss King!"

"Good morning, Mr. Golding! I just wanted to ask you if anything unusual had happened last night."

"Why do you ask that question?"

"I have good reasons for supposing something must have happened."

"You seem to know everything, Miss King. In fact, something did happen, even something terrible, and the author of it left no trace. A horrible crime."

"I'm going to come to see you immediately. I think I have certain information about it that I have from the criminal himself."

"Thunderation! Is that possible? In any case, I'll expect you, Miss King."

Ethel entered Golding's office 30 minutes later. She already knew about the night's event because the newspapers had put special editions for sale out on the streets recounting the horrible crime. The newspaper article they almost all printed read like this:

This morning, at about 2 a.m., a policeman—badge number 275—found the body of an elegant lady bathed in her own blood, in Small Street. The unfortunate woman had had her throat cut with a very sharp knife and her stomach too had been cut open so that the intestines were exposed. She no longer had money or jewelry on her, which proved that robbery was the reason for the murder. The victim has already been identified. She was Mrs. Carry, the wife of Holms Carry, well known in Philadelphia as a maker of machinery. She had spent the evening at Queen's Theater and had taken the shortest way back home on foot, as *she usually did. Mr. Carry has promised a $20,000 reward to whoever discovers the murderer.*

When Miss Ethel King arrived, Chief Inspector Golding was very upset. He had decided to put everything in motion to discover the guilty man, but he didn't know where to begin. He had no clues at all. Therefore he was waiting with the greatest agitation for the detective, who had told him she possessed information she had from the criminal himself. He knew Ethel King well enough to know she wasn't a woman to joke about such matters. And however strange that seemed to him, he didn't doubt that she had some clue.

He rushed up to her and shook her hand, saying:

"I'm very glad you're here, Miss King! I was eaten up with impatience because I'm convinced you're going to shed some light on this business."

"Exactly, Mr. Golding," Ethel replied, sitting down. "I've already told you that the criminal was kind enough to communicate certain little things to me."

"That seems to me hardly possible, Miss King," the Chief of Police said.

"It's nonetheless true, Mr. Golding. I owe this information entirely to the fact that I'm a woman. I have told you several times that my sex has more than once, remarkably, helped me to find certain criminals because these gentlemen, the rogues, couldn't imagine that a woman would ever risk hunting them down. Now if they learned that she had taken to the field, they would laugh and wouldn't deign to take precautions, certain that a woman couldn't collar them. You see, that's what happened today."

"You're probably right, and as unbelievable as your assertion had at first seemed to me, it now seems very plausible."

"Good! Have you already heard about the person who broke into my house last night to murder me, and that I arrested?"

"Naturally. You pulled off a masterly maneuver. Criminals ought to tremble when taking you on, Miss King."

"Dame, you have to protect your skin!" the detective retorted, smiling. "Listen carefully to what I'm going to tell you, Mr. Golding," she added in a serious tone. "The man responsible for the attack against me last night, the one who sent the dangerous bouquet you know about and the murderer of poor Mrs. Carry, are one and the same person."

The detective then handed him the letter signed Henry Alton, which he read with astonishment, after which he slapped his knee hard.

"Thunderation! You're right again, Miss King! This scoundrel must be dumb as an ox for his exploits and his luck in never being caught in Europe to have swelled him up with egotism and pride to the point that he makes fun of detectives and the police."

"That's the situation, and it's good that he's like that," replied Ethel, "otherwise, he would without a doubt be a little harder to catch."

"I'll heartily congratulate you Miss King if you earn the $20,000 reward the husband of the victim promises. But do you have a plan at the moment? Where do you intend to begin your investigation? What's the first thing that you're going to do?"

"Arrest the author of the crime!"

"But the job doesn't go so fast. You don't know where he's hidden or who he is."

"I can learn where he's hidden. I believe I know who he is."

"You know who he is? You can't seriously believe that signature Henry Alton is his real name?"

Ethel threw Mr. Golding a look that wasn't at all flattering, because the Chief flushed and mumbled some words of excuse.

"Let's drop that, Mr. Golding," Ethel continued in a colder tone. "I really want to tell you who the murderer is, although in my opinion, you should have known it as soon as you read that letter. You have certainly heard about a murderer who commits his crimes in the big European cities, principally in London, and mainly attacks well-dressed ladies. He always has the same method of operation. He starts by cutting his victim's throat, without a doubt to keep her from crying out, and next he cuts open her stomach. That last act seems to be the result of a special perversion, so that these murders committed for theft are also sadistic murders. In London and throughout all of England, this monster is known under a name which has become a source of fear; he's called Jack the Ripper."

The Chief of Police jumped up from his chair, exclaiming: "Why of course! I must have been mad not to have thought about that! Jack the Ripper is in our country! It was beginning to be too hot for him over there, and he came to our country. But I hope he won't last long!"

"You can be sure of it," Ethel answered. "I certainly even count on picking him up today, and to do that, I'm asking you to give me some men."

"Of course, you'll have whatever you wish, and I'll go with them. I want to be there when this fellow is captured."

"Now, would you have the man arrested last night in my house brought in?"

The Chief rang and gave the order to have the prisoner, John Nagaman, brought in.

"John Nagaman is a bird we've been following for some time already," he continued. "He has on his conscience several little murderous knife attacks, a few burglarized house safes, and other peccadilloes. I'm afraid he'll never again see the sweet light of liberty."

The man soon appeared, escorted by two policemen. On seeing Ethel, he let out a terrible curse.

"What do you want with me?" he asked in an angry and hostile voice.

"I would like to ask you—if it isn't presuming too much on your goodwill—to give us the name of the man who sent roses to Miss King yesterday and who sent you to murder her last night."

The prisoner laughed wickedly and threw a look full of hate at the detective.

"I won't say anything," he said. "Not a word. You'll never get his name. You'll never catch him, and he'll take terrible vengeance."

Ethel came forward a step and told him in a calm voice:

"At least tell me how much Jack the Ripper paid you to murder me."

These words had the effect of a thunderbolt striking the criminal, who trembled and turned wide-eyed toward the detective and stammered:

"You know…? You female devil!"

"Oh! Yes, I know that and even something else," Ethel answered. "I know that Jack the Ripper has been praised by his colleagues in America as a hero. His brilliance, I warn you, will tarnish quickly. He was told there was a female detective here. So he joked and said that in a few days Ethel King wouldn't keep his friends from doing whatever they liked. Isn't that right?"

"Who…Who told you that?" stammered John Nagaman, crestfallen.

"I have it from Jack the Ripper himself."

"From himself? Then he's been caught?"

"No, he just wrote me."

"Wrote? Then that's the biggest stupidity under the sun."

"You said it," the Chief laughed, giving the order to take him away.

"And now, get your men and follow me," said Ethel, full of confidence. "Ten men will be enough. Either I'm very mistaken or I'm going to have the pleasure of introducing you to my lover."

The End of a Criminal

When they arrived at the house on Dark Street, the men crept cautiously, one by one, into the back courtyard. Ethel King had preceded them and was waiting for them in front of the shed. She posted them behind the boxes and the other litter so that none of them were visible. Everything was done with the greatest caution and without any noise.

"Hide yourself also, Mr. Golding," she said in a low voice. "At any moment one of those rogues may put his nose outside, even though at this early morning hour they are all sound asleep in their den. Don't move before I give the signal—a whistle or a revolver shot. I'm going to stretch out on that pile of boxes so I can see in all directions without being seen."

From the position she had chosen she could in fact see everything, but she was mainly watching the shed where she was more convinced that the criminals were hiding since John Nagaman had changed expression when she had spoken to him about it.

Two hours were spent in waiting, when Ethel, who was beginning to feel the loss of sleep, felt a strange movement in the frame of the boxes on top of which she was lying. She came to a sitting position so as to take up less space and to be less easily seen. It seemed to her that someone was pushing about some of the boxes at the base of the pile, but slowly, without any noise, inch by inch. Little by little she saw an opening appear in the wall of the courtyard. Out of it there came a bearded man.

The man immediately began to push the pile of boxes against the opening. He must have found the pile heavier to move than usual, because he raised his head, and at the same time his eyes stared into those of the detective and into the barrel of the gun pointed at him. He was completely transfixed and incapable of uttering a sound. Ethel King jumped down lightly near him murmuring in a muted and firm voice:

"Silence, or you're a dead man!"

At the same time she motioned, and the Chief with two policemen ran forward and tied up the individual without giving him time to defend himself. While they were leading him away to a secure site, Ethel said to the policemen:

"My guess was right, as you see. Now we know the entry to the hideout. We're going in. I'll go first. Follow me closely to give me strong back up support."

The boxes were again moved back with all necessary precaution. When the entry was opened, Ethel King went in, followed by the Chief and his men. They first had to go down some ten steps, after which they came to a door with windows which was only pushed shut and through which there was a little daylight. Ethel pushed it half open and saw in front of her a sort of square subterranean room, rather small, the kind of cellar in which crime finds asylum and protection. A smoking lamp was hanging from the ceiling and lit somewhat a counter placed in the back where bottles and glasses were lined up between food stuffs of all kinds. Four men were stretched out on the bare ground, sleeping with closed fists.

Three of them had the dress and look of tramps; the fourth was rather elegantly dressed. In addition, his clean-shaven face was marked with the stigmata of all the vices and had, even in sleep, a ferocious and repulsive expression.

"Be careful, now, inspector," Ethel said in a voice as soft as a breath, pointing out the fourth sleeper. "That's Jack the Ripper. Let me go in first. You hide behind the shade of the wall, near the door. I want it to be his dear Ethel that Jack sees when he wakes. Your men will remain outside and come in at the first signal."

The detective advanced on tip-toes right up to the sleeper she was interested in, while keeping an eye on the three others. There were two revolvers near Jack that Ethel picked up and placed in her pockets. She looked a moment at the sleeping criminal, who wasn't aware of the kind of awakening he would have. Then she kicked him sharply with her foot, saying in a clear and distinct voice:

"Ho, Mr. Henry Alton, wake up! Your lover is here and this isn't the time to sleep. Come on! Stand up! Quickly!"

The man, sufficiently awakened by the kick she had given him, reached out with his hand for his revolvers near him. They had disappeared. He sat up as if moved by a spring and acted as if about to jump on the detective, but the revolver she was pointing at him held him at a distance.

"Good morning, Mr. Henry Alton, better known as Jack the Ripper," she continued. "How are you? Did you have pleasant dreams?"

However, the other three had awakened and gotten quickly on their feet, too surprised not to hesitate.

"Ethel King," one of them murmured in a frightened voice.

Jack heard it and recoiled.

"Ethel King," he repeated automatically.

"But of course! I'm the woman you're so in love with! Ah! Jack, Jack the Ripper. That did me good, to get a love letter. I was eager to know its noble and generous author and I've come to invite you to take a little walk. When we're outside, I'll tell you all of my heartfelt thanks for all the splendid roses you sent me yesterday and also all my gratitude for the messenger of love who visited me last night on your behalf! While we're waiting, let me ask you to leave in your belt the knife you'd like to draw. Be calm, or you'll be nothing but a cadaver yourself."

"Oh! You think you've got me," shouted the criminal, who had gotten over his surprise while she was talking. "Let's go, boys, kill that woman! Since she risked coming among us, we're going to celebrate my marriage to her in a way that will astonish her."

Just as the scoundrels raised their weapons, Inspector Golding rushed to Ethel's side, calling his men. A confused scuffle followed. Ethel had her arm grazed by a bullet. Jack the Ripper fought like a demon, slashing right and left with his knife; he wounded four policemen before they were able to subdue him. Of his three accomplices, one was dead, the two others wounded and lying on the ground.

No longer able to do injury, Jack threw terrible looks at Ethel King, who, without worrying about the blood flowing from the wound in her arm, stood near him, smiling.

Ironic and triumphant, she said: "Henry Alton has lost his bet. That doesn't matter. I believe it was a little inconsiderate of you to want to send me into the next world to better prove your love. You're nonetheless an unusual fellow and after your death, that you'll find, I fear, premature, your love letters will be one of the most curious ornaments of the Crime Museum."

The miscreant struggled in his bonds.

"Daughter of the Devil!" he bellowed. "I'll get revenge!"

"I've already been told that, or something like it, by Mr. John Nagaman, who is now under lock and key," Ethel answered. "Good health, Mr. Alton. I'm glad to have made the acquaintance of a man who was so attracted to me from the day he set foot on the American continent."

And turning toward the Chief of Police she added:

"You see, Mr. Golding, I've kept my word. The rest is up to you."

"And you've really well earned the $20,000," answered the Chief, giving her a warm handshake.

She then started back to her house, while Golding transported his prisoners to the holding cells.

Jack the Ripper was convicted of Mrs. Carry's murder. They found on him all he had stolen from the dead woman. His handwriting proved also that he was the instigator of the attack attempted against Ethel King. He was condemned to end his career in the electric chair. His accomplices, all criminals long sought by the police, got off with several years of hard labor, except John Nagaman, who was given life in prison.

The clever and daring arrest of the monster who had made the name Jack the Ripper grimly well-known, was to the great honor of Miss Ethel King, the female detective, and assured her a worldwide reputation at the same time.

4. THE SIGN OF THE DEVIL

Mrs. Minnie Willow

Mrs. Minnie Willow, a young widow, owned a pretty country house located in Swanborough, about 30 miles northwest of Philadelphia. She was noted for her wealth and her beauty. The evening parties she gave every week were regularly attended by a crowd of friends and acquaintances.

She naturally had an army of admirers, among whom were immensely rich land owners. So there was great surprise when the widow announced her engagement to a scientist with no fortune. The doctor, Ralf Arling, lived in Philadelphia. He did research in the natural sciences and had already published some remarkable works. During his research excursions in the area around Philadelphia, he had often passed through Swanborough and Mrs. Willow had invited him to her teas.

The scientist had soon fallen in love with the beautiful widow, who responded to his love.

The news of the approaching marriage of Ralf Arling and Minnie Willow had caused a lot of disappointments. The young woman had received many good wishes which didn't come from the heart. But she worried very little about it. Her love was enough to make her happy, and the visits of her fiancé, who came to see her several times a week, were always too seldom and too short for her taste.

It was a rainy autumn day, a Sunday. Minnie Willow, lay stretched out on a chaise longue, her gaze lost in the distance. Her marriage was to take place in ten days. She noticed her reflection in the mirror and sent it a happy wave.

"I'm beautiful!" she murmured softy with her red, well outlined lips. "And it's for him…for him alone!"

But her look halted at the clock and she trembled.

"My God! It's already 11:30 a.m.! And Ralf hasn't arrived yet? He usually arrives at 10 a.m. I hope nothing has happened to him! He promised me to be on time today."

At that moment, the front doorbell rang.

"Ah! There he is," the young woman said, breathing a sigh of relief. A minute later, the maid came to announce:

"Mr. John Gettys, the constable, asks if Madam can see him."

Minnie, disappointed, replied with irritation: "Have you forgotten my orders? I'm not at home for anyone…and most of all for that man I've never liked."

"Mr. Gettys insists; he's come, he says, for an important matter concerning Doctor Arling."

Minnie turned pale.

"Ralf!" she exclaimed. "The constable has come because of Ralf? What's happened? Show the gentleman in."

The maid left. Minnie automatically placed her hand on her breast to slow down the beating of her heart.

"What's happened?" she repeated. "Has Ralf been the victim of an attack?"

The constable came in, a strange smile on his lips. He was a handsome man, tall, with a good physique, and a carefully tended beard. He wore an impeccable jacket, patent leather boots, and carried a high hat in his hand. He bowed very low and simply said:

"Mrs. Willow."

"What do you want?" the young woman asked.

Gettys nodded and looked serious.

"I'm sorry to have to tell you bad news. You can't know Mrs. Willow, how long the road coming to you has seemed to me."

Minnie had become deathly pale. She crushed a batiste handkerchief in her clenched hand.

"But tell me then!" she exclaimed. "The facts, sir, get to the facts! Can't you see what state you've put me in?"

The constable was hesitating.

"My fiancé is he…is he dead?" continued the widow in failing voice.

"If that was all it was!" said Gettys, in a pitying tone of voice that made Minnie want to slap him.

"What worse could have happened to him? My Heavens, this isn't possible…no, a thousand times no."

"Unfortunately it is, Madame…Ralf Arling is charged with a burglary, for which he is wanted by the police."

Minnie stood as if petrified. The last drop of blood had drained from her face. She stood still, her eyes staring and haggard, her lips partially open; she didn't seem to understand what the constable had just told her. But suddenly, her look flashed, the red of indignation filled her livid cheeks.

"You're lying," she exclaimed. "Ralf Arling is incapable of a bad deed."

"Nevertheless what I've told you is the truth, Madam. Calm down, please, and control yourself. Alas! I can't change anything about the events. And please believe me, no one could deplore any more than I do that you have given your love to…someone unworthy."

"Mr. Gettys!" the young woman exclaimed angrily.

"Let me tell you everything without holding anything back. That's the best way to cure your broken heart. You will have to undergo a painful struggle, but it will be brief."

"Tell everything you want to, I won't believe you. I know Ralf's noble character too well to believe for an instant that he is guilty."

"But, Madam, at least listen to the facts! My superiors gave me the painful mission of telling you. I would wish with all my heart that Mr. Arling were innocent, but the circumstances are such that there can be no doubt."

The widow, who had stood up nervously at the constable's first words, fell back into a chair. She shook her head.

"I don't believe any of that story. Tell me, nevertheless, what you've been sent to tell me."

She pointed to a chair for the policeman, who began in a low voice.

"Last night in Philadelphia, while looking for a dangerous pickpocket, I passed by Alexander Street. A policeman came up to me and, very excited, told me that someone had just broken into the offices of Timbora and Son's factory. Obeying my duty as a policeman, I ran to the factory with the agent. On the way, he told me that, while making his rounds, he had noticed a light in the offices. He had immediately scaled the fence which surrounds the factory's grounds and hurried toward the building. He was afraid, with reason, that an intruder had broken in. At that moment, the light went out and a man jumped out a window and left running. The policeman shouted at him to stop, but the thief had agilely jumped the fence and fled too quickly for the agent to catch him. The man turned around for an instant when passing under a street lamp and revealed his features. He was blond, with a hooked nose. He had a beard and was wearing a soft hat. He was carrying a package under his arm."

The constable stopped to observe the beautiful widow. She was listening without flinching, a jeering smile playing across her lips.

"Go on!" she said.

"I went with the police agent to wake up the Director of the factory to tell him about the incident. He went with us to the offices and verified that the safe had been broken into. A little steel box holding $12,000 had disappeared. But here's the most significant thing. The investigation that I began on the spot led me to discover, on the ground, beside the safe, this little medallion."

Gettys took out a little gold medallion and presented it to Mrs. Willow. The young woman trembled and looked with astonishment at what the policeman had found.

"This piece of jewelry has a very unusual shape. I immediately had the impression of having seen it before. But where? I searched my memory: it was at your house...hanging on Ralf Arling's watch chain! My suspicion was transformed into certainty when, on opening the locket, I found inside your miniature portrait. Then I remembered the description of the burglar the policeman had given me: a blond man with a hooked nose, bearded, wearing a soft hat...No more doubt, the guilty man was Ralf Arling."

"No, it wasn't he!" Minnie exclaimed. "If you furnished me with a thousand other proofs, I would still repeat: He's not the one!"

"However, you'll certainly be forced to recognize that I'm right, Madam. I understand that it's hard for you to believe, but the facts are there."

"No, no, there's not a word of truth in all that!"

The constable looked at the widow angrily.

"Are you calling me a liar?" he demanded.

"No, but you're surely mistaken. If you knew Ralf as I do, you would know that he is incapable of committing a robbery."

"People sometimes have great illusions about a man's character. Remember the proverb: 'Still waters run deep.' "

"Don't insult Ralf! He's the best, the noblest man there is!"

"Hear more, Madam. My investigations finished, I returned immediately to Police Headquarters. Inspector Golding was there and I made my report to him. He ordered me to go to Doctor Arling's domicile and arrest him. The Doctor wasn't at home, but we made a new discovery in his bedroom which completely overwhelmed me. Ralf Arling had thought it wise to flee, but he had left the strong box stolen at the factory;

no need to say that the steel box had been forced open and emptied of its contents."

The constable stopped talking. Minnie remained mute, her regard lost in the distance.

"It goes without saying," the constable repeated, "an arrest warrant has been issued against Ralf Arling. His description has already been circulated in every direction."

The young woman stood up.

"Ralf is innocent," she said firmly. "He's the victim of a devilish plot. I'm convinced, sir, that Doctor Arling will prove himself innocent sooner or later and that the one who wanted to make him perish will be punished."

Gettys had immediately risen.

"I'm very sorry, Madam, that I'm the one fate has chosen to bring you this news. If you persist in believing in the innocence of your former fiancé, that's all to your honor for it proves your soul is noble and generous."

"My former fiancé? No, Mr. Gettys, you are mistaken. I'm more than ever attached to him, and I'll stay faithful to him until death!"

The constable shrugged.

"You will perhaps change your opinion when Ralf Arling is in prison."

"Ah! That's the last straw! Leave, Mr. Gettys. You're not the man to be considerate of a woman who is suffering. Leave me!"

As he was leaving, Gettys turned around one last time and said:

"You misunderstand my intentions, Mrs. Willow. No one wishes to see you happy more than I do. If you ever need a friend whom you can absolutely rely on, come to me. Goodbye, Madam."

He left and shut the door rather loudly.

Mrs. Willow remained standing some minutes in the same spot, deep in thought. Thoughts were whirling around in her head. She felt she was about to lose her mind, but the unshakeable confidence she had in the innocence of her fiancé sustained her. Obeying a sudden impulse, she went to the telephone. She had just had an idea which seemed to her to have been inspired by God himself.

She got connected to Ethel King, the famous Philadelphia detective. Ethel King was at home. Mrs. Willow told her about the visit from the constable and asked her to use her expertise to help remove the terrible suspicion weighing on Dr. Arling. The widow was deeply relieved when the master detective agreed to take charge of the case and promised to go to Swanborough with Charley as soon as possible.

A Consultation

For the clarity of the story, we must go back in time to recount some facts that were only revealed later by the confession of a criminal.

The evening preceding the events we have just reported, Friday, John Gettys had received a visit from Dr. Arling at his home. He was acquainted with him, having often encountered him at Mrs. Willow's teas.

"Sir," he said to him, "I believe my life is in danger and I've come to ask for your protection. If I've come to you instead of taking my case directly to the Chief of Police, it's because I wish to avoid troublesome publicity. On the eve of my marriage, I don't want the case to be spread about; not that I have anything to reproach myself with, but Mrs. Willow, my fiancée, might be sadly affected by all those stories."

Gettys looked at his visitor with curiosity.

"I'm listening, sir. What's it all about? Please believe that I would be delighted to render you service."

"Here it is, Mr. Gettys. For about a month, I've been receiving, every two or three days, threatening letters, in which I'm told that if I don't willingly give up Mrs. Willow's hand, a way will be found to prevent my marriage, even killing me, if need be."

"The devil!"

"I've brought you the letters that you can study at your leisure. Now, yesterday, on leaving my fiancée's house, I was crossing the Swanborough moor at nightfall to go catch the train when I heard a pistol shot and a bullet whistled past my ears. I didn't have a weapon. No one would have heard me in that deserted part of the countryside if I had called for help. Running away would have been as dangerous as facing my unknown aggressor. Therefore, I chose the wisest thing. I fell down as if I had been wounded. Then, hidden in the bushes, I crawled some 100 feet further on, where I remained crouching in a ditch hidden by the bushes. I owe my safety to this stratagem, because the criminal started to search for me. I saw him going back and forth at the place where he had seen me disappear. Finally, he passed very close to my hiding place muttering: 'It's too dark now. I can't find him. I'll come tomorrow morning at dawn.'"

"You were in fact in grave danger, Mr. Arling," said the constable, pretending to be very struck by the doctor's story. "Can you give me a description that will help me find your aggressor?"

"Yes, Mr. Gettys, precisely. As the murderer was walking away, I slid out of my hiding place and I followed him cautiously. He took a path that ended at a little woodcutter's cabin, about a mile from Swanborough. It appears that he lives in that little house. I saw him go in there."

Gettys nodded with a satisfied look. "Good," he said, "we'll take him in his lair. But it doesn't seem very likely to me that that individual was acting for himself. He must have been hired by someone to kill you. Can you point out to me the person from whom the threats you received came?"

"Not absolutely, unfortunately, sir. I have only suspicions; I will confide them to you on the condition that you promise me to keep them secret."

"We are friends, Doctor. You have earned my discretion."

Arling thought a moment. He finally said: "I had the misfortune to inspire a violent passion in a Russian dancer who was passing through Philadelphia. I did nothing to cause that, I assure you. I only met that woman, a certain Wanda Baranowsky, several times at evening gatherings. You have perhaps heard of her."

"Indeed."

"Well, that woman, scorning decency, made advances, that I naturally opposed with indignant reserve. I suppose that her love was transformed into fierce hatred. I can't say that the threatening letters came from her. The handwriting doesn't look like that of a woman. But I have an idea that they were inspired by Wanda Baranowsky. You will see that in one of those 'love letters' they threatened to 'carry my head to a person I had offended.' Until now I had considered that correspondence as a joke in bad taste, or, at the most, as an awkward stratagem to make me decide to give up a union that will be the happiness of my existence. But after my adventure of yesterday evening, the thing seems to me a great deal more serious."

The constable thought a few minutes and then stated:

"It seems to me difficult to implicate Wanda Baranowsky in this affair, at least so long as her accomplice hasn't been caught. So, the first thing to do is to get hold of your attacker. I'll be in Swanborough in an hour and I'll begin my investigation. I'll follow the criminal's trail and keep him from making another attempt on your life. I can't, however, arrest him just on the basis of your testimony. He wouldn't have any trouble getting released and returned to freedom, and everything would begin again. It will, therefore, be necessary for you to help me."

"I couldn't ask for anything better, Mr. Gettys. What must I do?"

"Return tomorrow evening, Saturday, at nightfall, to the spot where you were attacked on the Swanborough moor."

"Why's that?"

"I want the murderer to renew his attack, in order to catch him in the act."

Dr. Arling was perplexed.

"What? Isn't that quite dangerous?"

"Don't worry. I'll be on watch. I won't let the scoundrel out of my sight for a second, I swear to you. He won't give you a scratch."

The young scientist wasn't a fighter. He had perhaps never in his life handled a revolver, but he possessed that quiet bravery that is the panache of noble souls.

"All right," he decided, "I'll follow your advice." And smiling, he added, "I'm putting my life in your hands."

"It's safe there," the constable replied with a strange intonation which would have surprised a man less ignorant of evil than Arling was. "But I have one recommendation to give you. Don't talk about this to anyone, especially to Mrs. Willow. You would worry her without cause and perhaps put an obstacle in the way of carrying out our plan. Don't even say that you've come to consult me."

"It's agreed. Besides, I won't see Mrs. Willow until tomorrow morning."

Arling thanked Gettys warmly for his kindness in taking charge of his interests and left.

When he left, the constable began to pace up and down nervously.

"So that imbecile Bill Sandy missed his shot," he murmured. "He almost got himself arrested and me with him. But this time I'll succeed and I'll kill two birds with one stone. I'll have Minnie Willow's fortune and the good graces of Wanda Baranowsky."

Before going to Swanborough, Ethel King had gone to see Inspector Golding, with whom she was on excellent terms. She told him she had taken on the Ralf Arling case.

The inspector looked at her with astonishment.

"But that case is virtually closed!" he said. "Arling's guilt is proven. We have nothing more to do but proceed to the arrest of the guilty man."

Ethel had received sufficient explanations from Mrs. Willow not to blindly share the opinion of the Chief of Police.

"That doesn't matter," she said. "I want to go to Swanborough to see Doctor Arling's fiancée. I have an idea I'll learn something new."

"As you like, Miss King. But it seems to me the case isn't important enough to justify the intervention of an Ethel King."

"I don't share your opinion," the detective answered. "What's more important for a detective than to snatch an innocent person from dishonor?"

With Charley Lux, who had waited for her in the hall, she went to take the first train to Swanborough. The afternoon was already far advanced when they arrived at the little borough. They reached the somewhat isolated country house of Mrs. Willow.

"Ah! Miss King! Here you are!" exclaimed the widow. "You can't believe with what impatience I was waiting for you. Sit down, please. Let me describe the character of my fiancé and tell you about his present life."

Ethel and her cousin sat down facing Minnie and the latter cited haphazardly from her memories numerous facts from which it became apparent that the young scientist was a loyal, noble, and generous man, incapable of a bad act. Then she came to the terrible accusation the police had lodged against Dr. Arling. She repeated almost word for word the conversation she had had with John Gettys, the constable. The young woman frankly set forth to the detective the charges leveled against her fiancé. She finally let her indignation burst forth when she repeated Gettys insinuations that she would change her opinion when Arling was in jail.

"I swear to you, Miss King, my fiancé is innocent. I have hidden nothing from you. I could cite you a thousand traits of loyalty and generosity in Ralf."

"I've heard enough now, Mrs. Willow. I believe you and I entirely share your conviction. I can't believe in the guilt of a man like Dr. Arling. It's absurd to think that a young scientist can in this way, from one day to the next, become a common burglar."

The young woman took Miss King's hand in gratitude.

"How happy I am to hear you say that!" she exclaimed. "It's a great relief for me to finally find a sympathetic person who shares my conviction."

"Yes, I repeat, I share it entirely. But I now ask you, Mrs. Willow, to answer some questions. According to what you've told me, Constable Gettys maintains that he came to tell you about the situation, following the orders of his superiors?"

"Yes."

"Well, he lied. Neither the Chief of Police nor his subordinates have thought about giving him such a mission. But let's go on. Were you acquainted with Gettys before his visit to you today?"

"Yes, I invited him sometimes to my evening parties and he came to see me from time to time."

"Was he among the number of men who wanted to marry you?"

"He asked me twice to marry him."

"Did he seem to be very passionate?"

Minnie smiled tiredly.

"Oh! They all were! It's probably because of my fortune, Miss King, that I have so many marriage proposals."

"Your engagement to Dr. Arling must have caused many disappointments."

"You may say so!"

"Did any of your suitors who were turned down show resentment?"

"Yes, there were even some who reproached me bitterly."

"And John Gettys?"

"Some days after my engagement, he came to my house with the Doctor. He congratulated me, but it was easy to see that his compliments were not sincere."

"And today, did he speak to you about his love?"

"No, he just told me he would always be my devoted friend."

"The conduct of this constable seems very strange to me. In my opinion, it wasn't compassion that compelled him to come and tell you about the events; I have, instead, the impression that he experienced a feeling of triumph in telling you about them."

"There are so many incomprehensible things in this affair!" Minnie noted. "I can't explain how that locket was found in the offices of Timbora & Son, nor how they found the empty strong box in my fiancé's house."

At these words, the young widow placed Dr. Arling's locket in a dish.

"Ah! You have the medallion?" Ethel King questioned, surprised.

"Yes, Mr. Gettys forgot it. He had handed it to me. I kept it in my hand during our conversation and he didn't remember to take it back."

"Show it to me, please."

Ethel took the piece of jewelry and examined it carefully. She made a movement of surprise.

"Dr. Arling didn't lose this locket; it was stolen from him," she stated. "The link which held it to the chain has been cut with pliers. Look at it!"

"Then the factory burglar would be the pickpocket who robbed my fiancé!" Minnie exclaimed.

"Maybe. In any case, the discovery that I've just made conspicuously reduces the charges made against Dr. Arling. I'm going back to Philadelphia with my assistant to investigate at your fiancé's house. I also intend to pay a little visit to Mr. Gettys."

The detective consulted a timetable and found that the first train for Philadelphia didn't leave for another three hours. It was approaching nightfall. Ethel King certainly couldn't get back to Philadelphia before 8 p.m. After thinking about it, she decided to leave Charley with Mrs. Willow.

"I can't help thinking that there is, at the bottom of all this, a plot to prevent your marriage with Dr. Arling. Charley may perhaps find some interesting clue here."

Mrs. Willow naturally made no objection. She called the maid and told her to prepare two place settings for Ethel King and Charley Lux, who would dine with the widow.

At 7:15 p.m., as night fell, the car ordered from Philadelphia arrived. The driver rang the bell at the wrought iron gate to the garden. He knew he had come to pick up Ethel King. When the maid opened the door to him, he asked to speak to the detective immediately.

He was taken quickly to speak to Ethel King, who saw that he was very excited.

"What has happened to you?" she asked.

"Oh! It's terrible, Miss," the driver answered. "You're familiar with the road that runs between Swanborough and the area before it, on the Philadelphia side, a deserted place. There's nothing on the right or left but harvest fields or moors. From time to time there are also small woods. On leaving Philadelphia, I turned on the acetylene headlights of my auto and I started on the way at full speed. They had told me I was to pick you up, Miss King, and I thought you were certainly in a hurry. I had just gone past a wood, about a mile from here, and I was watching the open plain in front of me, when a man suddenly surged into my head-lights. He was carrying a shapeless packet on his shoulders. I saw him at the last moment when he was no more than 30 feet in front of the car. I hit my brakes and blew my horn.

"The man was frightened and jumped to one side; he stumbled and almost lost his balance. In order not to fall, he dropped his burden, which rolled onto the ground, sliding out of the canvas in which it was wrapped. I couldn't hold back a cry of terror in seeing clearly by my headlights the object the stranger had just dropped. I couldn't believe my eyes! It was the cadaver of a decapitated, half-nude man. I could clearly see the trunk bleeding from the shoulders. I almost fainted. I instinctively stopped. But at the same moment a voice yelled at me: 'Go on your way!' Shots from a revolver burst out behind me and some bullets whis-tled past my ears. I thought it prudent to flee. I drove my car as fast as it would go. I took only a few minutes to get here."

Ethel King had stood up.

"Come, Charley. It's certainly a matter of a terrible crime. Driver, take us as quickly as possible to the spot where that situation happened to you."

Ethel and Charley took leave of Mrs. Willow. That story by the driver had put her into an indescribable state of nerves. Five minutes later the automobile arrived with the speed of an express train at a turn in the road, very near a little wood.

"Look!...Look over there!" Ethel King suddenly shouted.

She pointed in the direction of an isolated barn, the outline of which could be vaguely distinguished some distance away. On the black mass of the construction an immense question mark lit up the night. That lu-minous sign produced a fantastic effect. The car stopped in front of the barn.

"Wait with the car," Ethel King ordered the driver.

She jumped onto the road with Charley and crossed the field which separated the road from the barn. At that moment, a country man, running, appeared in the headlights.

"In the name of heaven, come with me," he cried out. "Look at that brilliant sign. It was surely the devil who drew it there and the unfortunate victim he struck down is there."

Ethel King went forward with Charley and the countryman and arrived in front of the barn door where the question mark gave off a phosphorescent light. A decapitated cadaver was stretched out in front of the entry to the barn. It was naked to the waist. He had been left only with his shoes and his trousers. He had no ring on his finger; his pockets were empty; and the few clothes he was still wearing bore no mark whatsoever, nor anything in particular that could serve to establish the victim's identity. Ethel King turned her pocket electric flashlight on the decapitated man; she leaned over to examine him. The countryman was watching that scene, terribly afraid. He was constantly looking around him, as if he feared to see the devil appear.

"It's the devil who did that," he repeated. "He's the only one who could have done it. A man wouldn't know how to write with fire."

"This crime is the work of a man, and not of the devil," Ethel King said gravely. "Charley, we're not going to leave this county before we lay hands on the scoundrels who committed such an atrocity."

The young detective nodded silently. Ethel told the countryman not to touch the body before the coroner and the police had come to make their investigation.

"In the name of heaven! What are you thinking about?" the man answered. "I'll certainly be careful not to touch this dead man, because it was Satan that cut off his head, and if I touch him, the same thing will certainly happen to me."

Ethel King herself gave up trying to find a clue on the victim.

"The criminal wanted to cover his crime with a veil of mystery," she said. "In that way he was probably counting on arousing superstitious terror in the inhabitants of the countryside which would keep them from alerting the police."

With Charley she went back in the direction of the automobile, which was waiting at the edge of the road.

"Could you make out the murderer's features?" the detective asked the driver.

"No, I was going too fast and when I stopped my car I didn't have time to turn around. The bullets were already flying past my ears and I sped off. I didn't want to leave my skin here!"

Ethel King and her cousin began to search for tracks in the fields, using their electric pocket flashlights. They had come very near the barn, some 100 feet from the road, when they suddenly heard the roar of the automobile motor. The automobile had been put into gear and was driving away in the direction of Philadelphia.

Ethel King made a megaphone of her hands and yelled out:

"Where are you going? Wait!"

The driver didn't answer, but there was a cry, then an explosion. Some seconds later, the automobile picked up speed and moved away with insane speed.

For a moment, Ethel King remained struck with astonishment, then she exclaimed:

"It's the murderer! He attacked the driver and made off with the auto. Run after him, Charley!"

The young detective sprinted off. Certainly he couldn't dream of catching the car, but he wanted at least to make an effort not to lose sight of him.

Ethel watched him for a moment as he went down the road. She hardly expected that he would succeed in seeing the direction the murderer had taken. An idea came to her. She wanted to return to Mrs. Willow's house and telephone Philadelphia to ask the police to stop the car when it arrived in the city.

A Capture

Ethel King's conjectures were right. The driver was waiting on his seat for the return of the detectives, who were proceeding with their investigation. He saw the mysterious light shining on the barn and could not, any more than the countryman, keep from giving way to superstitious terror.

He felt the car suddenly shake on its shock absorbers, as if someone had just jumped on the running board. He didn't have time to turn around. A hand seized him by the throat and the cold barrel of a revolver was pressed against his temple.

"Start driving, if you value your life," a hoarse voice whispered in his ear.

The unfortunate man, more terrified than ever, engaged the clutch, and started the car forward. He had hardly gone a few hundred feet when he heard Ethel King's call. Then the poor devil cried out for help. That was his downfall; the murderer blew out his brains.

The driver fell over and the murderer took his place at the wheel. The man scarcely knew how to drive an automobile; nevertheless, he kept up the speed and, for the first minute drove without encumbrance along the road that ran straight for half a mile or so; but following that he came to a sharp turn. And that's where the inevitable catastrophe happened. The murderer wanted to turn, but he turned too suddenly and threw the vehicle into the ditch. A dull splintering sound rang out; the car turned over. The driver remained pinned under the car, while the criminal was thrown ten yards from there into a field and remained stretched out, unconscious.

Charley Lux, who hadn't given up the chase, had viewed the accident from a distance. He was pleased with the idea that the criminal would no longer escape him. Several minutes later he discovered the unconscious scoundrel. He was a poorly clothed, stocky man, with a brutish face.

In his fall he had been struck on the head and was bleeding profusely, but his heart was still beating. The detective tied his hands and then dressed his wound. He had scarcely finished when the scoundrel opened his eyes. The first thing he did was to utter a vicious oath.

"Swear if you like," Charley told him, while helping him to get up. "You've been caught and you'll get the punishment you deserve for your crimes."

He shoved him onto the road in the direction of Swanborough.

"Go on, walk. And don't try to get away unless you want to get a bullet in your shoulder."

The criminal hesitated a moment; on seeing the detective's weapon aimed at him, he thought it wiser to obey. He started down the road, followed by Charley Lux. The two men took the road to Swanborough together, and after walking a half hour they saw the lights of the village before them. During the walk, the prisoner had turned around several times, but he had watched in vain for an opportunity to escape; he always saw Charley Lux's lantern and revolver covering him. Attempting to flee seemed really too risky. In addition, he had a shoulder broken in several places. It hung down limp and was causing the scoundrel severe pain.

Charley and his prisoner were reaching the first houses of the village when they saw a vehicle drawn by two horses coming to meet them, with Ethel King and some police officers in it.

She had at first telephoned Philadelphia as she had intended to; then she had gotten in touch with the Swanborough police, and, as there was no automobile in the little village, she had rented a carriage. While the coroner and the two policemen went to examine the cadaver of the driver and that of the decapitated man, they took the murderer to the police station.

"What is your name," Ethel asked him.

The criminal didn't answer.

"You won't gain anything by refusing to talk. On the contrary, you have every advantage in making a complete confession. Who is that decapitated man you murdered?"

"I wasn't the one who killed him," the scoundrel protested.

"Who was it then?"

The prisoner remained stubbornly silent. Ethel pointed out:

"If you say nothing, everyone will believe that you're the murderer, and you won't escape the death sentence. On the contrary, if you're frank, the judges will be lenient toward you."

The scoundrel let himself be convinced. The pain he was experiencing, the consequence of his fall, contributed to wearing down his resistance.

"It was John Gettys, the constable, who forced me," he stammered. "I was at his mercy. Some time ago he caught me in the process of burglarizing a house. But instead of sending me to prison, he offered me my liberty on condition that I render him some services. I promised to do what he wanted."

"What is your name?" Ethel King asked for the second time.

"Bill Sandy."

"What were you supposed to do?"

"Dr. Arling, that you may know, came to Swanborough often. The constable commanded me to spy on him and to kill him when he crossed the moor on the way to the train station. Thursday evening I was hidden at the edge of a wood. I saw Dr. Arling pass by and I fired at him, but I missed. When John Gettys learned that, he went into a blue rage and he told me he would take charge of getting rid of Arling himself. He had thought of another plan.

"Yesterday evening I spied on Mr. Arling as he left his restaurant in Philadelphia, and I bumped into him as if by accident. On that occasion, I stole the gold medallion that he wore on his watch chain. Arling was supposed to come to the Swanborough moor and the constable had made an appointment with him. John Gettys waited for him along the road, in a deserted spot, and murdered him. It's the doctor's corpse you found in front of the barn. During this time, I was to carry out the burglary. I'm the one who took the strongbox from the safe in the Timbora and Son factory and left the doctor's medallion in the offices. I broke open the strong box and I took the money; that I kept for myself."

"But you left the empty strongbox at the doctor's house?"

"Yes, that wasn't difficult. I got into the house without any noise by picking the locks. I dropped off the strong box and left. In this way, suspicions had to fall on Arling."

"Why did Gettys have you take the decapitated body to the front of the barn?"

"He had learned, from the police in Philadelphia, that Ethel King had taken the case in hand. At that moment he was staggered and thought about fleeing. But he got the idea of mutilating the corpse. He went back with me this evening to Swanborough. We took the body out of a ditch where the constable had left it. Gettys himself cut off the head, that he hid in a travel bag. He went back to Philadelphia by the train. Me, I was told to carry the decapitated dead man to the front of the barn and to paint a large question mark on the door with phosphorescent paint."

"Why that stage setting?"

"To influence the superstitious country people."

"What did he want to do with the victim's head?"

"I don't know...Burn it probably."

"Are you supposed to go meet the constable?"

"Yes, at his house...to give him the news. He's waiting for me."

The scoundrel, who seemed to be suffering atrociously had a fainting spell and if the two agents hadn't jumped forward to support him, he would have fallen off his bench. The interrogation couldn't continue.

"Have...a...doctor...come," the criminal moaned. "I've now told...all I know..."

"Answer one more question," Ethel King insisted. "You wanted to use the automobile to get back to Philadelphia?"

"Yes."

"And you forced the chauffeur to drive, by threatening him with your revolver?"

"Yes."

"But when he cried for help, you killed him?"

"Yes, I was like a madman. I didn't know any longer what I was doing," Bill Sandy stammered.

Ethel King and her assistant decided to return to Philadelphia by the first train. It left in an hour. Ethel returned first to Minnie Willow's house to inform her, with the greatest consideration, of the tragic end of her fiancé.

Minnie's despair was heartbreaking. Ethel tried in vain to console her. However, when the first crisis of sorrow had passed, Mrs. Willow reflected on the fact that there was no absolute proof of Dr. Arling's death, since they had only the statements of Bill Sandy. She told that to Ethel King, who shook her head sadly, but didn't dare snatch that last hope from her.

Denouement

It was 3 a.m. when Miss King arrived at West Avenue in Philadelphia with her assistant. The house bearing the number 33 was a two-story building with a little garden in front of it. There was a light on the first floor, but the window curtains were tightly closed.

"He must be anxiously awaiting Bill Sandy," Ethel King observed. "When he sees me arrive in the place of that scoundrel, that will be a little surprise for him."

The detective, who was practiced in all sports, climbed over the wrought iron fence. Charley did the same and they both slipped noiselessly to the side of the steps.

"We're going to go into the house," Ethel said. "When I get into the room where Gettys is at this moment, you'll hide yourself behind the door and stay on watch to come in if need be."

She took out her master key and forced the lock. For a detective as experienced as she, it was child's play. A few minutes later, she went across the entry hall with Charley. The door to Gettys' apartment opened to the right. Ethel King took care of that obstacle as easily as she had the first. She pushed the door open cautiously, fearing it might hold an alarm system. But that was not the case. No tinkling troubled the profound silence which reigned in the apartment. Ethel and Charley slipped on tip-toes into the corridor and stopped in front of a door under which a thin ray of light filtered.

A huge fire was burning in the fireplace. John Gettys, sunk into a vast armchair, was looking at the flames, meditating. The expression on his face denoted extreme trouble. He was pale. From time to time a nervous tremor shook him. He was so absorbed in his thoughts that he didn't hear the door open slowly and someone enter the room. Ethel King entered on her tip-toes, behind the constable, and saw in the fireplace the remains of a skull that the fire had almost consumed.

Gettys suddenly snatched himself out of his revelry, looked at his watch and, worried, murmured:

"So late already! And Bill isn't here yet. Hopefully, nothing has happened to him!"

The constable got up nervously and he then saw Ethel King. He let out a cry of terror. But the detective bowed and said:

"Good evening," Mr. Gettys. "Don't be afraid. It's a colleague who's come to see you."

The rogue instinctively plunged his hand into his jacket pocket, but Ethel King had already put her revolver under his nose.

"Leave your weapon where it is! You wouldn't however want to kill a colleague."

The constable had to give up his intention. But his eyes glittered and he asked in an irritated voice:

"You are Miss King?"

"That's my name."

"How did you get in?"

"Through the door."

"Why didn't you ring the bell?"

"In order not to disturb you in your reflections, so much more so as you are busy with a case which must excite all your interest."

"What case?"

"That of the burglar Ralf Arling. I've come to talk over that case with you. You've already made some investigations that can guide me in my inquiry."

The rascal sighed with relief.

"I couldn't ask for anything better than to be of use to you, Miss King," he said. "Sit down, please."

Ethel King was playing, as if unconsciously, with her revolver.

"Ralf Arling is innocent, Mr. Gettys," she observed.

"How's that? I have gathered some crushing charges against him."

"That's true, Mr. Gettys. But we have arrested the real guilty person and he has confessed."

"You don't say! What's his name?" the constable exclaimed in a strangled voice.

"Bill Sandy."

Gettys tried in vain to force a smile.

"Bill Sandy," he repeated. "I don't know him."

"We found a decapitated cadaver on the Swanborough moor and we suspect that Bill Sandy knows the murderer."

"Ah! Did he tell you his name?"

"No, not yet, but it won't be long."

There were several seconds of silence, during which Gettys tapped his revolver in his pocket several times.

"I congratulate you on your success, Miss King," he finally continued. "But how can I help you?"

"You might be able, perhaps, Mr. Gettys, to turn the murderer over to me."

"On my word, no, Miss King. It's through you that I'm just now getting the first news of the crime. Have they identified the victim?"

"They suspect that it's Dr. Arling," Ethel continued.

The constable turned pale. The visitor continued in the most natural voice:

"You could perhaps tell me, Mr. Gettys, if the head these flames have almost devoured is that of Dr. Arling."

The rascal wanted to rise, but Ethel King's revolver held him in check.

"Don't move, Mr. Gettys. If you do, I'll be tempted to fire."

She turned toward the door and shouted:

"Charley! Come in!"

A minute later Charley Lux was putting handcuffs on the constable, who let out a terrible oath.

"What does this mean?"

"I'm arresting you in the name of the law, John Gettys. You're accused of having murdered Ralf Arling and of organizing the burglary of the Timbora and Son factory."

Gettys remained prostrate in his armchair.

"Ethel King," he said in a failing voice, "you can't know how passion can lead a man to the most insane acts. I love Mrs. Minnie Willow. I committed the crimes you accuse me of in a moment of madness."

Ethel King looked at the rogue coldly.

"If you're able to make a jury believe that, you may perhaps escape the gallows," she said. "But don't lull yourself with false hopes. I'm persuaded that you acted less through love than avarice. It was most of all for her fortune that you dreamed of marrying Minnie Willow."

No. 45 Chaque fascicule contient un récit complet. 10 Cts.

ETHEL KING
LE NICK CARTER FÉMININ

Le Lac solitaire.

«Accostons sans bruit, Charley,» chuchota Ethel King.

5. A MODERN SALOMÉ

A Series of Assassination Attempts

It was a cold autumn night. A closed automobile turned into Garden Street, one of the most beautiful streets in Philadelphia, and stopped in front of No. 77. An elegant gentleman got out of it and ordered the driver to wait. When he rang the bell at the pretty villa, a suburb clock slowly chimed the 12 strokes of midnight.

A window on the second floor of the little house opened and a young man asked:

"Who's there?"

"Someone who wants to speak to Miss Ethel King about urgent business."

"Just a moment."

A few seconds passed, then an electric light with a reflector attached came on over the door and threw a wave of light over the nocturnal visitor. He could thus be seen distinctly from the house of the famous detective.

Ethel King had adopted this arrangement to avoid receiving at home persons with evil designs intent on making an attempt on her life. It was only thanks to the precautions that she took that she had to that point escaped attempts made by her numerous enemies. The reflector allowed her to submit every visitor who came to the garden door to a preliminary examination.

Ethel King had noticed that a person driven by bad intentions, always made a frightened movement and instinctively tried to leave the field of light when the lamp was turned on.

The blond gentleman didn't move and at the end of a minute, the garden door opened. The visitor entered and went up to the top of the steps where he was met by Charley Lux, the assistant and cousin of the great detective.

He was taken into the office of Ethel King, who was seated at her desk, a revolver placed in front of her, within reach of her hand.

After the usual introductions, the man declared:

"My name is Paul Boyssel, Miss King. I'm French by birth and have only lived in Philadelphia for about a year. I'm Director of the Mercantile Bank."

"Please sit down, Mr. Boyssel. You come at a very unusual hour. I see that you are very pale."

"Indeed, Miss King...I've just had a great fright, and I admit that, for a moment, I completely lost my head. I saw no other resource but to come to you. I hope you will succeed in delivering me from the unknown persecutors who are dogging my steps."

"Ah! So you have enemies who are trying to harm you?"

"Who want to take my life, Miss King. It's a horrible thing to live under constant menace, to tell yourself that at any instant a man might rush up to you to stab you or blow out your brains; to think that a criminal hand could pour poison into your water or in your food, that in returning home you're perhaps going to find a bomb under your door."

"And you're living with that impression?"

"Yes, Miss King. It's true mental torture. That has gone on for some weeks and the police to whom I appealed several times, haven't been able to help me. They are as incapable as I am to lay hands on the mysterious persecutors."

"That's strange," said the detective. "Would you be kind enough to tell me in detail about the attempts you've been the victim of so that I can get as clear as possible an idea of the situation?"

"Gladly, Miss. As I have already told you, I have been in Philadelphia only a year. Before that, I lived in Paris. I resigned from the situation I occupied there to take that of Director of the Mercantile Bank that a friend in New York helped me get here."

"Had you written previously to that friend that you intended to emigrate and would be glad to find a position in the United States?"

"Yes."

"And why did you leave France?"

Paul Boyssel blushed slightly and answered with embarrassment:

"I prefer not to explain myself on that subject, Miss King. The reasons why I decided to become an ex-patriot are private."

"As you wish. But tell me what has happened to you here,"

"I'm very happy with my new position, which gives me a salary greatly superior to the one I earned in France. In addition, I have become very quickly accustomed to the American way of life, and I was the happiest of men when these persecutions began."

The narrator paused and Ethel King took advantage of the pause to ask:

"Are you married, Mr. Boyssel?"

"No. I'm 32 years old, but I'm not thinking yet of getting married...But, to get back to my story. Let me tell you that one night, six weeks ago, returning home I found on my desk a scrap of paper with these words: 'Prepare yourself. Your death has been decided.' "

"Do you still have that note?"

"Here it is."

The visitor took a little square piece of yellowed paper out of his billfold and held it out for the detective. Ethel examined the unusual missive. The words were written in pencil; the letters, separated one from the other, were slanted to the left.

"The writing is disguised," Ethel King noted. "It's impossible to say if it was written by a man or a woman. Nevertheless, I'm well versed enough in handwriting that I can draw some rough estimate from this simple line about the character of its author. The person who wrote this to you is energetic, passionate, not very sensitive, and possesses a propensity to cruelty, which in addition is shown in the way the sentence is written."

Boyssel looked at the detective with bewilderment.

"You can see all that in that written line?"

"Definitely, Mr. Boyssel. It often happens in our profession that we have to examine anonymous letters and a good detective must have studied graphology."

"But you said that handwriting is disguised?'

"Yes, that jumps out at you. However, it's useless for a person to falsify his handwriting. He can't entirely suppress certain characteristics which still give an idea of his character. But, let's go on. What did you do when you found this note?"

"At first I didn't attach any great importance to it. I made my butler undergo a strict questioning. At the beginning I thought he had allowed himself to play a bad joke on me. But I soon dropped that idea. That man has been in my service since I arrived in Philadelphia. He's a devoted boy, faithful and serious, incapable of such a silly act. However, apart from him, no one else can enter my apartment during my absence."

"May I ask where you live?"

"72, 33rd. Street, the second floor. My windows look out over East Park."

"Could someone not have gotten into the apartment through the window?"

"Yes, they could. I was even convinced that my enemies had entered that way.

"The day after I received this threatening note, I was almost the victim of the first attack, just as I was entering the Mercantile Bank. It was 9 a.m. The large vestibule was empty. I put my foot on the first stair step to mount to the second floor, when I suddenly saw a hand come out from behind a column and point a revolver at me. Fortunately, I had the presence of mind to jump to one side. That movement saved my life. The bullet whistled in front of me without hitting me.

"My assailant shot twice more; however, I had hidden behind a column. Then I saw a man wrapped up in a huge overcoat, pulled up right to his ears, and wearing a felt hat with wide rims which hid his face, run across the vestibule. I ran after him, but he was more agile than I was. I lost trace of him. The bank employees, excited by the gun shots, started searches which found nothing more.

"The criminal had escaped. As you can well understand, I called in the police who started an investigation but didn't manage to arrest my assailant. They didn't know how to make anything of that anonymous letter."

"I can easily believe it," Ethel King observed. "You're the one responsible for their lack of success, Mr. Boyssel."

The visitor looked surprised.

"Why's that?"

"We'll return to that question shortly," the great detective replied. "First tell me what happened to you afterward."

"There were several other attacks against me. The next one happened a week later. My enemies sent me a package through the mail. My butler, whom I had told to open it, thought he heard a weak tick-tock on the inside. I rushed to carry the package to the police. It was a bomb! The scoundrels had missed their target once again.

"But they didn't get discouraged. One evening when I was absent, two weeks ago, my butler, who had to write a letter to his parents, sat down at my desk, even though I hadn't given him permission to do so. He had sat down without closing the blinds or the curtains. Suddenly a shot was fired from the house across the street. The bullet came through the window and struck him in the head.

"James Billing, that's his name, fell over unconscious, and when I returned I found him bathed in his blood. I am persuaded that bullet was meant for me. The murderer, posted in the house across the street, seeing a man sitting at my desk, thought that it was me. Fortunately, my servant's wound wasn't serious. In this case again, all the police investigations were in vain. They investigated the house across the street, but didn't find anything. There was a vacant apartment on the second floor. The author of the attack must have gotten in there."

"They didn't turn up the slightest clue? Not even footprints?"

"No. They just found an open window."

"That's too bad," Ethel King murmured. "You should have contacted me at that time. If the criminal had left footprints, the comings and goings of the policemen would have blotted them out. It's a waste of time for me to investigate that house."

"The last attempt was made last night. I went to the club, but, feeling tired, I left about 11 p.m. On returning home, I saw nothing suspicious. James was already in bed. I remained several minutes in my study, then I went into my bedroom. I started to get undressed when I noticed something. It was something insignificant in itself, but I found it unpleasant because it upset my habits.

"My servant hadn't prepared my bed by removing the coverlet. I could have taken the trouble to lift it off the top of the bed myself, but I'm a little cranky and I make it a principle not to let my butler get by with anything so that he doesn't, in the long run, pick up the habit of negligence. I went out into the hallway and called James. He answered me immediately. Two minutes later, he was in my bedroom. I showed him my bed and reproached him for his forgetfulness, but he lifted his arms to heaven and swore by all the gods that he had removed the coverlet, as he did every evening before going to bed.

"I remembered my enemies. Was there again another bomb under the coverlet?

"I took a revolver out of the night stand and ordered James to pull back the coverlet carefully, and then to immediately jump back. The event should prove to what extent my prudence was justified, because, when the servant pulled back the coverlet, two poisonous snakes hidden under it, raised up hissing.

"Both of us let out a cry of terror. Giving way to my first emotion, I fired several times and killed one of them. Just as I fired my last bullet, my bathroom door suddenly opened. A masked man with a raised knife jumped out into my bedroom and threw himself on me. I instinctively jumped back, but I managed to grab the man's wrists and thus avoided the mortal blow. I fought several seconds with the villain. My butler, who had recovered from his stupor, intervened. He picked up a chair and used it as a bludgeon. The murderer, finding he was no longer the strongest, dropped his knife, jerked loose from my hold, and jumped out the open window. He slid down using the lightning conductor cable and took to his heels.

"James and I looked at each other, terrified. Finally, I armed myself with a cane and killed the snake, which was still in the bed. After that, I made the decision to come see you, Miss King, because the regular police are incapable of protecting me. I have unlimited confidence in you."

On the Trail

The great detective had gotten up and was walking up and down.

"Will you help me, Miss King, in my fight against my persecutors?"

"Yes, but on condition that you tell me everything without reserve."

"But I have told you everything," the young man replied.

"You've told me what has happened to you here in Philadelphia. You've been silent on what made you decide to leave France. Now, I have a feeling that the enmity of your enemies began in Paris and not in the United States."

Boyssel lowered his head.

"But I swear to you, Miss King…"

"It would be better not to swear anything. Either you tell me why you left France or I refuse to take on your case."

The visitor hesitated a moment and then said in a worried voice:

"All right, Miss King, since you insist, I'll tell you that story. I don't like to tell it because I know it doesn't show me in a good light. Here it is!

"Three years ago, in Paris, I met a Russian dancer, an adventuress. She was beautiful. As to her character…my word, Miss King, it was almost like that of the one you sketched from the handwriting of the anonymous letter.

"I fell in love with that woman. What can I say about that love? That sacred name can't apply to a passion like mine. An absolute vertigo took hold of me. I lost the use of my reason. I was mad about Wanda Baranowsky and, I must admit, she responded to my passion."

Ethel King seemed surprised. She knew Wanda Baranowsky was in Philadelphia because that woman had been indirectly involved in a case the great detective had had to solve. There had even been serious suspicions about the Russian dancer, but as they possessed no proof against her, she was easily vindicated.

"I gave up everything for Wanda," Boyssel continued. "I neglected my business. I displeased my superiors; I went into debt to satisfy my mistress's caprices. My creditors were hounding me; my possessions were seized. The bailiff became a frequent visitor to my house. I began to realize my folly, and little by little, I came to discern Wanda's true character better.

"One fine day I decided to break it off. That took place following a quarrel I had with the dancer in the presence of her brother. It was in vain that Wanda declared to me that a child was to be born from our love. I told her straight out that our liaison was over.

"That decision was painful to me but I still had enough mind left not to spoil hopelessly all the rest of my existence.

"Wanda showed the baseness of her character. She called me the vilest insults and her brother called me a rogue. Carried away by anger, I struck the Russian. The next day, he sent me his seconds as witness to a duel. A meeting with pistols was agreed on and two days later I killed the brother of my former mistress. I was arrested and brought to trial. My lawyer obtained my acquittal, but I lost my job and I found only a badly paid position in a small bank. It goes without saying that I didn't like my new situation, and I feared Wanda Baranowsky's revenge.

"So I wrote to my friend in New York, and, as he had influential relatives, he was able to get me the position of Director at the Philadelphia Mercantile Bank. I breathed a sigh of relief when I left Le Havre on the steamer that would take me to America.

"I hadn't let it be known where I was going. There were scarcely a few friends who knew my destination. I began work enthusiastically. I became a different man. I was completely cured of my insane passion for Wanda Baranowsky. Nothing remained but for me to repent of my past mistakes.

"There you are, Miss King. Now you know everything. You will understand why I don't like to speak of the motives which forced me to leave France. But it's better, I agree, that you know about it."

Ethel King had listened in silence. After a moment she said:

"Wanda Baranowsky has learned that you are in Philadelphia. She has followed you to take revenge on your abandoning her and for having killed her brother in a duel."

"However, I haven't seen Wanda once in Philadelphia," Boyssel answered.

"Nevertheless, she's here. It so happens that I had indirect business with her. If you had followed the news items in the newspapers, you would have read her name there. A terrible crime instigated by that woman was committed lately. They were unfortunately unable to bring sufficient charges against her to convict her. I hope this time, with your help, to free society of that dangerous creature. Wanda wishes your death and she has faithful followers that she has charged with murdering you. Until now you have miraculously escaped all her attempts. But your former mistress won't become discouraged. Her first failures only excited her rage. She will put everything in operation to annihilate you. Be on your guard. I'll try to save you from your terrible enemy, but I can't promise you immediate success. A new attack might very well be directed toward you before we have taken effective measures against your persecutors."

"Naturally, Miss King, I never go out without a weapon. From now on, every evening I'll search my apartment to be sure an assassin isn't hidden there. My butler will sleep in my bedroom. We both sleep very lightly. We will wake up at the slightest noise."

"Good. Take every imaginable precaution. First of all, I'm going with you to your apartment to inspect the area; then I'll get to work."

The house where Paul Boyssel lived on the second floor, was an elegant building inhabited only by rich people. The Frenchman paid the coachman and went with the detective to his apartment. The police, alerted by James Billings, were there. They had to finish their investigations. Mr. Golding, the police Chief, who had come in person, told Ethel King that he had discovered no interesting clue. He was staying, however, to help in his friend's investigation.

Ethel King first questioned the butler.

"Did you hear nothing suspicious this evening before going to bed?"

"No, Miss. That would have put me on my guard. Since my master has been harried by mysterious enemies, I've been extremely cautious."

"In your opinion, how did the murderer get into the apartment?"

"He climbed up by the lightning rod cable and jumped into the bed-room through the window."

"Did you see his face?"

"No, he was thin and of middle height, almost like you Mr. Boyssel."

"So you didn't notice anything suspicious?"

"Nothing. But when Mr. Boyssel got me out of bed to tell me I hadn't turned back the covers of his bed I had a presentiment of danger. I told myself that it was probably a new criminal attempt against my master. What happened following that certainly proved that I wasn't wrong."

"Listen carefully. Here's an important question. Have you noticed, in the last few days a very beautiful woman who would have come to wander around the house or who appeared interested in Mr. Boyssel in whatever way?"

The butler shook his head.

"No, Miss."

"No one came to the door during your master's absence to ask for information on his habits?"

The domestic reflected a moment.

"Tell me, James, the Director of the Mercantile Bank observed, didn't you speak to me once about an insurance agent who came to get information about me?"

"Yes, I did, in fact, sir. He was a thin man, clean shaven. He said he came to speak to you about life insurance. He asked me all kinds of things. He especially wanted to know if you had a mistress. I finally showed the fellow the door."

"But he had probably learned what he wanted to know," Ethel King said.

"Yes, I must admit that the scoundrel got me to talking. He present-ed himself so cleverly!"

"If we arrested the aggressive fellow who came to your door, we would perhaps recognize in him the one who claimed to be an insurance salesman."

Ethel King pursued her investigations, but she found nothing either that put her on the trail of the criminal. She would have put surveillance on Wanda Baranowsky—she knew her address—but the Russian woman had moved since the previous affair. She must have entrenched herself in the hideout she had chosen, since no one seemed to have seen her again.

"I don't see anything else to do except to have Wanda Baranowsky looked for all over Philadelphia tomorrow," Ethel King whispered in Boyssel's ear. And she added out loud:

"I advise you not to spend the night here. It would be a great deal better if you went to stay in a hotel for some time."

"I'll take your advice, Miss. I too believe I'll be too exposed by staying here. Besides, my apartment is going to stay under surveillance by the police."

"No, that's not necessary," she said, and speaking to Inspector Golding, she said:

"I'll ask you to remove your men, inspector. That apartment is actually the bait by which we can hope to catch the murderers. If we scare them with a great deployment of police, they won't come."

"It will be as you like, Miss King," the Chief answered.

"I know by experience that you never make a decision lightly."

"Let's leave now. I'll watch the house from the outside," the detective said. "As for the butler, he can go to bed in his own bedroom without worrying. No one will harm him."

James was brave. He made no objection. He retired into his bedroom while Ethel King went down the stairs with Paul Boyssel, Golding, and the policemen.

The Frenchman again pointed out to Ethel King the hotel where he intended to register, then he walked away rapidly, while the inspector returned to the police station with his agents. Ethel King went to sit on a bench at the entry to East Park. From there, she could watch the door of the house and windows of Boyssel's apartment.

An Atrocious Crime

Ethel King had been at her post for an hour when she saw a man turn the corner of 33rd Street and approach No. 72. That individual gave the impression of being an elegant gentleman. As he passed under the street lamp, the light fell on his face and Ethel King couldn't hold back an exclamation of surprise. She had just recognized Paul Boyssel.

Why was the Frenchman returning to his house after having spent an hour at the hotel? The great detective thought for a moment of going up to him and asking him for an explanation. However, Ethel King changed her mind; the young man must have forgotten something. The detective didn't want to be seen under any pretext, because it was possible that the criminals were in the neighborhood. She therefore remained on duty where she was and decided to wait until Boyssel came back down. She was sure no one had again entered the house.

James, the house servant, had stretched out on his bed fully clothed. The idea of remaining alone in an apartment where the owner was the target of persecutions by a band of murderers caused him anxiety he couldn't control. He had armed himself with a revolver. He held it in his hand, not turning loose of it for an instant. The poor devil couldn't sleep. He tossed and turned nervously in his bed. From time to time, he lifted his head to listen. And although he had locked the door of his bedroom, he couldn't throw off a feeling of terror. He heard 2 a.m. strike at the clock of a faraway church. The sound had barely receded when he sat up in his bed, his hand clinched on the butt of his revolver.

He had distinctly heard a noise in the corridor, as if someone had opened the door. He was not mistaken. The door closed again and steps could be heard in the hallway. James was brave; once his first emotion had passed, he got up, lit a candle, and opened the door. His revolver in one hand, his candlestick in the other, he went out into the hallway. The door to his master's office was ajar and let filter through the light from a lamp with a rose shade which was lit on the work table.

James slipped noiselessly up to the door and looked through the crack. He made a movement of surprise on seeing a man walking up and down in the room. He pushed open the door and exclaimed:

"Ah! Mr. Boyssel, you've already returned. I thought that you were to stay at the hotel."

James saw his master recoil with astonishment.

"It's me Mr. Boyssel," he said to reassure him. "It's not an intruder."

The Frenchman had recovered. He made a sign to his domestic to leave and told him in an almost inaudible voice:

"I didn't stay at the hotel; I had second thoughts. Go back to bed, James."

"But, Mr. Boyssel, if something happened to you…"

"It's all right…leave me alone…I'm not afraid…"

"But nevertheless, I can't…"

"Go back to bed, I tell you."

These words were also pronounced in an indistinct voice, but in a sharp tone. The butler left, shaking his head. So what was wrong with his master? James found him strange, unusual, and Boyssel never spoke so low and curtly.

James Billing sat on the edge of his bed to think. He would never have gone back to bed at any price. He wanted to be ready to intervene if something happened to his master.

For what reason had Boyssel left the hotel to return to his apartment? Perhaps he had made a new plan with Ethel King. But why did he come back alone? The butler searched his brain in vain to find an explanation for his master's conduct. And suddenly a strange circumstance struck him. He knew that Paul Boyssel, when he left was wearing a gray suit, but the one he was wearing now was black. Why had he changed suits before returning to his apartment? He hadn't taken a valise with him. Where had he procured this suit that James had never seen him wear?

It was probably on the advice of Miss Ethel King that Boyssel had acted in this way. James had a respect without limits for the famous detective, whose cases he followed with great interest in the newspapers. He didn't doubt that Ethel King would shortly succeed in getting rid of his master's terrible enemies.

"She's decided it's to be this way," he murmured. "I don't understand why she's taken this measure, but Ethel King knows what she's doing. I'll get an explanation of the mystery later."

He interrupted his thoughts and raised his head. He quivered with terror. He had just heard, coming from the office, a plaintive moan, followed by a death rattle. For a moment he was paralyzed with terror. What had happened? Had a crime been committed? Had Boyssel been cut down by his ruthless enemies?

Still armed with his revolver, the butler rushed toward the door, but just as he was about to open it, he heard a small mechanism click over. Someone had turned the key in the door from the outside! He was locked in his room. Then he was no longer in doubt that something had happened in the apartment.

James Billing was desperate. Sunk in his own thoughts, he had not heard any criminal footsteps approach his door and activate the lock, so as to prevent him from going to help his master. On the other side of the hallway, separated from him only by two doorways, Paul Boyssel had just fallen by an assassin's bullets, without his prisoner butler being able to do anything to help him. That thought put James in a mad rage.

He threw his whole strength against the door, which moved, cracked, but it was solid. It gave way only after several minutes of effort. He was sweating profusely. When one of the panels finally broke apart, he felt on the point of falling from exhaustion. He put his arm through the hole he had broken in the door. The key had been removed and James was forced to enlarge the opening to get through. He was able with some trouble to climb through the hole and run to the office door. That one was locked from the inside.

"I have to get inside! I must!" James exclaimed.

He ran to get a box of tools from the kitchen. He wanted to get into the office however he could. He seized a pair of pliers and started to work. He still kept his revolver close at hand, since the murderer might at any moment leave suddenly to attack him.

The faithful servant placed the end of his pliers between the door and the door frame and pushed against it with all his strength. Little by little, the panel came apart. Finally James could put his crowbar into the opening. He gave a violent push and the door gave way.

James Billing stood up on the threshold. Then a terrible cry rose to his lips.

His eyes opened wide in horror. He stretched out both his hands as if to push away the atrocious vision open before him. His master was sitting in the chair in front of the desk...his master...decapitated!

The body was leaning backward. A red stain was spreading between the shoulders. The blood had flowed onto the rug and formed a big pool. The victim's clenched hands were holding onto the desk. The knife with which the assassin had delivered the fatal blow was still planted in the shoulder of the poor man. The scoundrel, his crime accomplished, had still had the sinister courage to cut off the cadaver's head to carry it away as a trophy.

James remained struck with astonishment for a moment at the sight of this horrible spectacle. The test was too harsh, even for this brave man. He had just experienced terrible emotions and the physical efforts he had made to get into the office had exhausted him.

An inarticulate moan escaped his lips and he fell down unconscious.

The other people in the building had heard the commotion and they hurried to call the police. James had scarcely been unconscious for a few minutes when two policemen came to ring at the door, and getting no answer, forced the lock. Followed by the neighbors, they entered the room and discovered the decapitated body and James, still unconscious.

Those present at that horrible discovery cried out in horror. No one doubted that the body without a head was that of Paul Boyssel. It was known, in the building, that the Frenchman was pursued by implacable enemies and that the police had made, in that regard, several fruitless investigations. Thus the assassins had succeeded in putting their ghastly plot into execution despite everything. They had triumphed and, as the pinnacle of their cruelty, they had carried off their victim's head.

Naturally, immediate investigations were begun. They searched the house from top to bottom. They made the rounds of the neighborhood, the telephone and the telegraph offices in every direction. An hour later, hundreds of policemen formed a unit and left in search of the head of Paul Boyssel.

As in the former occasions, all that zeal was useless; the searches brought no results. The information obtained from James Billing, whom they had brought back to consciousness, furnished no useful clue. His story only confirmed the general opinion, which was that the body was that of Boyssel. Nevertheless, Inspector Golding couldn't explain how the murderers had accomplished their goal while Ethel King was investigating the case. What had the famous detective done?

A Sinister Present

Ethel King had remained on the park bench to observe Paul Boyssel's house. She saw the light go on in the office. She was expecting her client to come back out, but 30 minutes passed and Paul Boyssel still didn't reappear.

She began to get worried. What could have made the Frenchman decide to return to his house when she had advised him to take refuge in a hotel! She was very curious. Finally, no longer holding back, she resolved to go up to the apartment to get an explanation of that bizarre circumstance. As she was going to get up, she suddenly saw the office window open. A man's silhouette was framed in the light. The man put his leg across the window sill, grabbed the lightning rod cable and slid to earth.

Ethel King was frozen with horror. The man who had just descended into the street was certainly not Paul Boyssel. He had neither his height nor his shape. He was without a doubt the murderer.

The individual had raised his overcoat collar and turned down the borders of his hat. It was impossible to distinguish his features. He must have gotten in from the back side of the house. Ethel King was very worried. She feared that a crime had been committed, that Paul Boyssel, called back to his apartment by inexplicable motives, had been killed by his enemies. The great detective hadn't been able to prevent the catastrophe and that was what caused her the most grief.

The man, who had just descended from the window, walked rapidly down the street. Ethel King hesitated a moment. Should she, first of all, enter the apartment to see what had happened? No, the criminal was escaping her. She must take to her heels. She rushed off in pursuit of the fugitive. She was a past master of the art of shadowing criminals. Besides, the criminal didn't know he was being followed. He walked faster without turning around.

Ethel King noted a fact that heightened her fears. The stranger was carrying a packet under his arm. The object was wrapped in a piece of oilskin. Several times, the man readjusted the folds of the canvas, as if to keep something from falling out of the package. But he didn't completely succeed.

Ethel King suddenly noticed drops of blood on the sidewalk pavement in front of her, and from this moment she saw more as she continued her pursuit. Passing down a dark street, the criminal stopped, put his packet down on a bench and wrapped it with more care. That time his efforts were successful, since Ethel King saw no more drops of blood on her way.

The man reached the railroad station on Girard Avenue. Ethel King entered the ticket area almost at the same time as he did and heard him ask for a ticket to Wynnefield, a suburb of Philadelphia. The train was supposed to depart in 15 minutes. As there were some travelers on the quay, Ethel King took the opportunity to look closely at the criminal. She saw that he wore a long black beard and that he had long hair.

He was seated on a bench and hugging his packet as if it was a precious object. Ethel King walked slowly up and down the quay without seeming to notice the criminal. He appeared very sure of himself. He didn't think he was being watched.

When the train came into the station, he waited until everyone had boarded, then he sat down in a second-class compartment. Ethel King was in the same car as he. She was watching him while appearing to read a newspaper. The man's eyes were gleaming with triumph.

Ethel King was devastated, which rarely happened to her. If her conjectures were correct, if the unfortunate Frenchman had been murdered, she felt herself, in a certain measure, responsible for his death. He had contacted her with confidence and she had promised to protect him. And nevertheless she had not prevented his enemies from striking him down. If she had listened only to her indignation, she would have aimed her revolver at the scoundrel and she would have invited him to open his package. But she controlled herself, knowing very well that the man was only an instrument in the hands of Wanda Baranowsky. He was without a doubt going to see that woman with a demon's heart.

At the end of 20 minutes, the train stopped at the Wynnefield station. The stranger got off. Naturally Ethel King continued to shadow him at a distance. The man walked across the whole suburb and finally stopped in front of a pretty country house surrounded by a large garden and with a conservatory beside it. He opened the wrought iron gate with the key he had on him. Ethel King made a quick tour of the garden and scaled the fence which separated the villa from an empty field.

The detective had not noticed that she herself had been followed from Philadelphia by a man who kept himself cautiously at a very great distance. This man had also come to Wynnefield by the train, but he had gotten into another compartment. He got into the garden through the same pathway as Ethel King, who was cautiously slipping toward the house, hiding behind trees and bushes. She saw the criminal ring the bell at the front steps.

It was already becoming daylight, the heavens turning pale and the first rays of sunlight coloring the east. A maid came at the end of several minutes, answering the doorbell.

"Ah! Mr. Petroff, it's you," she said, on opening the door. "What is it you wish?"

"I must speak to Wanda Baranowsky. Announce me."

"But Madam is in bed. She's asleep," the maid objected.

"That doesn't matter. Wake Miss Baranowsky. Tell her that it's I and that I'm bringing total victory. I guarantee you that she'll get up immediately and will even give you a good tip."

Ethel King hadn't lost a word of that conversation. She judged by the stranger's accent that he too was Russian and she told herself that he must be one of those seeking the dancer's hand. She wanted at any cost to get into the house. This was not easy to do. The servants were already awake and she greatly risked being surprised if she tried to enter through a door.

While walking around the villa, looking for an entry, she found a window in the conservatory open. She climbed across the window sill and hid behind a huge plant. She remained motionless a long time, listening. The conservatory's decoration denoted great luxury. The paths, covered with colored gravel twisted between beds of rare flowers which gave off delightful perfume. A statue rose here and there among the greenery. Jets of water gushed from fountains where gold fishes were swimming.

Ethel King walked on the edges of the flower beds to avoid the sound of gravel crunching under her feet. She slipped to the door separating the winter garden and the house. She was about to enter the house when she heard footsteps. She jumped quickly backward and crouched behind a plant.

It was just in time. Petroff had just entered. He still had his packet under his arm, but he had taken off his overcoat and hat. He held in his left hand a silver platter like those used to serve drinks. Ethel King was very curious. The Russian disappeared behind a huge plant and she didn't dare approach to see what he was doing. In a few moments, Petroff reappeared and began to walk about in the pathway. He was smiling and murmuring unintelligible words, as if experiencing diabolical joy and could hardly wait for the arrival of the mistress of the house.

Finally the door to the winter garden opened. A tall and elegant woman entered. It was Wanda Baranowsky. She was really a first class beauty and Ethel King immediately realized that that woman was perfectly capable of making a man insane with love. An inflexible will could be read in her dark eyes. Her whole aspect expressed cruelty, but that only made her more exciting. In all her bearing, that woman had something majestic. You felt she was accustomed to commanding. She approached her morning visitor haughtily and greeted him with condescension, like a princess.

"Ah! Good Morning, my dear Petroff," she said. "You had my maid awake me by announcing total victory."

He took her hand and placed ardent kisses on it. Then he looked at her, his eyes shining with triumph and replied:

"Yes, I have indeed been victorious, my dear Wanda."

The dancer sat down on a bench and looked at the Russian with curiosity.

"It's very daring on your part to affirm such a thing. You know what I mean by victory."

The scoundrel burst out laughing.

"Yes, I know, naturally," he answered.

Then he approached the young woman and said to her, his voice hoarse with emotion:

"Do you remember, Wanda, when we were seated side by side on this same bench two months ago and I begged you to give me your love? You spurned me and your cruelty plunged me into despair."

"Yes, I remember."

"And when you saw to what mental tortures I was prey to, you told me there was one way to conquer you, body and soul."

"I remember that."

"Is it true? Repeat to me what you said then."

The Russian woman stood up. Her face took on a hard, haggard look, which brought to mind the head of Medusa.

"Yes, I'm going to repeat it," she replied. "I shouted to you then: 'Bring me the head of my mortal enemy, the Frenchman, Paul Boyssel, who abandoned me and who killed my brother, and I will belong to you, body and soul.' "

"Yes, that's what you said to me, and it was for me like an order from on high. I don't hold back from anything to conquer you, because you are everything on earth for me. Will you keep your word, today, Wanda?"

"Do you doubt it? I will love passionately the man who avenges me on my mortal enemy."

The criminal let out an exclamation of joy.

"Is that the truth?" he cried out with rapture.

"The truth," she assured him. "Go and accomplish the mission I gave you. Then I will belong to you. But I must tell you that another like you is looking to merit that prize. The actor, Fortino, also wishes to earn my love. He has sworn to me to kill the damned Frenchman."

"He won't succeed in doing that because I have already fulfilled my mission."

The young woman stood up excitedly.

"Petroff…you…you were able to do that?" she cried out. "I don't dare believe it."

"I have taken vengeance on Paul Boyssel!"

"When?" the Russian woman asked in a state of unimaginable excitement.

"Tonight. He was seated at his desk. I plunged a knife into his heart and I've brought the proof of what I claim."

The young woman fell back onto the bench and said:

"That's good. Show me that proof."

He went to get something behind the huge plant and came back, carrying his victim's bleeding head on the silver platter.

"Here's the head you asked me for, dear Wanda."

The Russian woman had turned pale, but soon the color returned to her cheeks; her eyes were shining; a diabolical smile formed on her lips.

"Finally," she murmured, "finally my vengeance is satisfied."

Ethel King couldn't wait any longer. She jumped out from her hiding place. She shook with horror at the sight of the spectacle before her. It was a second Salomé that she had in front of her.

So the scoundrels had managed to assassinate the unfortunate Paul Boyssel!

Wanda and Petroff didn't notice the detective. The Russian was contemplating Wanda Baranowsky and the dancer couldn't take her eyes off the bleeding head. Then Ethel King brandished her revolver at the two scoundrels and shouted to them in a harsh voice:

"Don't make a move! In the name of the law, I arrest you! You'll pay for this atrocious crime on the gallows."

Petroff dropped the silver tray with his horrible trophy. Wanda turned pale and was dumbfounded on seeing the detective. Ethel King was herself terribly excited, because she now had the proof that Paul Boyssel had been murdered.

"Scoundrels," she said, "I couldn't keep you from killing your victim, but I will at least watch to see that you receive the punishment you deserve for your crime."

At this moment a male voice was heard through the winter garden window.

"There's a mistake, Miss King; I'm still alive. That's not my head!"

At these words, Paul Boyssel jumped through the window.

Ethel King looked at him, mute with astonishment. She didn't understand how that man could be standing safe and sound before her, when a decapitated head whose features so much resembled his, was lying there on the path.

Wanda Baranowsky had become sick. Petroff was trembling all over. Suddenly he jumped toward the head and picked it up. He tore at the hair, which came lose, the beard, which came off.

"Great gods!" the scoundrel stammered. "I made a mistake. That's Fortino, the actor."

He dropped his victim's head and did not try to defend himself when Ethel King came forward to put handcuffs on him. Ethel also handcuffed Wanda Baranowsky and asked Paul Boyssel to go for the police.

The two prisoners, against whom the severed head constituted an overwhelming charge were soon behind bars. The next day they found Wanda Baranowsky lifeless in her cell. She had taken poison to escape hanging. Petroff's confessions finished clarifying the circumstances of the drama. Wanda Baranowsky had two men who loved her with an insane passion. That hellish woman had known how to nourish her two lovers' passion without giving anything to either of them.

The two worshipers were Wassily Petroff, an enormously rich Russian, and Fortino, the actor. Wanda wanted to make them the instruments of her vengeance. She had sworn that she would belong to the one who brought her Paul Boyssel's head. The two insane men had tried everything to satisfy the horrible caprice of their mistress. The Russian had first of all shot at Paul Boyssel in the lobby of the Mercantile Bank. The first attempt having failed, he posted himself in a vacant apartment in a house across from that of the Frenchman. He had shot at James, that he had seen at his master's desk and that he had taken for Boyssel.

As for the actor, Fortino, he had slipped into Boyssel's apartment and put the two poisonous snakes in his bed, and then hidden in the bathroom. Fortino had taken imprints of the locks of the house and had false keys made. His first plan abortive, he had conceived a refined one. The same night he had disguised himself to look like Paul Boyssel, put on a false beard and a wig, and with clever make-up made his face to resemble that of the Frenchman. In this way he counted on being able to enter the house without any obstacle. The butler himself would take him to be his master. If he didn't find Boyssel, he would wait for him and his victim could no longer escape him.

The actor had been the victim of his own stratagem. Petroff had entered from the back of the house and had murdered Fortino, whom he took to be Boyssel.

Wassily Petroff was condemned to death and finished with a rope around his neck.

As for Paul Boyssel, he was forever rid of his dangerous enemies. He adequately proved his gratitude to Ethel King, the great detective.

ETHEL KING
LE NICK CARTER FÉMININ

Le Maléfice.

Ethel King n'hésita pas; elle tira et Bob s'écroula, tué sur le coup.

6. A CRIMINAL ASSOCIATION

Dreaded Enemies

Ethel King was at an evening gathering in the home of Mr. Dooner, a rich Philadelphia industrialist who was giving a brilliant reception at his private townhouse on 35th Street. The famous detective, who had for many years maintained an excellent, friendly relationship with the Dooner family, had gladly accepted an invitation to the party. Our heroine was the object of great consideration by the hosts and their guests, because everyone had heard her exploits praised.

To judge by her grace, her friendliness, her feminine charm, you would never have supposed that Ethel King, in the exercise of her profession, frequented the dregs of humanity when necessary and she could, when she had to, accommodate herself to the mores and manners of the most inferior classes.

It was already 7 p.m., but no one among the guests was yet thinking of leaving. The evening parties at the Dooner's were always so pleasant that they lasted well into the night.

Ethel King was talking with some ladies when a butler came up respectfully.

"A gentleman is asking to speak to Miss King about urgent business," he said. "He's waiting for Miss King in Mr. Dooner's office."

The servant held out a visiting card on which the young woman read:

Harry Sweed, Police Inspector, Camden.

The great detective didn't hesitate to answer the visitor's appeal. When Ethel King went into Dooner's luxurious office, a slender man with a clean-shaven face, rushed forward to meet her. She had been acquainted with the inspector for a long time. She exchanged a cordial handshake with him and asked:

"What brings you here, Mr. Sweed? You find me very curious."

"I went to your house, Miss. They told me you were at an evening party at the Dooner house," answered the policeman. "The case that brings me is so serious that I couldn't wait there; I've come here. Pardon me for having chased you to your friends' party. You probably know that

Camden's security has been troubled for some time by a gang of scoundrels with incredible daring. A great number of shops have already been pillaged by the criminals. The last one was that of a small jeweler, who, ruined by the burglary, had to file for bankruptcy. But the thieves, not satisfied with breaking into houses, attacked passersby with weapons at night, in the street. The city police are up to their eyeballs in work. We've had to double the sentries. The bad neighborhoods are constantly patrolled. Nevertheless, despite my efforts, I haven't had the slightest success to record; not one of these rascals has fallen into our hands.

"Now, here it is that Browning, the well-known industrialist, has just been murdered, two hours ago, in his yacht, in Camden. The unfortunate man was coming back from a cruise. He was on board alone, with a sailor. The murderers pulled off their job just as the yacht docked. The sailor was struck from behind and lost consciousness. As for Browning, he was found stabbed repeatedly in his cabin. As in the preceding cases, the criminals didn't leave any clues. Nevertheless, I don't doubt that this crime must be attributed to the gang that has so long infested Camden. The scoundrels have reached an unheard of impudence. They commit their crime almost under the eyes of the police. There actually is a station on the quay, not 20 paces from the spot where Browning's yacht was moored. Nevertheless, the police on duty weren't aware of anything. When the sailor, who had a serious head injury, regained consciousness, he dragged himself as far as the station and made his statement.

"We again find ourselves faced with an enigma. But this time, I've had enough. We have to be done with it, whatever the cost. That's why I've come to beg you to take charge of this case. If someone is capable of unmasking the villains and handing them over to justice, it's you!"

"I'll try, Mr. Sweed," Ethel King answered. "So you don't have a clue that will let you pick up the trail of these rascals?"

"No, the sailor didn't see anyone. The criminals slid into the boat without making any noise."

"I want, first of all, to examine the place of the crime," declared the great detective. "I'll be down there in an hour, at the latest, Mr. Sweed."

The inspector, delighted with Ethel King's consent, thanked her warmly and took leave of her.

The young woman returned to the drawing room and explained to the mistress of the house that she had to leave immediately. She told Mrs. Dooner about Browning's murder. The news spread immediately among the guests and caused great excitement.

The first thing that Ethel King did was to return to her house on Garden Street and change clothes. She woke up her assistant, Charley Lux, and told him to get dressed and join her as soon as possible in Camden, where Browning's yacht was moored. As for herself, she got back in her car, had herself driven to the ferryboat on the Delaware River, and embarked for Camden.

Inspector Sweed had pointed out to her the exact location of the yacht's quay. It was almost 1 a.m. The streets were deserted. Snow fell and a glacial wind whipped the flakes against Ethel King's face. The young woman could see only several feet in front of her. In the storm, the street lamps were scarcely giving off any light, resembling pale, trembling stars.

Ethel King had been making slow, difficult progress in a southerly direction when she heard hurried footsteps behind her, the sound deadened by the snow. She tried to turn around, but at that same instant she felt herself grabbed by the throat and brutal hands pulled a sort of hood over her head.

She tried to cry out; the heavy material muffled her voice. She estimated that there were at least three of her aggressors. Despite her resistance, the thieves tied her feet and her hands. She was now stretched out on the snow, not even able to see what was happening around her. The sack they had tied over her head made breathing very difficult. The men picked her up and carried her. She tried to orient herself, but that was almost impossible. She was aware that they were carrying her into a house, that they went down a corridor and descended a stairway. Finally, the smell of mold coming to her nostrils, made her conclude that she was in a cellar.

Her captors deposited her on the ground. Ethel King heard the buzzing of voices, but couldn't understand the words. A little later, they picked her up to place her on a bench, her shoulders leaning against the wall. She was aware that another person was seated next to her.

They finally took off her hood. She looked first of all to her right and recognized Inspector Sweed, bound as she was. The two prisoners found themselves in a spacious cellar where chests and bundles were stacked up. It was probably there that the thieves stashed their loot. A large gasoline lamp fixed with a white metal reflector spread rather bright light into the room. The cellar had no exit except a large door reinforced with iron. There was no window.

Four badly clothed men with menacing faces were watching the captives. The room was furnished with a rickety table and some worm-eaten chairs. Some straw mattresses lined up in a corner served as beds for the thieves.

One of the thieves, a tall, gawky fellow with a brutal expression swaggered in front of the prisoners.

"Good evening, Mr. Sweed; good evening, Miss Ethel King. How do you like it here?"

Sweed tore furiously at his bonds.

"Turn us loose immediately," he shouted, "or you'll suffer the consequences of your unspeakable act."

Four bursts of laughter answered him.

"That would just settle your case, Mr. Sweed, if we untied you and put a revolver in each of your hands. Then you would arrest us and we would all go to prison."

"You're villains!"

"...that you'd really like to grab. Since you really wanted to get to know us, we didn't want to refuse you that satisfaction any longer, because we're considerate of the police. Unfortunately, you'll pay dearly for the pleasure of having seen us; you'll pay for it with your lives. But I think that you wouldn't want to hold it against us, because we have conducted ourselves toward you as perfect gentlemen."

Sweed was very pale. He threw desperate looks at Ethel King, who remained impassive.

"Until now, Mr. Sweed, you weren't dangerous for us, the criminal continued. Your efforts only amused us. The measures you took were too clumsy to frighten us. I can tell you, just between us, that more than once I had a drink with the good policemen that you set on our trail and told them the most outrageous stories. Most of your policemen are as stupid as you are, Mr. Sweed. In spite of everything, we had you watched, because it could happen that you, by chance, might have an idea of genius. You know what they say: 'Even a blind hen can find a grain of wheat.' And you've found that grain this evening, Mr. Sweed. When you came to the yacht to investigate, you were beside yourself and paced up and down the deck like an enraged tiger. Before long, however, you calmed down and sent your men out in all directions, as you never failed to do in similar cases.

"We didn't miss any of that. We were watching you. At a certain moment, deep in your reflections, you didn't move; then you struck your forehead as if you'd just had an idea. You muttered something between your teeth, and you at last went to the embarcadero to arrange the boat's passage to Philadelphia."

The prisoners had listened without saying a word, but at that moment Sweed exclaimed with rage:

"May the Devil take you! So you were close to me then?"

"One of us was hidden in the little boat beside the yacht and was watching you with a spy glass. I myself followed you to Philadelphia and saw you enter Garden Street. Now we knew very well who lived at No. 77 of that street. I understood that you had really had a good idea that time. You wanted to solicit Ethel King's help. Ethel King is an adversary to be taken into account. We've always told ourselves that our job would become dangerous the day that spy took up our trail, and in that case, we would need to take the necessary steps.

"The opportunity presented itself. You didn't find Miss King at home, Mr. Sweed, because she was at Mr. Dooner's home. I followed you there; I heard you talk to the doorman. You returned to Camden; we were on your heels, and when you had reached the quays to return to Browning's yacht, we were sure of picking you up tonight to enjoy your nice company. It was the same for Miss King as for you. Her assistant, Charley Lux, was supposed to follow her. He too will soon be ours."

Sweed gritted his teeth.

"Yes, yes, I understand you," the thief sniggered, "the surprise isn't agreeable. It's really too bad; the one time you have an intelligent idea, to see it made useless like this. It's sad to think that Ethel King, the master detective without an equal, has let herself be taken so easily."

"What scoundrels you are! Even so, Ethel King will bring an end to you," Sweed shouted with indignation.

"Tomorrow, when she's dead? Her ghost will appear to take us to prison!"

Bursts of loud laughter greeted that outburst. Ethel King, who hadn't yet said anything, calmly observed:

"Why are you laughing? My revenge will come sooner than you think."

The gang bombarded her with sarcasms and the leader declared:

"You'll stay here. We intend to amuse ourselves this evening with a little target practice. You'll look a little different then. I'll bet you'll be crying and begging us to stop."

"I'll take that bet," the young woman answered. And speaking to Sweed, she added:

"Calm down, Mr. Sweed. These rascals aren't worth the trouble of getting into such a state, because they are of unimaginable stupidity. I have never seen such fools."

"How dare you talk to us like that?" one of them screamed.

Another pulled out a knife and made as if to jump on Ethel King, but his comrades held him back.

"Not yet," they shouted, "we first have to make her pay for the insults she's just thrown in our face. Wait until Glensing and Parrish are here. Then we'll get to work. I'm going to fetch them; they're probably at Thornton's on the other side of the Street and won't guess that we've gotten hold of our most dangerous enemy."

With these words, the leader started toward the door with one of his accomplices.

"Watch our two prisoners carefully!" he again cautioned the others before leaving.

The door shut noisily. The two thieves who had remained to guard their captives took chairs and sat down beside the bench on which Ethel King and the inspector had been placed, their hands and feet tied. The scoundrels were determined not to stop watching their victims for an instant.

A Surprise

Ethel King pretended not to hear the sarcasms the criminals were hurling at her. She looked at the inspector and smiled.

"Well, Mr. Sweed, what do you think? Shall we stay here?"

The policeman sighed.

"What a question!" he said. "What can we do? We can't do anything to try to escape. But I'm sure our agents are looking for us. They'll come here and then too bad for these rascals!"

"They'll never find this cellar, even if they looked for it until the day of judgment," one of the criminals continued. "No, no, you're lost without any hope. In an hour you'll be nothing but cadavers!"

Ethel King greeted these words with an amused peal of laughter which disconcerted the two criminals. They couldn't understand how a woman could still laugh in such a desperate situation. Inspector Sweed looked at the great detective with admiration.

"I'm amazed at your calm, Miss King," he said. "To look at you, you wouldn't think we were in terrible danger."

"That's no longer the case," Ethel King replied in the most tranquil tone. "I don't know who could keep us from getting out of here."

The two criminal exchanged an astonished look and then one of them sneered:

"I believe Miss King has lost her mind. Fear has made her mad."

"Unless she's trying to scare us," the other one noted. "But she won't succeed. She can't escape death."

"We're all mortal, gentlemen," the young woman declared in a sarcastic tone. "But if you imagine I'm going to end my existence tonight, in this cellar, you're committing a huge error."

"Oh? And so what will you do?"

"I'm going to arrest your gang, and I'm going to begin with you."

The two scoundrels bent double with laughter.

"You want to arrest us? That's priceless! We're really curious to see how you're going to go about it. Come now, Miss King, the incomparable sleuth, the biggest star in the detectives' heaven, arrest us!"

"As you like. In the name of the law, I arrest you. Put your hands in the air!"

The young woman had spoken in a sharp, incisive voice. At the same time, she had freed her arms that the thieves had tied behind the back, and was pointing two revolvers at the criminals. They yelled out in fear and rose hastily, turning over their chairs.

"Raise your hands in the air," Ethel King ordered for the second time.

One of the scoundrels obeyed, but the other swore an abominable oath and reached for a weapon in his pocket. Without hesitating, Ethel King pressed the trigger and a shot echoed from the ceiling. A bullet pierced the hand the bandit had carried to his pocket and wounded him in the stomach. He fell down, moaning.

"The next time I'll aim for the head," the young woman said coolly.

She put one of her revolvers in her pocket while keeping the other pointed at the second criminal standing in front of her, his hands in the air and trembling all over. With her knife she cut the cords holding her feet; then she freed the inspector who had watched that rapid scene, mute with astonishment.

"Will you please take care of tying up these two rogues, Mr. Sweed," she said. "Don't be afraid to tie them tight."

While Ethel King continued to watch the bandits, her revolver in her hand, Sweed took care of tying them up and soon the scoundrels were lying beside each other on the floor. Then the young woman looked at the inspector, smiling.

"What do you say about that, Mr. Sweed?"

"I don't understand it at all; it's almost as if you were gifted with supernatural power."

"Is that so? Nevertheless, the explanation is simple!"

Ethel King pointed out the spot on the wall where the thieves had placed her. Just above the bench there was an old rusty nail. While exchanging ironic comments with the criminals, Ethel King had rubbed the cords holding her wrists against that nail and had succeeded in breaking them down. She had done this so cleverly that her guards hadn't noticed anything. They also hadn't seen her take her revolvers out of the secret pocket in her skirt.

"You see, Mr. Sweed, I owe my freedom to that nail. It goes without saying that the thieves, who've lodged in this cellar for a long time, knew of the existence of that iron point. Nevertheless, they sat me down in that spot. I was perfectly correct in maintaining that those pigs have no equals for stupidity."

"You're indeed right," the inspector answered. "Miss King, you're admirable!"

"Let's leave these scoundrels here, temporarily, and send the police to watch them. As for us, let's go with some agents to the Thornton bar. We'll probably nab the rest of the gang there. You see, Mr. Sweed, these people, who thought they were so wicked, made their capture easy."

The bound thieves shouted with rage; the wounded one writhed in pain; but Ethel King and the inspector didn't pay any attention. The door wasn't locked and so they climbed the stairs to the top, where they found a second door, open like the first. They entered a corridor without a window. Ethel King turned on her pocket electric flashlight. This passage measured about 13 feet in length and ended at a battered dirt wall. A ladder was placed under a big trap door which could be seen on the ceiling.

The inspector climbed up the ladder and raised the panel. He looked out cautiously at first and told his companion in a low voice what he saw. The trap door led to a deserted stable. The top of the trap door was covered with hay, which hid it from indiscreet investigation.

There was nothing surprising in the fact that the thieves believed they were safe in this hideout. They left cautiously through the trap door and closed it behind them. The stable opened onto a deserted courtyard. Sweed and Ethel King could reach the street without any trouble. They found that the building was No. 59 on Federal Street in Camden, east of the port. The Thornton Bar the thieves had mentioned was on Cooper Street, a quarter of an hour from there.

As soon as he was in the street, Sweed blew a whistle to call policemen. He sent some of the agents to the hideout and ordered others to go find backups. He gave the order not to take the two prisoners immediately to the station, but to wait for that until their accomplices in the bar had been arrested.

The reinforcements the inspector had ordered were not long in arriving, and the police then started toward Cooper Street to Thornton's Bar .

A Partial Success

On the way, the little group met Charley Lux, who had arrived from Philadelphia, going along the quays to meet Ethel King at Browning's yacht. He heard the story of the adventures of his cousin and of Sweed with astonishment, and trembled at the thought of the dangers they had run.

The policemen approached Cooper Street in little groups so as not to draw attention. Ethel King was well acquainted with Will Thornton's bar as was the inspector. The establishment was only frequented by the worst elements of Camden. The room, in a deep cellar, was packed every evening with a mass of dubious people.

The police frequently went down into that tavern to make arrests; but they had to go there in force because the clients had often opposed the representatives of the law. The dangerous scum who frequented the saloon were always armed, so that bloody brawls were not rare. In the present case, they were trying to arrest four thieves, and that operation promised to be very hazardous.

"There are certain to be 50 hoodlums at Thornton's Bar at this hour," the inspector declared. "Not a single one of them would hesitate to take on the defense of our thieves. We must expect a battle."

Ethel King thought a moment.

"No, Mr. Sweed, in this case," she finally said, "we're going to act in such a way that this situation will end without combat, or if we're absolutely forced to come to blows, we'll arrange it so the encounter isn't murderous."

"That's easy to say," Sweed answered. "How will you manage it?"

"I have a plan. I'm going to my little apartment on Front Street; then, when I'm disguised, I'll go into the establishment, alone at first. I hope to find a way to make the weapons of these rogues harmless."

The inspector looked at Ethel with admiration.

"I would very much like to see how you'll do that."

"That will depend on the circumstances. As for you, Mr. Sweed, you take care of surrounding the house. Watch the main entry as well as the courtyard, but try, temporarily, to see that no one notices the presence of policemen. Your men can reach the courtyard by going through the neighboring houses and scaling the walls and the fences."

"Perfect. I'll give my orders in that way. I myself will be part of the group watching the house from the rear."

"Listen to me again. You will probably hear some revolver shots in the saloon, and even a real fusillade, but don't let yourself get excited by that and come into the room. A pistol shot is not a signal to you. But if I whistle, come in with your men through all the doors at the same time. I'll point out to you the ones you should arrest."

"I'll follow your instructions, Miss, but let's hope that none of the criminals escape us."

"Yes, let's hope so," Ethel King answered. "To tell the truth, there's no way to know if Will Thornton has set up secret exits in his establishment through which his clients can escape unseen. In any case, I'll do the impossible to see that no one slips through our hands."

The young woman left after having ordered Charley to join the policemen who were supposed to watch the principal entry to the bar. She went quickly to her little apartment on Front Street and proceeded to completely transform herself. She metamorphosed into a young man of doubtful elegance, put on a glossy black jacket, an old pair of boots, a sportsman's hat of a greenish color, under which she could hide her thick hair. Her false collar wasn't immaculately white and her tie was of an indefinite shade,

In addition to her usual weapons, she stuck an antique two-shot pistol in her pocket. She put on makeup to appear paler, and glued on a thin mustache so cleverly that even the sharpest eye wouldn't have been able to detect the fake. To complete her character, she provided herself with a cane. She had taken less than 30 minutes to complete this disguise. She looked at herself in the glass with satisfaction. She told herself that the criminals would surely not recognize her.

Ten minutes later, she turned into Cooper Street and checked to see that the policemen in charge of watching the bar were well hidden. Charley was in front of the establishment's main door, in an obscure passage. On seeing someone arrive, the young man told himself that that person must be his cousin. It was impossible for him to recognize her at first, but he was expecting to see her in disguise and, looking closely, he noticed that the character was exactly the same height as Ethel King.

The character opened the door of the bar and entered. The bar's atmosphere was heavy with thick tobacco smoke. Almost all the tables were occupied. There was a clientele of about 60 persons of the two sexes. Brutality, the absence of scruples, could be read on all the faces. Among those people, there probably wasn't one who had not had a taste of prison.

Ethel King walked calmly past the rows of tables and immediately aroused the clients' attention. They had never seen this young man in the bar, and a new-comer was always the object of careful examination.

"Well! Who's this greenhorn?" someone shouted loudly. "What's he doing here?"

Ethel King had noted the thieves she was looking for, but she passed in front of them, pretending not to see them. She smiled and nodded to those throwing jibes at her. She went to the bar and asked for a whiskey. The waiter questioned her while waiting on her.

"So who are you? I've never seen you here before."

"That's not surprising," she answered him. "I'm from Baltimore. I've only been in Camden two days."

"What's you trade?"

"Oh! I have a good one. If the police here aren't too hard, I'll do a good business."

The bar waiter winked, a sign he understood.

"Ah! I understand," he said.

But Ethel King shook her head.

"I'll bet anything you like that you can't guess what I am," she said. "What you're thinking is completely wrong."

"Really? You surprise me. Then why did you mention the police?"

"Well! In a lot of cities, things are immediately stirred up if you fire some revolver shots in a saloon."

"I'm not following you. Do you like to handle a revolver that much?"

"But of course. I'm a marksman by profession."

"Professional marksman? Thunderation! Then you must be extremely good at it!" the man, clearly struck with respect, exclaimed.

"On my word, yes I am. Would it be possible for me to give a showing here?"

"Naturally! Amusements always go over well."

"But if the police hear shooting, would they try to interfere?"

"Bah! The police don't come near this place. The policeman who entered to shut down the demonstration would be thrown outside immediately."

"Well, in that case, I'll begin. I can tell you, without bragging, I'm the best marksman in the world," Ethel King declared, straightening up proudly.

The bar manager addressed the drinkers in a loud voice.

"Ladies and Gentlemen, we have with us, an extraordinary man, an incomparable marksman. The master offers to give us a demonstration of his skill and I think that you would all like to see him exercise it for you."

"Oh! Very good! Marvelous!" they shouted from different directions.

"I'll give a dollar!"

"Me too!"

"I first want to see what he can do!"

Ethel King took out of her pocket a small coin attached to the end of a string. She went to fix the string under the top of the back door frame, so that the coin hung across from the hinges. Then she exhibited her two-shot pistol and returned to the other end of the room, against the table where the four thieves were sitting.

"Ladies and Gentlemen, I'm going to show you proof of my skill, but before that I invite the persons present to try their skill against me. I claim there is no marksman here who is my equal!"

She waved about a $50 bank note.

"I promise to give this $50 bill to the one who, from the place I'm standing, can shoot the string from the edge of the coin."

There was a general brouhaha; men stood up, a revolver in their hand. The four thieves came forward first, Johnny, their leader, at their head.

"I'm going to try to win that money," he shouted.

He raised his revolver and fired, six times, one shot after the other. The bullets drove into the door without hitting the string. A burst of laughter greeted that failure and everybody began to fire. The establishments' clients came one after the other to stand at the spot indicated and to discharge their weapons. The door was soon as full of holes as a sieve, but not one had hit the target.

Ethel King had wanted to force the criminals to fire their revolvers. She knew by experience that most of them didn't have extra ammunition.

A voice rang out: "It's your turn now! Shoot, young man! Let's see if you aren't bragging and if you are as clever a marksman as you say!"

"Just a moment," Ethel King answered. "I'm going to go see if one of you hasn't nicked the string."

She went to the door and pretended to look at the improvised target. But she suddenly opened the door and putting her whistle to her lips, blew a long blast. The spectators didn't at first understand what that meant, but as soon as the doors let in policemen, a concert of howls broke out. Ethel King's clear voice dominated the tumult.

"Halt! Don't anyone move! The first one who tries to resist is a dead man! We're here to arrest four thieves. We won't bother the other clients."

A Saloon Battle

These words did not calm the uproar. No longer able to use their firearms, the criminals brandished their knives.

Ethel King made her way toward the table where Johnny and his friends were sitting.

"I'm arresting you!" she shouted.

There was a rush forward. Inspector Sweed and the dozen policemen pushing through the crowd behind the young woman were separated from her. Ethel King, pushed back against the bar, saw herself threatened by lifted knives. She pressed the trigger of her revolver; one of her attackers rolled to the floor, moaning. But several hands paralyzed her right arm, forcing her to release her weapon. She fired with her other revolver she was holding in her left hand and a second attacker fell. Then the disguised detective jerked loose and jumped on top of the bar to escape the knives directed toward her stomach.

That melee had lasted only a few seconds. At the other end of the saloon, Sweed and the police were resisting as well as they could the assault of the frenzied gang, which was trying by any means to force them into the courtyard.

The criminals were making projectiles of everything that fell into their hands: beer tumblers, saucers, platters rained down on the agents. Fortunately they frequently missed their target and caused as much harm to the other hoodlums as to their adversaries. The women, most of all, were enraged. They climbed up on tables and threw glasses and bottles in all directions.

"Down with the cops! Kill them! Bleed them!" they bellowed.

Several policemen had already been wounded and Sweed was beginning to wonder if the affair wasn't going to end with the massacre of all his companions.

"Shoot into the pack," he ordered, so as to give a little more room to the little troop.

Shots rang out and the wounded's cries of pain mingled with the criminals' vociferations of rage. In a moment of panic, the gang retreated to the back of the room where Ethel King was isolated in the middle of her enemies. The tables were overturned, dragging down in their fall those who had used them as a platform and made a barricade in front of which the policemen were forced to stop.

Sweed was in mortal worry about the fate of Ethel King. He heard revolver shots at the back of the saloon and surmised that the great detective was in the process of fighting a desperate battle.

The criminals, at first disconcerted by the fusillade, had regrouped on seeing the policemen held back by the obstacle formed by the stacked up tables and benches. They posted themselves behind the barricade and defended it furiously against their adversaries.

Sweed was panic-stricken.

"Charge, boys! Charge!" he was repeating mechanically.

But it was impossible for the agents to obey him. They had trouble holding back the unleashed rabble and instead of charging, they had to clear a way to pass through.

Ethel King looked down on the crowd of her enemies. The bar waiter, who was still behind the bar counter grabbed her by one of her legs and pulled her backward so roughly that he caused her to fall on her side between the counter and the wall.

"Cop spy!" he bellowed, "I'll split your belly!"

He grabbed a heavy earthenware jug which contained lemons and was placed under the table and brandished it as if to crush the young woman. She could hesitate no longer. In her fall she had lost one of her revolvers but she still had one. She aimed it at the man. A detonation sounded and the scoundrel collapsed, shot dead with a bullet between the eyes. Ethel King jumped up with a bound and threatened the howling crowd with her weapon.

"The first one who comes near me, I'll make him share the same fate at that rascal," she shouted.

She had lost her cap in the fight, and her hair had come undone.

"It's a woman!" one of the thieves exclaimed.

"Ethel King!" roared Johnny's voice.

The scum remained stunned for a moment; then the clamor began again, more enraged. The women heaped curses on the policemen.

"I'll have her hide," Johnny was still shouting in the middle of the tumult, and he made a motion to throw himself on Ethel King, but others did the same and there resulted another jostling for position.

"Kill Ethel King!" shrieked the scoundrels.

There was a frenzied rush forward.

Ethel King still had four shots left in her revolver. That wasn't enough to fight against such a troop of ferocious beasts. The young woman really wanted to pick up the revolver she had dropped but didn't find time; if she had taken her weapon off the gang for a second to stoop down, she would have lost the last chance to hold off the criminals.

"The first man who tries to jump on top of the bar is a dead man!" she shouted, as she backed up against the shelf holding bottles, glasses, and carafes.

The furious mob hesitated for a moment, then surged to the right and left to surround the lead top bar. The detective could not, especially with a single revolver, stand off her enemies from all directions at once. She noticed that the clients of the establishment were divided into two groups, one trying to grab her, the other fighting foot by foot to prevent the police from coming to her aid. An empty space remained in the middle of the room between the two. Even the tables and benches had been picked up and carried to the barricade to re-enforce it.

Ethel King, seeing herself on the point of being taken, instinctively adopted the only method she had to escape her assailants, at least temporarily. She fired a shot at the group pressing against the bar to force them to spread out a little. She got to the top of the bar, jumped, and came down lightly in the middle of the room, in the unoccupied section.

The situation, nevertheless, remained most critical, since the young woman was exposed to the fury of the criminals, without any protection, and without a means of retreat.

Her exploit of agility was greeted by angry cries, and, in an instant, Ethel King again saw herself threatened from 20 sides at once.

Sweed and the policemen had seen their ally at the moment she jumped on top of the bar. Conscious of the terrible danger she was in, they redoubled their efforts. The barricade defenders, distracted by what was happening behind them, resisted more weakly. The police took advantage of that fact to push aside the tables and benches, which turned over noisily. With revolver shots and clubs they cleared a passage through the crowd and reached Ethel King, just as she, after tenacious resistance, was about to succumb under the sheer weight of numbers.

"Thank God!" Sweed shouted, his voice trembling with emotion. "You're safe and sound, Miss King! If something had happened to you, I would never have forgiven myself for having let you risk this dangerous situation."

The police were answering with gun shots a new assault by the gang. Resistance suddenly ceased. Mad panic seized the criminals when they realized that the police were definitely the stronger.

"Where are our fellows?" the inspector asked.

"Follow me!" Ethel King shouted.

She broke through the crowd in the direction of Johnny and his accomplices. As the police were guarding the bar's doors, the panic-stricken clients looked for refuge under the bar, in the cellar, on the little stairway that led to the second floor. The floor was littered with the dead and wounded. A gaslight had been broken in the course of the fight and continued to burn, throwing out a great high flame which threatened to set the ceiling on fire. Suddenly the sound of a breaking window resounded in the room.

"They're getting out by the window!" Ethel King shouted.

Favored by the confusion, Johnny and his friends, hidden by the crowd, had reached a casement window and escaped through it. Two policemen stationed in the street tried to stop their flight. Cries of rage and then revolver shots rang out from the outside. Despite the policemen's efforts, Johnny and one of his accomplices managed to get to safety by making off as fast as their legs could carry them.

As for Glensing and Parrish, they remained in the power of the authorities. Parrish had been grabbed by the police just as he jumped through the window, and Glensing had fallen back into the room, wounded by a shot in the leg. Most of the clients slipped away. The battle had cost the lives of six criminals. There were about ten wounded. The operation had only half succeeded. Johnny, the head of the gang, had slipped through the net with one of his accomplices. Even so, the inspector and Ethel King were nonetheless satisfied. Sweed very much admired the great detective's idea. If the criminals hadn't discharged their weapons before the fight, it would have been a great deal more deadly and might have cost the lives of several of his men.

The next morning newspapers published long articles on what had happened in Will Thornton's famous bar. The criminals who were arrested were stubbornly mute. They would say nothing of their criminal activities or of Johnny, their leader.

Decisive Victory

Three days had passed. Ethel King hadn't stopped working on the case, but until then she hadn't succeeded in tracing the two last members of the gang. She was aware that the most important capture was that of Johnny. So long as this miscreant remained free, he wouldn't have any trouble finding other accomplices to continue his criminal activities. Ethel King's and Charley Lux's searches in Philadelphia saloons continued to be fruitless. It was necessary to wait until the scoundrels committed a crime which would furnish a clue.

At noon on the fourth day, Inspector Sweed called the detective to the telephone.

"Miss King, I would be obliged to you if you would come to see me immediately, at my private residence. I want to bring you up to date on a new, very important, incident, which has given me something to think about."

"Is it about our gang?"

"Yes."

"Good! I'll be at your house in an hour!"

The great detective finished lunch quickly and an hour after the telephone conversation, Ethel King entered the inspector's office.

"I'm very relieved that you answered my call, Miss King. The audacity of this scum goes beyond anything anyone can imagine. It's outrageous!"

"You're intriguing me."

Sweed took an open envelope from his desk and handed it to his visitor.

"Read, Miss King."

The detective first considered the rough handwriting of the address: "His Excellency, the famous police inspector, Mr. Harry Sweed, Camden."

Then she tore open the letter, unfolded it and read:

Very Honorable Mr. Sweed,

You will be surprised when you see our signatures at the bottom of this letter. But we want to write to you to express our gratitude to Miss King and you. You let us escape from Will Thornton's bar and we're persuaded that you're bitterly disappointed about that. But it won't do you any harm. Disappointment is good for the health. Besides, we have to recognize that Miss King's ruse was very clever.

We're using this letter to tell you goodbye, because we count on leaving Camden and Philadelphia very soon, never to return. However we want to send you a message which will certainly cheer you up. We have formed the project of carrying out, before we leave, a burglary which will make us rich to the end of our days. So, be on your guard, Mr. Sweed. You may succeed in pinching us. In order for you not to waste your time, we're confiding to you that it's in Camden itself that we intend to operate. Unfortunately, we can't give you the exact address, but we don't doubt that we'll meet you on the premises. Thanks to your talent, you'll discover, I'm sure, the house we intend to honor with our visit.

So, then, au revoir. *Please accept the expression of our devotion, of our gratitude, and of our highest regard,*

Johnny and Fred. "

"What impudence!" exclaimed the inspector while Ethel King looked at the letter in silence.

"Yes, it's always that same stupidity that the cleverest criminals can't help committing," the young woman answered. "I think this is exactly what will let me nab our fellows."

Sweed shook his head.

"But in the name of Heaven, how will you go about it?" he asked. "These scoundrels must have made their plan very well. Think of the size of our city! It would be useless for me to put all my police in service. I couldn't watch all the streets. How can we know in what section of the city the thieves intend to operate? They are so sure of their facts that their making fun of me is an added insult."

Ethel King kept all her calm.

"This letter didn't come through the mail?"

"No, it was a rather well dressed man, clean-shaven, with reddish hair, who brought it. And you'll see just how far the scoundrels will push their impudence. The individual asked to see me on an urgent matter concerning the thieves. My valet advised him to go see me at my office, at the Prefecture of Police, but the man insisted on my seeing him, at my private house. My valet went into an adjacent room to telephone me and tell me about the visit. I told him I would come immediately. But when the valet returned to my study, the man had disappeared and this letter had been left on the table."

Ethel looked around the room.

"You have only one person in your employ, Mr. Sweed?"

"Just one man, yes. I also have a housekeeper and a maid, but they weren't there, neither of them, when the letter was delivered."

"It's unusual that the criminal asked to talk to you. He could just have simply delivered his letter and gone away."

"Perhaps he believed that I was at home and proposed to assassinate me if I received him."

"That hypothesis is not unlikely, but I have another opinion about it."

The young woman looked at the sheet of blotting paper spread out on the desk. A smile played over her lips.

"Well, Mr. Sweed, put everything in motion to thwart the scoundrels' intentions."

"I'll do it, Miss King. My agents will keep watch tonight. And you, Miss King, will you help me?"

"I already have my own theory. I can't tell you about it for the moment, Mr. Sweed, but if my conjectures are confirmed, I'll turn the thieves over to you this very night. You must promise me, however, to spend the night at the Prefecture of Police and not take part personally in the investigation."

"That was my intention. I'll hold myself ready at my office to receive my men's reports and give the necessary instructions."

"Good. I will perhaps succeed. If I call you, Mr. Sweed, come running without losing a minute. I imagine you'll be very surprised."

"I'll come; I promise you," the inspector declared, and saw Ethel King out.

She returned to her house and told Charley Lux about the unusual discovery she had made at the inspector's house.

"The thieves intend to burglarize Sweed's apartment," she said. "I deduced that from several clues I turned up. We'll prepare a surprise for the inspector. I want him to find the thieves in handcuffs tonight in his own house. We must proceed with caution, because Sweed's servants will surely raise the alarm if they notice anything. I'll get into the inspector's house at 11 p.m. The thieves certainly won't come before midnight.

"You, you'll stay down below, hidden across from the main door. It's possible that the scum have found accomplices and placed lookouts. In that case, you'll go immediately to get policemen to arrest them. If you see the scoundrels enter, follow them as far as the apartment. We'll then catch them between two fires."

The bandits hadn't indicated to Sweed in their letter that they would commit the burglary during the coming night, but it was easy to guess that they would take advantage of the inspector's absence. Sweed, troubled by the letter, would take important precautions that night and would certainly not be at home. The burglars could work without being disturbed.

Sweed was very rich. The study where he worked, which also served as a library, contained two small, well stocked safes. If the criminals managed to break into them and steal the money and valuables, they would make a clean sweep of a very respectable fortune.

Ethel King and Charley got on their way a little before 11 p.m. and soon arrived in Camden, in front of Inspector Sweed's house. The highly placed official occupied the whole second floor. His apartment was richly furnished.

Charley Lux hid on the other side of the street in a dark corner. Ethel King opened the door with a skeleton key. She entered, closed the door without any noise, and climbed the carpeted stairs. She stopped on the second floor in front of Sweed's apartment. She doubled her precautions. It took her more than 15 minutes to pick the lock, finally the bolt moved silently.

On entering the corridor, the young woman thought she heard a slight noise. She stopped to listen, holding her breath. Were the burglars already working? She placed her ear on the study door, but she no longer heard the noise. She turned the door knob cautiously, opened the door slightly and looked in. A feeble light was coming from the street through two big windows. Ethel King pushed the door a little further open and took two steps into the room; she intended to hide behind a tall writing stand to wait for the burglars.

At that moment she was aware of something like a man's breath and muffled footsteps to her left. She raised the lantern that she already had in her hand, and put her finger on the trigger of her revolver. She told herself that the burglars, already in the apartment, had noticed her entry and had prepared to attack her. She had to prevent them. She pressed the switch on her lantern and a ray of light cleared away the shadows.

Ethel King hadn't been mistaken. A man was crawling in front of her, a knife in his hand. Before she could do anything to defend herself, she felt an iron hand strangle her neck from behind. She didn't lose her head, however. She shot twice at the criminal crouching in front of her, in whom she had recognized Johnny. The scoundrel, who was going to launch himself upon her, rolled over, letting out a loud cry. Ethel King forced herself downward at the same time. The burglar who held her by the throat was seated on top of a stand of sorts. By throwing herself to the floor, the young woman pulled him down with her, forcing him to release his hold.

Ethel King got up immediately. She brandished her revolver at her adversaries.

"Don't move or I'll blow your brains out!"

The scoundrels didn't dare make a movement. The gunshot had awakened the servants. The women cried out in fright. The valet came running. He was no little surprised to see Ethel King and the two burglars. Charley Lux arrived in his turn and took charge of securing the prisoners. Johnny was wounded, but it was thought wise to handcuff him anyway.

Ethel King went to the telephone and asked Inspector Sweed, who was still at the Prefecture, to return home. Sweed exclaimed in surprise and declared that he would come immediately. He was on the spot 15 minutes later. When he learned what had happened, he could hardly believe it. He shook Ethel King's hand warmly.

"But how did you do it, Miss King? How did you know that the burglars would come to my house tonight?"

"That wasn't hard to guess. Something at first seemed suspicious to me. The criminal who came to your house, and that your servant has just recognized as one of our two prisoners, instead of immediately presenting his letter, had himself taken into your work room, claiming to need to speak to you about an urgent matter. That individual simply wanted to find out the layout of the place. He quickly drew a sketch of your office. I noticed that while I was looking at a piece of blotting paper that was on your table. Having finished his sketch with pen and ink, the scoundrel dried it on your blotting pad, and the lines are reproduced there. That clue oriented my deductions, and I came tonight with my assistant to arrest the criminals. You can see that I had a lucky inspiration!"

The burglars roared with rage, but their shouts and their oaths didn't keep the police from taking them to the station. It was found that the criminals had broken into the apartment by leaning a ladder against the kitchen window that had been left open.

Johnny Break—that was the name of the gang's leader—pressed with questions, made a complete confession. Ethel King soon located his domicile, where they found a part of his stolen goods. The rogue admitted his guilt in the murder of Browning and in several other crimes which brought him the death penalty. His five accomplices were sent to prison for long years.

7. THE BLOODY WHITE ROSES

A Cry of Distress

Ethel King was working at her desk in her pretty Philadelphia villa on Garden Street. It was near midnight and the wind was shaking the windows of the house. Charley Lux, the young cousin and assistant of Ethel King, had been in bed a long time, as had the housekeeper. But Pluto, the young woman's faithful Great Dane, was stretched out at his mistress' feet and raised his intelligent eyes to her from time to time.

Ethel King had finally put down her pen and placed the report she had just finished into an envelope when the telephone rang. The detective picked up the receiver.

"Hello, this is Ethel King. Who's speaking?"

A desperate voice, a woman's voice, answered.

"Miss King? Miss King? Is that you?"

"Yes. What is it? Hello?"

"Come quickly. Help me...Bring Harold, my husband...He's at the Union Club."

"I'll rush there now. What's your name? Where do you live?"

"I am..."

The name wasn't pronounced. A piercing cry rang through the telephone.

"Hello!" the troubled detective cried out.

No answer. Ethel King tried to get the operator, but it was more than a minute before the telephone operator deigned to communicate with her.

"Please, Miss, tell me the name of the person I was just talking to."

"I'm sorry, I don't know anything about that. I've had so many communications since then."

"Think back. It's a matter of something serious...perhaps of a murder!"

A soft exclamation of fright was followed by a short pause before the telephone operator declared:

"I'm sorry, but I absolutely cannot give you that information."

Ethel King, understanding that she wouldn't obtain anything from the employee, hung up the telephone.

"There's nothing more for me to do but look for this Harold who's at the Union Club," the detective resolved out loud. "That's not the easiest thing, since there are a lot of societies in Philadelphia called the Union Club!"

She got dressed to go out and hurried first to the police, where she obtained a list of Philadelphia clubs. Then she began to get into communication successively with the different "Union Clubs" that had a telephone. She succeeded at the fourth telephone call. It was a society of sportsmen, whose headquarters were on Vine Street.

"Have all the members of the club left?" Ethel King asked.

"No, Miss, there are still some gentlemen playing billiards."

"Do you know a member whose first name Harold?"

"Harold? Oh, yes, Mr. Wallis, of course."

"Is he married?"

"Yes, and not for very long. He gave a party at the club six months ago on the occasion of his marriage. He's still here, playing a game of billiards."

"Good. I need to speak to him about an urgent matter."

"Should I call him to the telephone?"

"No, but ask him to wait a moment. Tell him that a lady, who absolutely must see him will come to meet him at the club. I'll be there in 15 minutes at the most."

"Good. I'll deliver your message, Miss."

The club's administrator, who had answered Ethel King, went into the billiard room and approached an elegant young man with an attractive appearance.

"Mr. Wallis."

"What do you want with me, Mr. Miller?"

"A lady has just telephoned. She says she absolutely must speak to you and that she will be here in a quarter of an hour."

"A lady?" asked the young man. "Could that be my wife?"

"Certainly not, since she asked if you were married."

"This is bizarre! Who could that woman be who wants to speak to me at such an hour?"

"She'll be here soon, and you'll learn what it's about."

"You're right."

Harold Wallis went back to his game, but he was distracted. He, who ordinarily was so skillful, missed all his shots. He was worried. The presentiment of a misfortune was oppressing him.

Finally the administrator called to him:

"Mr. Wallis, the lady is here. She's waiting for you in the reading room."

The young man passed into the library where he found himself in the presence of a slim young woman dressed simply and elegantly.

"Mr. Wallis?"

"I am Mr. Wallis," the young man answered, bowing. "To whom do I have the honor?"

"My name is Ethel King."

Wallis gasped in surprise.

"Ethel King! Then you're the famous detective?"

"I am, in fact, a detective."

"And you come to see me? You need to see me about an urgent matter? My God! So what's happened? Is it about my wife?"

"Don't get excited like this, Mr. Wallis. I was called on the telephone at midnight by a lady, but I can't confirm that it was Mrs. Wallis. When she wanted to say her name, she was interrupted. I heard a loud cry; then there was silence. It's quite possible that someone has harmed the person who called me. They at least kept her from finishing her conversation. Do you have a telephone in your apartment?"

"Yes, in the bedroom."

Ethel King repeated what the unknown woman had said to her.

Wallis, panic-stricken, shuddered. "It could very well be that it was Irma. Oh! I can guess…that odious letter! My poor wife has been the victim of an attack! Come, Miss King, come quickly. We may arrive in time to save her."

"Just a moment! Let's be sure, first of all, that it really was Mrs. Wallis who called me to help her. What is your telephone number?"

"12456."

"I'm going to telephone that number. If the telephone is in your bedroom and your wife is at home, she'll answer, won't she?"

"The telephone isn't exactly in the bedroom, but in a booth which is separated from it by a little glass door. Sometimes my wife is a very light sleeper. The ring of the telephone always wakes her."

Ethel King went to the club telephone and asked for telephone number 12456. But she listened in vain; she received no answer.

"Give me the telephone," said Wallis, trembling all over. "I don't understand this at all. She must be there."

He had no more success than Ethel King.

"Something has happened!" he exclaimed in a hoarse voice. "Let's hurry, Miss King!"

He was deathly pale; all his features showed anxiety.

"We don't have a minute to lose," Ethel replied. "Where do you live? Mr. Wallis?"

"478 Walnut Street, on the right bank of the Schuylkill River, at the other end of the city."

"Let's take a cab."

Wallis went out first, in a very understandable state of excitement. With Ethel he reached the closest cab station.

"A five dollar tip! Burn up the pavement!" he shouted to the cabman and jumped into the carriage.

The cabman whipped up his horse, which left at full speed. While the vehicle was rolling along, Ethel King advised:

"I beg you, Mr. Wallis. Get hold of yourself. It won't do any good for the coachman to urge his horse to go faster. It will take us a good 30 minutes to reach your house. And in that length of time you can furnish me a lot of important information."

"Ask me. I have entire confidence in you, Miss King. I have often talked about you with my dear wife. That's probably why Irma thought about calling you."

"You've been married six months?"

"Yes."

"Do you have any enemies?"

"I don't know of any."

"Is that really true?" the detective insisted.

"Yes, yes, I assure you."

"I had at first thought that a burglar had gotten into your house and that your wife had been awakened by the noise. But you made a remark that modified my opinion."

"What remark?"

"When I repeated to you what your wife had said to me over the telephone, you exclaimed: 'The odious letter!' Would you explain that letter to me?"

There was a moment of silence. The man hesitated. Finally he replied in a strangled voice.

"I can't tell you."

"Why?"

"Because I don't want to tarnish in your eyes my dear wife, who is purity itself."

"I am asking from a completely objective point of view. Besides, you may believe that you won't have to reproach me for indiscretion. If a crime has been committed and you want to help me find its author, you must be entirely frank with me."

"That's not possible!" the young man stammered.

"You must, however," the detective insisted.

"Let's wait, Miss King. If a crime has really been committed, I won't hide anything from you. But if we're alarmed by mistake, I prefer to be silent."

Ethel was content with the response and, dropping that subject, asked: "You're in business?"

"I own a little ceramic manufacturing business on Brown Street."

"Do you go there every day?

"Yes, I'm there every morning from 9 a.m. I go home at 1 p.m., and return to the factory at 4 p.m. I always stay there until 7 or 8 p.m. When I go to the club, I go straight there without first going home. It rarely happens that I stay at the club as late as today. It was bad luck. If I had gone back earlier, I would probably have prevented a catastrophe."

"Has your wife seemed to you to be upset, worried?"

"No…However, to be frank, I must say that for a month or two, she has seemed less happy than usual. I questioned her several times on that subject, and she blamed this change in mood on neuralgia. I called in a doctor who put her on a diet and her condition seemed to improve."

"Did you establish some connection between that change in mood and the letter to which you referred?"

The young man trembled.

"I never thought about that," Wallis murmured, more troubled than ever. "My God! Could it be possible? But no! A thousand times no! Irma is so pure, so good; her love for me is so deep! She is incapable of such a thing!"

Ethel King thought she had guessed the content of the letter that Wallis refused to show her.

"Irma seemed so happy again today," the young man said despondently. "I had brought her a beautiful bouquet of sweet smelling white roses, and she was as happy as a child; she thanked me effusively; she hugged me. And now! Mercy! When I think…that I'm perhaps going to find her bathing in her blood…"

He didn't finish. And he covered his face with his hands, trembling throughout his whole body. The trip finished in silence. The cab finally reached Walnut Street and soon halted in front of No. 478, a small three-story town house. The raised first floor was reached by stone steps. The door was closed and there were no lights anywhere.

As the cab went away, Harold Wallis looked at the door a moment, trembling.

"Great God! What are we going to see?" he murmured. "Will I find my wife alive, or is my happiness destroyed?"

Ethel King took the unhappy man's arm.

"Courage, Mr. Wallis. Whatever happens, stand firm!"

She climbed the steps with Wallis, who opened the door.

The Bloody Roses

"Where is the bedroom?" Ethel King asked.

"On the second floor. Irma must be there. I can't believe something bad has happened to her."

Harold made an effort to master his emotion.

"Come, Miss King."

He climbed the steps four at a time to the second floor. Ethel King had trouble keeping up with him. She heard him open a door violently and saw him switch on the electricity.

A piercing cry rang throughout the house, then the sound of a fall. When the detective crossed the threshold of the bedroom, a terrifying spectacle met her eyes. Harold Wallis had fainted beside the bed. The one he loved so much had disappeared. There was no longer anything on the sheets but a bouquet of white roses stained with blood.

Ethel King took a carafe of water which was on the bedside table and splashed Wallis' face. He wasn't long in coming around. The young man opened his eyes and at first looked around him with amazement; then his memory returned and he got up with a stifled cry.

"She's not here, Miss King. She's been murdered. That blood on the roses; it's my wife's…"

The detective made the unhappy man sit down.

"Get hold of yourself. I don't believe that Mrs. Wallis is dead!"

"What! You still have hope, Miss King?"

"Yes, I tell you again, your wife is alive. My job now is to find her and bring her back to you. As for the scoundrel who took her from you, I'll deliver him to justice."

"But how can you be so positive?" Wallis asked incredulously.

"If the criminal had killed the young woman, he wouldn't have taken the trouble to carry away the body. No, in my opinion, he wanted to hold Mrs. Wallis alive in his power."

"Why? Is it for a ransom? Oh! I'll gladly pay whatever they ask of me, provided my dear Irma is returned to me."

"It's possible that someone wants to extort money from you. But it's equally possible that a man has become madly in love with Mrs. Wallis and has kidnapped her."

Wallis pressed both hands on his chest.

"My God! You're right! The letter! That miserable letter..."

"Well! Don't wait any longer! Show it to me."

"Here it is!" The young man took his billfold from his pocket and drew out a crumpled paper. "This is an anonymous letter that I received two weeks ago. I didn't attach any importance to it at the time."

Ethel King unfolded the sheet of paper and read the following:

Mr. Harold Wallis
Industrialist, 56 Brown Street
Philadelphia
A friend is giving you this advice in your interest. Your wife no longer merits your confidence. She is deceiving you. She has already received someone at night. She has been seen. Don't let yourself be ridiculed.

X.Y.

"Did you show this letter to your wife?" Ethel King asked. "Or did you speak to her about it?"

"No, I considered it an infamous calumny against an irreproachable creature. In my eyes, to attach the least importance to such a letter would have been to insult Irma. My dear wife is incapable of doing what she's accused of."

"I believe you, Mr. Wallis. I am persuaded that your wife has been taken against her will. If that were not true, she wouldn't have telephoned me to come help her. Nevertheless, circumstances oblige us to take into account that letter which might have some bearing on the case."

"I understand, Miss King."

"Do you perfectly understand Mrs. Wallis' past?"

"Absolutely! Nine months ago she still lived with her mother at Wayne Junction. I became engaged to her a year ago."

"Where did you meet your wife?"

"She was the cashier in my factory. Her beauty, her sweetness, charmed me. I asked her mother, a very respectable old lady, for her hand. The family had been rich in the past, but the father, before his death, had made unfortunate investments and lost almost all his fortune. Irma's mother died nine months ago, and, as my fiancé would be alone after that, we decided to marry as soon as possible. The private ceremony took place last July. We were both infinitely happy. I know Irma's heart was totally mine."

"The young girl hadn't had any attachment before knowing you?"

"No, I'm certain of it."

Ethel King proceeded to an investigation. She first entered the little telephone booth. She couldn't hold back an exclamation of surprise.

"Look, Mr. Wallis. This door has been broken down. The glass is in pieces. The young girl probably took refuge here and locked the door. That was when she telephoned me. But the criminal broke down the door with his shoulder."

Ethel King then turned up traces of blood on the floor. A curtain had been snatched down. There was a piece missing from it. Not having turned up any other clues, Ethel King telephoned the police. She then went back into the bedroom and picked up the bouquet of roses.

"This is unusual," she murmured. "There is no trace of blood on the sheets. Only the flowers are stained with it. It has to be deduced that the scoundrel dipped them on purpose in the blood and then placed them on the bed."

Fifteen minutes later the police arrived with a young Commissioner who began investigations. Seeing the bloody roses, he stated the opinion that Mrs. Wallis had been murdered, and that her corpse had been removed. Ethel King let him continue as he liked and consoled as well as she could the poor husband who had been again plunged into despair by the Commissioner's declarations.

After having gone through, with no result, the rooms on the second floor, Ethel went down to the first floor. She wanted, first of all, to establish how the criminal had left the house with his victim. The door opening onto the little garden was open. Ethel King took advantage of the fact that the Commissioner and the policemen were busy in the bedroom to go on with investigations. She went into the garden, her flashlight in her hand. The ground was soft and wet because it had thawed after a heavy snow fall. Ethel King had no trouble in discovering the criminal's footprints, leading in two directions, coming and going. Those he had left when departing were deeper, and the detective concluded that he must have been carrying a heavy burden.

The man had obviously crossed the fence at the bottom of the garden. He must have had a great deal of trouble scaling it with his victim on his shoulders. Ethel King examined the planks of the enclosure one by one and discovered some strings of gray wool which had gotten stuck on a rusty nail. The detective put these bits of wool in her purse. Then she took the exact dimensions of one of the footprints. That done, she jumped the fence with the agility of a professional athlete and landed in the neighboring garden, which had large, well cared for gravel paths where the steps were hardly visible. In all, the young woman succeeded in following the criminal's trail only as far as Samson Street.

"If the scoundrel carried his victim any further, he had to have used a vehicle," the detective was thinking.

The abductor had regained the street by going through the grounds of a little villa at No. 291 Samson Street. Following her investigations, Ethel discovered that the scoundrel, by going through the center of the city, had arrived at the garden of a little townhouse situated to the left of Wallis' house. The trail suddenly stopped under a portico, to which a trapeze was suspended.

"This is unusual," Ethel King murmured. "It would seem that the criminal took his precautions to throw off searches."

The first steps of the trail had been imprinted very deeply. They were even marked better than those the kidnapper had left in leaving with his human burden. Neither were they exactly under the portico.

Ethel King directed her flashlight onto the footprints.

"It would seem that the criminal got here by jumping," she mused.

Her glance fell on the trapeze, then was carried to the wall of the townhouse, which was three yards from there. She noticed that one window on the second floor was open.

She went across the garden, scaled the wrought iron fence, to come down again on Walnut Street. She was now in front of No. 477, the house next to that of Harold Wallis. She rang at the door. Moments later, a window on the second floor opened.

"What do you want at such an hour?" a man's voice demanded.

"Let me in," Ethel King answered. "It's a matter on which a human life depends. I absolutely must talk to you."

"Who are you?" the man, suspicious, continued.

"I'll explain myself when you've let me in. In the name of Heaven, hurry!"

There was something in the detective's voice which decided the man to obey.

"All right, be patient a moment. I'm coming down."

The door to the steps opened in a few moments. The man first stopped at the threshold of the door and threw the light from his lamp on his visitor's face. Ethel King saw that he was holding a revolver.

"Don't be afraid," she told him. "I'm Ethel King."

"Really! Then come in. You're welcome. Tell me the reason for your visit."

He conducted the young woman into a luxurious drawing room where he turned on the electric lights.

"I know you by reputation, Miss King, and I'm ready to help you any way I can. Has a burglary been committed in a neighboring house, or even in mine?"

The man questioning Ethel King was an old gentleman with a white beard and a very likeable face.

"No, Mr..."

"Oh! Pardon me, Miss King. I forgot to introduce myself. I'm James Green, the owner of this house."

The young woman bowed, smiling.

"No, Mr. Green, there hasn't been a burglary in your house, but a criminal has broken into No. 478."

The old man exclaimed in horror.

"At Mr. Harold Wallis' house?"

"Yes, a kidnapping took place at midnight. Mrs. Wallis has been forcibly abducted."

"That's not possible! That charming young woman! Oh! How I pity that poor Harold. We see each other frequently; they are such likeable people! But how can I help you?"

"I believe the abductor passed through your house before committing his crime."

James Green made a movement of surprise.

"Through my house?" he exclaimed with amazement. "Excuse me, Miss King, I take that to be inadmissible."

"We're going to see. I would like to ask you some questions. Your answers will show me if my suspicions are justified."

"Ask away, Miss King. I myself am impatient to know if you're right."

He lit a cigarette and sank back into his armchair.

Important Revelations

"The façade of your house has six windows facing the garden on each story, doesn't it?"

"That's correct. However, two of the windows on the first floor are replaced by doors. One leads into the vestibule, the other into the laundry room."

"I'm talking about the second floor. Into what bedroom does the second window open, counting from Wallis' house?"

"Into the bedroom of my renter, Mr. Rooding."

"Ah! You have a renter! What sort of man is this Rooding?"

"You don't suspect him, do you?"

"Please, Mr. Green. Answer my question. I can't talk about suspicions yet."

"Well, John Rooding made an excellent impression on me, although I know very little about him."

"What's his profession?"

"I have no idea. I believe he is very rich."

"Then why is he renting this bedroom? Couldn't he rent an entire house?"

"It's only a temporary lodging, he told me."

"How much is his rent?"

"Eight dollars a week."

"What's he like?"

"He's a handsome man. He has very dark, curly hair. He wears a black, well-trimmed moustache, which goes very well with his olive complexion. He has a rather long face with brilliant black eyes."

"Does he seem to be a passionate man?"

"Oh, yes," Green answered. "He gives that impression."

"Do you know the address of his real home?"

"No, I've never asked him for it. I had no interest in that."

"How long have you rented that bedroom to him?"

"For about a month. He sends me the money punctually by mail every Monday."

"Does he often sleep here?"

"Two or three times a week."

"Is he here tonight?"

"I don't believe so. He always makes a lot of noise when he comes in, letting the door slam and making noise on the stairs."

"Why do you rent to him? You aren't that hard up, are you?"

"Certainly not. But he came to ask me to give him that bedroom, telling me that he had a great desire to have a place to stop off in this street and he had found nothing available. Since I didn't need that room, I gave it over to him."

"Ah! I understand! It was very important to this gentleman to live, not only in this street, but also near house No. 478."

"So you suspect him, Miss King?"

"Indeed. Your answers have confirmed my opinion. I will ask you now to take me to the bedroom in question. I would like to examine it."

"But what if Mr. Rooding is up there! He could have come in without my hearing him," observed the old man.

"He did come in without your hearing him, Mr. Green, and I'm persuaded that he avoided making any noise so as not to betray his presence."

"Then he's still there?" exclaimed Mr. Green?

"No, he has, if I'm not mistaken, left his bedroom in a somewhat unusual way."

"What way?"

"We'll see that upstairs."

The old man took the initiative and led Ethel King to the second floor. He found that his renter's bedroom door was locked.

"The key isn't in the lock," he said. "That's a sign Mr. Rooding isn't in his bedroom."

"So, he's in the habit of locking his door when he goes out?"

"Yes, the maid can't clean his bedroom except when he's there."

"Has your maid ever let slip any remark allowing you to suppose that she had noticed anything extraordinary about Mr. Rooding?"

"Never."

"Do you have another key to this door?"

"No. We can't go in, Miss King."

"Oh! Yes, we can," the young woman answered, smiling. "For detectives, there's no lock that will hold, Mr. Green."

She took a bunch of lock picks out of her pocket and had soon opened the door. Green went in first and turned on the electric lights. He exclaimed in surprise. Miss Ethel King said coolly:

"That's just what I thought."

A polished pole about 12 feet long was placed on the floor. One of the ends, turned toward the window, was fitted with an iron spike.

"I'm going to explain to you, Mr. Green, how Mrs. Wallis' abductor got out of this bedroom. He calculated everything to throw off the police, but he was wrong to think he could deceive an individual even a little observant."

She went to the window and looked down into the garden. The light from the bedroom lit up the top of the portico.

"You see, Mr. Green," Ethel King said, "Rooding used that pole. He hammered the end fitted with a spike into the beam of the portico and fitted the other end on the window ledge. Then he slid slowly and cautiously along this improvised bridge to the portico. Once seated on the beam, he threw the spike into the bedroom, then descended to the trapeze suspended there, gained momentum and jumped a certain distance."

"But why did he do that?"

"To make his trail impossible to follow. A lot of people would let themselves be taken in, that's certain. But the presence of the portico and the open window on the second window of your house struck me. From those facts, I drew the conclusions that led me here."

"You're incomparable!" Green exclaimed. "I'm also persuaded now that Rooding is the criminal."

"I hope to lay hands on him soon."

Ethel King began a minute inspection of the bedroom, but discovered nothing important.

"Nevertheless, he couldn't hide that spike from the maid who cleaned his room," Ethel King observed. "Is that girl your only servant?"

"Yes, but on major cleaning days I have other women come in to help her."

"Then that servant is the one who does everything?"

"Yes, she's the one who does the cooking and takes care of the house."

"What's her name?"

"Martha Lockwood."

"Is she pretty?"

"No, but she has an almost exaggerated gaiety."

"I understand. The handsome Rooding didn't have much trouble drawing her into his net. Wake that girl up, please, Mr. Green. Have her come down immediately to the drawing room!"

"As you order, Miss King."

Mr. Green climbed up to the third floor, but Ethel King went back down to the first floor, where she waited for Mr. Green. When he rejoined her, she showed him the anonymous letter that Harold Wallis had received.

"Do you recognize this stationery?" she asked him.

"Absolutely, that's the one I use."

"And the handwriting?"

"I have never seen it before."

Asked by the detective, he read with astonishment and indignation the few lines addressed to Wallis.

"That's an infamous calumny! Mrs. Wallis has never done anything to justify such accusations."

"I know that," Ethel King declared, "but I presume your maid can inform you as to the author of that letter."

The servant entered the drawing room five minutes later. She was a robust, red-cheeked girl who might have been 28 to 38 years old. She had a short, pug nose, and she squinted.

"What's happening that's making me come down in the middle of the night?" she asked.

"I'm from the police," Ethel King said seriously. "I have some questions to ask you."

"From the police?"

The maid turned pale and sank into the chair that the detective pointed out to her.

"You don't need to be afraid. If you tell me the whole truth, nothing will happen to you."

Martha Lockwood was somewhat reassured.

"I haven't done anything wrong either," she said impudently. "You don't have anything to reproach me with."

"Really? Think about it, Martha Lockwood."

"No, no, I haven't done anything."

Then Ethel suddenly put the anonymous letter under the maid's nose.

"And who wrote this letter?" she asked her in a sharp voice.

Martha Lockwood lost her composure.

"I don't know anything about that," she stammered.

"So admit it," the detective continued. "If not, I'll be forced to arrest you and take you to prison as an accomplice of the criminal, John Rooding."

The girl cried out in terror.

"John Rooding, a criminal? Oh! That…that's my death!"

"Answer me now. Who wrote this letter?"

"Me!" the maid answered, bursting into tears.

"Why?"

"Oh, I had reasons for doing it. John Rooding deceived me. He started an affair with the beautiful Mrs. Wallis."

"Tell us everything!"

The maid started a story interspersed with sobs.

"The first time John Rooding came here, he paid attention to me and told me I was the most beautiful girl he had ever seen, that no one had ever made such an impression on his heart."

"You naturally believed him? "Ethel King asked, throwing a furtive glance at Mr. Green.

"Why would I not have believed him. I'm not ugly and Mr. Rooding was so nice to me! I was completely happy when he told me he wanted to make me his wife."

"So, he promised you marriage?"

"No doubt of it."

"After that you didn't say anything about the spike that you saw in his bedroom."

"Ah! You know about that?" Martha exclaimed. "He made me promise not to say anything."

"Yes, we know about that. So this Rooding completely dominated you. He flattered you and kissed you and you believed everything he told you."

The maid let out a deep sigh.

"Yes, at first, but after two weeks I didn't have the same confidence in him."

"Why this change?"

"I was always asking him who he was and where he lived in town, but he refused to answer me."

"And nevertheless you believed in his sincerity," exclaimed James Green in a tone of reproach.

"Alas! Mr. Green, love makes you blind," Martha said, weeping. "And John is such a handsome man."

"Have you attempted to find out his address?" Ethel King asked.

"Yes, it bothered me too much. One morning when he left at daybreak I followed him."

"Ah! A good idea! Rooding didn't notice you?"

"No. I had taken my precautions so that he wouldn't recognize me. I hid my face under a big shawl. John didn't think that I was following him, because he didn't turn around once."

"Good! Where did he go?"

"He reached the Market Street station and took the train to 10th Street on the other side of Schuylkill River; then he walked as far as Filbert Street, where he went into a beautiful house. I went in also, but the concierge stopped me. When I asked him if the gentleman who went in ahead of me was the owner of the house, he answered 'yes' and added that if I wanted something from Mr. Allamore, I would have to come back another day.

"I became panicky. The thought that John Rooding had introduced himself to me under a false name shattered me."

"Did you take down Mr. Allamore's address?"

"No, but I can find the house again."

"Good. You'll take me there as soon as it's daylight. And, now, tell me how you came to write that letter to Mr. Wallis."

"I once saw John slip into the Wallis' house at night. I stood at my bedroom window. He used his pole to reach the portico; then he jumped to the ground. He went into the garden of the house next door. Then, driven by curiosity, I went out by the little courtyard door and went to look through the windows of the Wallis' house. There was a light in the ground floor room. I saw John Rooding kneeling in front of the beautiful Mrs. Wallis."

"And what was Mrs. Wallis' attitude?"

"I can't say. My eyes became blurred by tears and I returned quickly to the house. It was well that I did, because Rooding got out of the Wallis house through a window on the first floor and went across the gardens in the direction of Samson Street. I was desperate, and at the same time indignant against Mrs. Wallis. I sat down at my master's secretary and

164

wrote the anonymous letter that I addressed to Mr. Harold Wallis at his factory to be sure that it got to him."

"And you didn't say anything to Mr. Rooding?"

"Since then I've never had the opportunity to speak to him in private; otherwise I would have told him what I had in my heart."

"Forget that rascal, Martha," Ethel King advised. "He's unworthy of your regrets. After tomorrow he'll be in prison. And now, come. You're going to show me the house of Mr. Rooding, or Allamore. The scoundrel has forcibly abducted Mrs. Wallis and is undoubtedly holding her prisoner. We must snatch his prisoner from him!"

"What are you saying?" Martha Lockwood exclaimed. "He took that lady away in spite of herself? Oh! He has to be made to pay for that. I'm ready to go with you, Miss, and I want that rascal to know that I was the one who helped you."

While the maid dressed to go out, the great detective went back to the Wallis townhouse, took some of the bloody roses, rolled them into paper, and put them under her arm.

Arrest of the Kidnapper

Day was breaking when Ethel King arrived with the maid in front of No. 57 Filbert Street.

"That's John Rooding's house," Martha stated.

The door wasn't yet open; the concierge wasn't yet at his post. Ethel had requisitioned a policeman who was on guard in the street. She had shown her detective's badge and identified herself. She picked the lock, which required some time, but the door finally opened and the young woman went into the entry hall with her companion. She mounted to the second floor and found John Allamore's name on the main door of an apartment. Ethel tried again to use her lock picks to open, but her attempt failed. The lock was secured by a special device.

"Hide in the stairwell," the detective said. "I'm going to ring the bell. Wait until I call you."

Martha and the policeman obeyed, and Ethel King pushed the doorbell. After a moment of silence, she heard the sound of someone opening a door in the apartment and a voice asking:

"Who's there?"

"A lady who wants to speak to Mr. Allamore about a very urgent matter."

"He's not seeing anyone."

"Too bad for him! I've come to help him. Will you let me in?"

"Then what's it about?"

"It's concerning a matter only Mr. Allamore and I know about."

"Wait, I'll open."

Locks squeaked and a man looked distrustfully through the half-opened door. There were lights in the entry. Ethel put her foot between the door and the door frame. Given Green's description to her, she had immediately recognized the handsome man with an olive complexion, curly hair, and a jade black mustache. She quickly put a revolver under the criminal's nose.

"Mr. Allamore, or John Rooding, as you're pleased to call yourself, you're under arrest! This is Ethel King speaking to you."

The man stepped back, terrified, and the young woman followed him into the back of the antechamber. He stopped there, dismayed.

"Ethel King!" he exclaimed. "What do you want with me?"

The detective pointed to a bandage the man had on his left hand.

"I know about the circumstances in which you hurt your hand. That's what I've come about."

"What are you saying?" exclaimed Rooding, making an effort to regain control of himself. "You're about to commit a ridiculous mistake and an injustice!"

"Not at all. You know very well why I'm here."

Ethel King took the little packet out from under her arm, letting the paper fall off it, and presented two white roses stained with blood.

"Do you recognize these roses?" she asked in a cutting tone.

"No, I've never seen them before," he stammered.

But his whole attitude belied his words.

"The blood these roses are stained with comes from your hand," Ethel King said severely. Mrs. Wallis wounded you when you entered her house to kidnap her."

The scoundrel burst out in rage.

"I don't know anything about it! I don't want to know anything about it!" he bellowed. "Leave me alone! I don't know Mrs. Wallis!"

The detective didn't move her revolver aside.

"Your lies won't help you any, Mr. Allamore. Give in to the inevitable. That would be the best way to predispose the judges in your favor."

The man lifted a chair and brandished it.

"Leave here or I'll kill you!" he screamed. "You wretch! You've come to steal my happiness from me."

"Take a single step and I'll shoot," Ethel King answered coldly. "Hey! Policeman! Come here!"

Then the scoundrel lost all control of himself. He jumped toward Ethel King, who avoided him by jumping to one side because she didn't want to kill him. As he was turning around, the policeman arrived and grabbed him by the arm. A short struggle ended in the defeat of Allamore. The appearance of Martha Lockwood on the threshold had finished him.

"Where is Mrs. Wallis?" Ethel King demanded.

As the prisoner didn't answer, the detective began a search for the young woman and found her, desperate, locked in a padded cabinet where her cries couldn't be heard.

Irma's joy, when she heard she was free to return to her husband, can be imagined. Her eyes flashing with indignation, she approached Allamore, who almost fainted on seeing her.

"Miserable creature!" she shouted at him. "I have no pity for you. You deserve your fate!"

"Irma," Allamore moaned. "I only acted out of love for you."

"For love? The man who truly loves is incapable of torturing the object of his passion in this way. No, it was a perverse desire driving you, nothing else. Policeman, take that man to prison!"

Joseph Allamore made a movement as if to throw himself out the window, but the policeman restrained him and led him away.

Ethel King took a cab with Mrs. Wallis, while the maid returned by the train. On the way, the young woman recounted to the detective what had happened.

"He's insane," she said. "His passion for me is true dementia. I met him two years ago when I was still living with my mother in Philadelphia, on Diamond Street. I met him at a ball. Since that time, he has pursued me. At the beginning I rather liked him, but his impetuous passion finally put me off. He frightened me and I sent him away rather harshly.

"As my mother and I were afraid of reprisals, we moved to Wayne Junction and I took a job as a cashier at Mr. Wallis' factory. Allamore had lost trace of us. But his passion didn't cool off. He searched Philadelphia and its suburbs to find me, and finally discovered me when I was already the wife of my dear Harold.

"One evening, when I was waiting for my husband in the library of our house, Allamore came in to me through an open window. You can judge what my terror was! He threw himself at my feet and begged me to follow him if I didn't wish for his death. He would probably have used violence against me if the sound of a key in the entry door had not announced my husband's arrival.

"Allamore threatened to kill me if I said a word to Harold. Then he jumped out the window and disappeared. I went up to my bedroom and invented an excuse to explain to my husband my prolonged stay in the library.

"Last night Allamore came into my bedroom and dragged me away by force. I first took refuge in the telephone booth and called you to come help me. But the scoundrel broke down the door and made short work of my resistance. He cut his hand when breaking the glass.

"He picked me up unconscious and carried me to his house by automobile. He wanted to force me to give up my husband to belong to him. But I would rather have been killed than submit to that infamy."

The vehicle had reached Walnut Street, in front of the Wallis' townhouse. Harold's joy was as great as the amazement of the Commissioner, who had already ordered the garden dug up to find Irma's corpse.

Joseph Allamore, who was really almost half-mad, was confined to an asylum for the insane, where he died some months afterward.

8. A DAY AMONG THE FEMALE MONSTERS

A Cry of Distress

Ethel King stopped at the door of an elegant house on Samson Street in Philadelphia and rang the bell. When the servant came to answer the door, she asked:

"Is Mr. O'Beering at home?"

"Yes, Madam."

"Then give him my card, please. I wish to speak to Mr. and Mrs. O'Beering on an urgent matter."

The servant went to tell his employer and soon returned to show the detective into the downstairs drawing room.

Ethel King found herself in the presence of a lady dressed in dark clothing, whose face, framed by white hair, expressed goodness, and of an old gentleman with a grave and dignified demeanor.

James O'Beering greeted the detective with a great deal of kindness and invited her to sit down.

"I'm very pleased to see you in my house, Miss King. You've probably come about that swindling business we were the victims of."

"Indeed, Mr. O'Beering. I would like to ask you to give me precise information on that story. I was absent a week from Philadelphia. On my return, I learned through Inspector Golding that you had come up against persecutions by a gang of criminals. Since this wasn't the first job by these swindlers. I thought it was my duty to try to put an end to their shameful exploits."

"Mr. Golding did, in fact, tell us that he was trying to interest you in this case," O'Beering commented.

Mrs. O'Beering gave a discouraged smile.

"The information that we can furnish you with, is, unfortunately, very incomplete," she said. "We've already given them to the police, and nevertheless up until now the investigation hasn't progressed."

"I will ask you, even so, to recount the facts, as you know them, to me."

"We will do that very willingly," the gentleman declared. "You begin, dear Ellen."

Ellen O'Beering began:

"Here's how it was. A week ago, I had told our chauffeur, Hinricks to have our automobile coupe ready at 6 p.m. I wanted to go to a seamstress I use from time to time. She lives in Camden, on the other side of the Delaware River. It was a dark and rainy autumn day and night was falling when I left the house. The automobile made the trip to No. 292 Oxford Street rather quickly. My chauffeur waited for me down below with the car while I went upstairs to my couturiere. I stayed an hour in the house and when I came back down, it was completely dark. I hurried because I was afraid of being late for supper. There was fog and the nearby street light didn't light up the shadows.

"The chauffeur, seeing me come down, started the motor and settled in his seat again. I ordered him to return home as soon as possible. He grumbled an unintelligible answer. I got into the dark coupe and the automobile started off.

"At that same instant I noticed that I wasn't alone; a black form was crouched in the foldaway seat. Fear froze me. I wanted to cry out, open the window, but I had scarcely started a gesture when the shadow threw itself on me. Two bony hands seized my throat. There was a menacing whisper in my ear.

"I uttered a stifled cry and I lost consciousness. Where did they take me? I couldn't say."

Ellen O'Beering shuddered at the memory of those experiences. At the end of a moment she continued.

"When I came to, I was stretched out on a kind of litter made of straw and filthy rags. A strong odor of mold rose to my nose. There was an almost impenetrable darkness in the space where I was imprisoned. I stood up, crying out in fear. I was in a cellar containing nothing but the pallet on which I found myself. The only exit was a massive door, reinforced with iron. The light came from a smoky lantern hung on the wall.

"I hadn't yet had time to think of my horrible situation when the door opened and let in some creatures whose aspect increased my terror even more. There were four old women with bestial faces, dressed in rags. Their vulgar features expressed brutality, hate, cruelty. They came up to me and one of them began to speak.

" 'Good-evening, My Lady,' she said in a mocking tone. 'We're glad to find that you have recovered your spirits, because you're going to be able to leave this magnificent drawing room which you don't seem to like very much.'

" 'What have I done to you?' I cried out. 'Why have you brought me here?'

"The four shrews burst out laughing and a big ruddy-faced one answered:

" 'Times are hard. We're forced to invent a way to earn money if we don't want to die of hunger.'

" 'What do you hope to gain. I don't have any money on me.'

" 'But you can get some for us. You have only to write to your husband to ask him to send us a ransom of $5000. As soon as our emissaries have received that amount, we'll set you free.'

" 'Never,' I shouted, and I at first opposed with stubborn resistance their bad treatments and their threats. But at the end they beat me with so much brutality that I fainted a second time. They threw me down on the pallet where I stayed for long hours. When I awoke I tried to call for help, but not a sound could go across those thick walls. I struck in vain with all my strength on the closed door.

"The brutes left me two days without food or drink and when they came back in sniggering, I lay helpless on my pallet, my resistance was broken. They renewed their threats and their bad treatment and I finally agreed to write what they dictated. I begged James to pay the money as soon as possible, because I felt I was on the point of death.

"The wretches came back in the evening; they threw themselves on me and beat me senseless with clubs. When I regained consciousness, I was in the alley of a private house on 47th Street, and as a consequence, near Samson Street and my house. I got up painfully and called a policeman who brought me here. They had given me my liberty because my husband had paid the ransom demanded.

"I had to stay in bed three days before I was almost over the terrible tortures which had been inflicted on me."

Ethel King had listened in silence, only letting an exclamation of indignation escape from time to time.

"Oh! The wretches. These harpies won't escape punishment," she exclaimed. "I'll do everything to locate them and put them out of a state to do any harm."

"Yes, yes, Miss King. I ask you to do that," Mrs. O'Beering continued. "I don't wish any harm to those like me, but such criminals merit punishment that will set an example."

"They will get it. And you, Mr. O'Beering, what do you have to say about this business?"

171

The gentleman, whose wife's story had plunged him into extreme nervousness, was pacing up and down in the drawing room. He came and stood in front of the detective and declared:

"I don't know very much, Miss King, unfortunately. I can give you only insignificant clues. My wife's disappearance, as you might think, plunged me into despair. I alerted the police; I got in touch with detectives, but they didn't manage to find Ellen.

"They picked up my unconscious chauffeur under a coach doorway on Oxford Street. He had a deep wound to the head. When he regained consciousness, he recounted that he had walked up and down on the sidewalk while waiting for my wife to return and he had received a formidable blow on the head without seeing the author of the attack.

"The criminal had taken off his overcoat, his cap and his glasses. My wife had no idea that it wasn't our chauffeur that got behind the wheel.

"The auto was found that same night abandoned in a small street, the third from here, going toward the center of the city. You can judge my sorrow when I knew that all the circumstances indicated that Ellen had been the victim of a gang of scoundrels. I despaired of ever seeing her alive again.

"The next evening I received a letter through the mail in which I was told that my wife was in a secure place and well guarded and that she would be set free if I agreed to pay a ransom of $5000. An emissary was to come the next morning to pick up the sum in carefully packaged bank notes. If I refused to comply with that requirement, Ellen would die."

"Do you still have the letter?"

O'Beering took out of his pocket a dirty sheet of paper on which were traced a few hardly legible lines in deplorable handwriting. The ink was pale, as if someone had mixed water with it.

Ethel King read that brutal missive and asked:

"Then what did you do?"

"I informed the police and the next day when the emissary arrived he was arrested."

"That was a mistake."

"Yes, but Inspector Golding thought he was doing the right thing. The individual arrested was a hoodlum about 20 years old, badly dressed and uncouth. He claimed that his name was Tom Kensing and that he was a day laborer. If he's to be believed, a passerby approached him in Diamond Street and asked if he wanted to earn an easy $5.

"He eagerly accepted and was given the mission of going to my house to get a tied up package and take it to Jim Tornelly's saloon on Lombard Street. We couldn't get anything else out of him. The police have kept him under arrest, but they will probably be forced to release him for lack of proof, even though he gave me the impression of being a scoundrel of the worst sort."

"I'll question that man. They should have left him free and followed him. That would have been a great deal smarter," Ethel King declared.

"That's exactly my opinion," O'Beering said. "That arrest produced no result. They sent disguised agents to Jim Tornelly's saloon in vain. They found no suspicious individuals in the establishment.

"Another night went by. Hundreds of policemen and detectives spread out in search of my wife but their efforts were fruitless. The next morning a boy about 15 years old came to my door. He brought a letter requiring an answer. That was the letter that Ellen's tormentors had made her write. A postscript in the handwriting of one of the wretches told me to give the money immediately to the messenger, or if I didn't, my wife would be executed the same day.

"What was I to do? I didn't want to go to the police again. Their repeated failures had made me lose all confidence in them. I therefore made a package of the bank notes and gave them to the young boy with the intention of following him. But I had scarcely put the package in his hand than he ran off and disappeared from sight before I had seriously thought about following him. I understood that all searches would henceforth be useless, and I resigned myself to wait here, in mortal agony, for the return of my dear Ellen.

"The day went by, however, without bringing her back to me. I began to despair again. I had informed the police of these last events. Toward midnight I was still in my office, almost insane with sorrow, when someone rang at the door. A policeman brought my wife back half dead. You can imagine what our reunion was like.

"The maid helped Ellen get to bed and I had our doctor called. My wife's body was covered with bruises and bleeding stripes, traces of the wicked treatment that those wretches had inflicted on their victim.

"My indignation knew no limits. I expressly asked the police to find the criminals and bring them to justice. At present, Miss King, all my hope resides in you. I beg you to put these ferocious beasts away so they can do no more harm, because they will try to renew their hideous crime."

Ethel King stood up.

"I will proceed immediately," she answered. "If I succeed in ridding society of these harpies, that will be one of the greatest successes of my career."

She turned toward Mrs. O'Beering and added:

"So, you don't have any idea of what neighborhood or what gang held you prisoner?"

"No, I was unconscious when they took me to that cellar and when they brought me out of it."

"Neither can you give me a description of your jailors?"

"I only recall well the feature of the one who spoke to me. She was a fat woman with a puffy face and filthy skin. Her eyes had a greenish tint. She had full lips. Her hair was untidy; her hands large and red. She had a small, snub nose."

"These women didn't call each other by their first names in front of you?"

Mrs. O'Beering thought a moment.

"I don't recall, however…it seems to me I heard the name Jenny. But I don't know which of the four women it applied to."

"What kind of weapon did the wretches threaten you with?"

"They beat me with scrubbing brushes and clubs and threatened me with knives. One of them even suggested throwing me into boiling washing water."

Ethel King made a gesture of satisfaction.

"Now there's a clue all right."

O'Beering and his wife looked at the detective in astonishment.

"How's that?" the gentleman exclaimed.

"Oh, yes! You said a while ago, Mrs. O'Beering, that the head of the gang had red hands. The threat to throw you into boiling washing water, the fact of having beat you with scrubbing brushes, leads us to conclude that the four wretches are washerwomen."

"Ah! Now I remember," Ellen exclaimed. "When the women opened the door, I thought I smelled the odor of soap. That fact struck me, now that you call attention to it."

"In that case, my hypothesis is becoming almost a certainty. Good-bye, Mr. and Mrs. O'Beering. I don't despair of finding in the immense city of Philadelphia a washerwoman named Jenny."

A Fruitful Interrogation

Edith King went immediately to the police to see Inspector Golding.

"Well!" he exclaimed when she entered his office. "Have you been to see James O'Beering? The case doesn't look good, does it? The two spouses' information doesn't furnish the slightest clue, unfortunately."

Ethel King smiled.

"I hold another opinion, Mr. Golding."

The official looked wide-eyed at his visitor.

"What!" he exclaimed. "You've been able to deduce something serious from what they said?"

"I believe so."

"What is it?" the Chief of Police asked, anxious to know.

The young woman warded off the question with a gesture.

"I can't say anything yet," she declared calmly. "I would first like to get authorization to interrogate the prisoner, Tom Kensing."

"Do what you like, Miss King. If you really possess a clue that will allow us to find the criminals, hurry, because I was told this morning about the disappearance of a young girl, and I believe that this new horrible crime must be attributed to the four shrews."

"Who was it?"

"Miss Maud Sutter, the daughter of the well-known banker. The father, who is in despair, came to see me personally and begged me to get his child back. He offered to pay out a huge amount of money."

"Miss Maud Sutter," Ethel King repeated thoughtfully. "Isn't she that somewhat too emancipated young girl known for her eccentric behavior?"

"Yes, that's the one," Golding replied. "And it's also due to odd behavior that she must have fallen into the hands of the gang. Yesterday she was in Wharton Street, at the house of a friend, Miss Rysing. She had ordered her chauffeur to come pick her up at 10 p.m. with the car. The man wasn't on time, which infuriated the young girl. In her impatience, she declared that she would walk the long distance from Wharton Street to Lehigh Avenue. Miss Rysing tried in vain to make her give up that idea. Miss Sutter even refused to let a servant go with her, and since at 10:30 p.m. the chauffeur still hadn't arrived, she left without waiting any longer. She hasn't yet returned home."

"I think that if Maud Sutter has had the same adventure as Mrs. O'Beering, she'll be wiser in the future."

"That's my opinion," Golding said approvingly. "Besides, up until now I've kept the incident secret and seen to it that the newspapers don't talk about it. I wanted to first wait for the result of your visit to O'Beering and his wife, to see if you would obtain some important information. Since this seems to be the case, please tell me if you think it necessary to send a note to the press concerning the disappearance of Miss Maud Sutter."

"Not at the moment. I want first to proceed to the interrogation of Tom Kensing. After that, I'll tell you what seems preferable to me."

The famous detective went to the holding cells, where, on her request, they took her to Tom Kensing's cell.

The man, dressed in rags, had a vulgar expression and a treacherous look. He was walking up and down in his cell whistling. A key grated in the lock and the jailor let the detective in.

Tom raised his head, surprised, and shouted:

"Goddam, better and better! Now I even receive ladies in my prison. I'm curious to know what this one wants with me."

The young woman waited until the jailor had left, then she spoke to the prisoner.

"I'm Ethel King," she said with composure.

"Ethel King," he repeated.

He had obviously not expected to hear that name. He showed a certain worry. He gave the young woman a sheepish look.

"You know why I've come," Ethel King said.

"No, I don't know that," he grumbled in a not very confident voice. "I'll certainly be released. I can't be punished for having been a delivery man for an unknown person."

"Don't lie," Ethel King said with such firmness that he lowered his eyes.

Kensing's embarrassment lasted only an instant. He shrugged and sneered.

"You're trying to intimidate me, but you won't succeed. I'm innocent. Things happened like I said."

Ethel King didn't get upset.

"How stupid you are!" she said coldly. "Your accomplices didn't let you off. They've thrown all the responsibility on you."

The man recoiled a step and swore.

"Goddam! If that was true!" he exclaimed.

The young woman began to laugh.

"That's already a confession," she said. "You know more about it than you claim. But persist in your lies if you want to. Your stubbornness will, I guarantee you, get you some years more."

"I won't add a word. What I said is true. Believe it or not; it's all the same to me."

He sat down on the bench, hid his face in his hands, and remained motionless. Ethel King stayed planted in front of him. A minute went by in silence. Then the man lifted his eyes and shook his fist when he saw the detective's mocking smile.

"The Devil! What more do you want with me?" he shouted. "Since I've told you I won't answer you; leave me in peace."

"Very well. I'm going to walk over to the cell of fat Jenny, the laundress. Her statements are so clear that we don't need your confession."

When Ethel King named Jenny the laundress, rage tore apart the prisoner's features. He became livid, then the blood flowed into his face and he turned purple. He jumped up and walked about excitedly in his cell like an enraged lion.

"Really!" he exclaimed. "So you know everything. We've been betrayed! That Jenny Burde, that I had so much trust in, has handed me over. Oh! The pig! But I want..."

But he stopped, looking with hate at Ethel King.

"So you've won! You've picked up the trace of Jenny. You've discovered the secrets of the Norris Street laundry."

"Absolutely!"

The man raised his fists.

"Demon! I'll strangle you!"

He wanted to throw himself on the young woman, but she was already threatening him with her revolver.

"Stop!" she said in a sharp voice. "One step more and you're dead!"

The rogue stopped as if rooted in his steps. His chest heaved convulsively. Ethel King retreated as far as the door and knocked to tell the jailer to open for her. When she had gotten out and the jailer had closed the door again, Ethel King opened the grill in the door and said to the prisoner, who was still planted in the middle of the cell:

"I'm going now to the Norris Street laundry. Not one of the four women has been arrested yet. I didn't even know that they were laundresses and that one of them was named Jenny Burde. But, thanks to you, I've learned some very interesting things. I think it won't be too difficult for me to rid society of your infamous gang. A thousand thanks, old fellow!"

The grill closed. The criminal had remained as if petrified on hearing that he had betrayed his accomplices without intending to. When he understood that Ethel King had tricked him, he threw himself against the door with a cry of rage and hit his fists against the massive panel as if he wanted to knock it down. Ethel King paid no attention. She returned to Inspector Golding's office.

"Back already?" Inspector Golding asked. "Wasn't I right? Either this Tom Kensing is innocent or he's diametrically the opposite and a stubborn fellow."

"Oh! No. On the contrary, he was completely frank with me," the young woman said, smiling. "I learned everything I wanted from him. I have the firm hope, Mr. Golding, to shortly deliver to you, tomorrow probably, that infamous female quartet and their accomplices."

"That's marvelous! If you do that, Miss King, you will have solved a difficult problem in the most brilliant fashion. And I can tell you that you have once again shown us up, the regular police, I mean."

The young woman was content to smile. She took leave of the inspector and returned to her home to confer with Charley Lux, her cousin and assistant, on the steps to be taken. It was a matter, first of all, of finding the Norris Street laundry where Jenny Burde was employed.

The Laundry

Norris Street, on the east side, is one of the shortest streets in Philadelphia. The old houses which line it are occupied by a lower class population and people are stacked up by the hundreds in one single building. The police descend frequently into these houses, which often serve as hideouts for the worst criminals.

Jenny Burde's laundry was located at the back of No. 66, in a narrow and dark courtyard. She had only an impoverished clientele. However, there was no shortage of work. The establishment had no fewer than three washerwomen who worked all day at their vats.

The washroom was located in the cellar. The first floor, with its three rooms, served as living quarters for the owner and her employees.

In addition to the washroom, the basement contained other rooms which the laundress always kept locked.

Ethel King had first concentrated her inquiries in that part of the street which she knew was badly inhabited, and she had quickly learned of the laundry's existence.

There was a lot of activity in the washroom. The four women were occupied scrubbing linen, but it was easy to see that they had no taste for the work. They often left their washtubs and went into the neighboring room where there were bottles of brandy lined up with all kinds of delicacies.

The washerwomen were already greatly under the influence of alcohol. They were laughing, exchanging dirty jokes, and singing. They were not getting through a lot of work. The afternoon was already far advanced. One of them shouted:

"That's enough for today. I'm tired of working like a dog for a few miserable pennies."

"You're right, Jenny," another one answered. "We must get busy to pull off some more good jobs. After that we'll be able to retire."

"Be patient! This won't last much longer, Nanny," the woman responded. "When we let out the one who's inside right now, that will be at a good price. The situation is excellent, you can take my word for it, and I think that afterwards each one of us can retire with our $10,000 in our pockets."

Shouts of joy erupted, and the four women chanted in triumph. At that moment, the door leading to the courtyard opened suddenly and the washerwomen hushed. An ill-kempt, dirty man entered, stopped and looked around at the women with confusion.

"Is she here?" he asked, out of breath.

The laundresses looked at each other with astonishment, and Jenny answered.

"Who are you looking for?"

"My sister."

"Look at the four of us. Do you recognize your sister?"

The women burst out laughing.

"That boy could be our son, but our brother, never!" one of them observed.

"What's she like, your sister," Jenny asked.

"You won't betray us?" the young man asked, looking at the four women with distrust.

"Come now, why would we do that?"

"Will you protect us…and…"

He hesitated.

"But, go on then, speak!" Jenny exclaimed. "If it's the police you're afraid of, you're safe with us."

"Really?"

"You can certainly believe me when I tell you so. We aren't exactly the friends of the blue tunics and when we can play them a bad turn, we don't miss doing it."

The adolescent breathed easy.

"I believe you. I can see by your face that you can be trusted."

"Thanks for those good words," Jenny said, laughing.

"The police are, in fact, on our heels. We've run like crazy."

"What did you do?

He was silent a moment and looked the washerwomen up and down. Then he said:

"It was in the street. We roughed up a lady a little. She's probably taking a trip to eternity."

He had said these last words in an almost inaudible voice, backing off toward the door, as if afraid that the laundresses, on hearing his confession, might cry out for help. But Jenny told him:

"Stay. We won't betray you. We'll hide you and your sister."

"Then this isn't a trap?"

"No, certainly not!"

"I'll go back out to the street to look for my sister. I saw her hide in that courtyard. Can I bring her back with me?"

"But naturally."

"If you protect us, we'll give you a nice present."

A burst of laughter greeted that promise.

"You! What do you want to give us?"

The adolescent looked offended and replied:

"Do you really think I don't have anything? You're making a big mistake. I've just taken something very beautiful from the lady."

"And what's that?"

"Do you want me to show you what I'll give you?"

"But, of course! Show it!"

The young criminal rummaged in his pocket and brought out a bracelet set with diamonds.

"Here's what you'll have. That's worth at least $2000."

The women's eyes gleamed with covetousness.

"Then come back with your sister," the four women exclaimed with one voice. "You don't have anything to be afraid of. On the contrary, I think we'll get on very well."

The young man nodded in satisfaction and replied:

"So much the better. Let's hope I can find Mary, and that she hasn't fallen into the hands of the police."

He went out the door and climbed up to the courtyard. Some ten minutes went by and the adolescent reappeared accompanied by a girl with a more than neglected appearance. She was pale and seemed very excited. The young man came in quickly, while the girl stopped, trembling, on the threshold.

"Here we are. This is my sister Mary."

"So come in, Mary!" Jenny exclaimed. "You don't need to be afraid."

The girl still hesitated.

"I don't know. You're laundresses…You won't betray me?"

"No, what the devil! Hurry up, or the policemen will pinch you."

"Do you have a safe hiding place for us?" the girl, still distrustful, asked.

"Naturally, and one even better than you imagine."

At that moment heavy footsteps resounded on the courtyard pavement.

"There they are, the police!" the trembling girl cried out. "Oh! Hide us! Hide us! We're lost."

The steps approached the stairs. Jenny ran to the door at the back and opened it.

"Quick! Get in there! Don't make a sound!"

The adolescent hid in the cellar with his sister and Jenny locked the door. Then she returned to her washing vat, and the four women began to work with scrubbing brushes and beat the clothes as if they still had a great deal of work to do.

The door to the courtyard was pushed open and a policeman appeared on the threshold.

"What! Still at work?" he shouted.

"But, of course. We have a lot to do."

"Have a young man and a girl by any chance come down there to you? We're looking for them because they murdered someone."

"Oh! Murdered!" Jenny exclaimed, shivering in horror. "That's terrible! Even so, there are some bad rascals on this earth! Try at least to see that those there don't escape you!"

"So, you haven't seen them?"

"No, we would tell you if we had. There's no place in our business for such scoundrels."

"If you see a suspicious person, warn the police immediately," the policeman said.

"Don't worry; but I don't think anyone will have an idea of coming down here."

The policeman saluted and left.

However, a curious scene was taking place in the neighboring cellar. When the door had closed, that place was completely dark. But the girl took a flashlight out of her pocket and turned it on. The ray of light fell on the row of food and drink.

"They lead a life of Lucullus here," the woman said in a low voice, "but that will end in tears and gnashing of teeth."

There was a bolted door at the back. The girl approached it and placed her ear at the keyhole. She shook her head when she heard stifled sobs.

"She's inside there, Charley," she murmured. "We're in the gang's hideout."

The two who were pretending to be murderers were none other than Ethel King and Charley Lux. After what she had learned, Ethel King could have requisitioned help from the police and raided Jenny Burde's establishment, but she preferred to go about it differently. She was afraid that the shrews had imprisoned their victim in a secret hideout where someone who didn't know about it would not have been able to gain entrance. If the women had been arrested, they probably would not have betrayed their secret, and the unfortunate prisoner would be dead of starvation in her hidden cell.

Ethel King could now ascertain that the door to the cellar was not hidden, but she was nevertheless glad that she had first entered alone in the place.

At the end of an hour, Jenny again opened the door to the laundry.

"The danger is past," she said. "You are absolutely safe; the police won't come back."

The washerwoman told what had happened, exaggerating the conversation with the policeman. Ethel King thanked the woman warmly, and shook her red, somewhat swollen hands.

The description Mrs. O'Beering had given of the leader of the gang fit Jenny Burde completely. She had a puffy face, a grayish complexion, green eyes, untidy hair and full lips.

The women stopped work and passed into the middle cave where they began to drink and eat. They invited their guests to partake of the food and drink.

"What do you think? Why don't you stay here all the time," suggested Jenny, on whom the alcohol was having more and more effect.

"Stay here all the time?" Ethel King replied. "But that can't be."

"And why not?"

"Because you can't require my brother to help you with the washing, and because I myself don't feel I have any taste for that job."

The women laughed.

"It's not in the washing you can help us. You can be useful in another way," Jenny said mysteriously.

Ethel King pretended great curiosity.

"Another way? So you have another profession?"

"Oh, yes, and a very lucrative one, I hope you may believe it. However, to exercise it you have to have a big conscience, as you yourselves do. It's a matter, in fact, something like what you did this evening and which almost got you caught."

"Ah! So that's it!" Charley exclaimed. "Then I'm for it and I bet that my sister will go along too."

"Why not? The essential thing is that it brings in money."

"Good Lord!" Jenny said. She went into a corner of the cellar, dislodged a loose stone from the wall and took several stacks of bank notes from the hole and showed them to her new friends.

"Look! Here's what that brings in," she said. "Are you in?"

"That goes without saying. But now tell me, what it's all about."

The horrible woman leaned over to the detective's ear and whispered.

"We lock up rich people here in our cellar and keep them prisoner until we've been paid a fitting ransom to give them their liberty."

"And if you aren't paid?"

The old woman laughed silently and diabolically.

"In that case, the prisoners don't leave here alive."

"All right, but how do you manage to bring them here without anyone knowing about it?"

"We go about it very cleverly. The last time we had to do the job all alone, because Sam Workman is in prison."

"Sam Workman? Who's that?"

"My son and our assistant," another woman declared.

"And why is he in prison?"

"Because he was the messenger. We put him in charge of going for the ransom, but he was arrested. Naturally they don't have anything against him. He said that he had received the commission from someone he didn't know who came up to him in the street. They will be forced to release him."

"That's very clever," Ethel King said. "So you now have a bird in the cage?"

"Yes, there, behind that door," Jenny whispered in the ear of her new accomplices.

"Who is it?"

"If we only knew!"

"What! You've kidnapped someone and you don't even know who it is?"

Jenny's eyes gleamed with rage. "She won't say. But no matter how stubborn she is, we'll certainly make her talk."

"How will you do that? So you haven't yet tried?"

"Yes we have. We picked up that little girl not far from Line Street. It was between 11 p.m. and midnight...nobody in the street...I slipped up behind the young girl and, wham, a nice little tap on the back of the head made her see 36 candles.

"We carried her here through the courtyard and we threw her in there on the pallet. When she regained consciousness, we asked her to tell us who she was, but she refused to answer. We wanted to jump on her to give her a good thrashing, but she drew a revolver and pointed it at us. We beat a fast retreat. The rogue fired, but fortunately didn't hit us. We had time to go outside and lock her up."

"How long has she been here?"

"Since this morning."

"What have you decided?"

"She may be sleeping now. We want to slip inside without making any noise and take away her revolver."

"And if she's not asleep?"

"We'll let her stay locked up until hunger and fatigue wear down her strength. Then we'll make sure of her."

Jenny went to listen at the door of the cell, and not hearing anything, she whispered:

"She seems to be asleep. I'm going to try to open the door."

"Hand me the key," Ethel King advised. "I have some experience in the art of opening locks without making any noise."

"Goddam!" Jenny exclaimed. "You seem, like a remarkable customer!"

She rummaged in her pocket and held out the key to the detective, who used it with remarkable skill. No grating, no click broke the silence. Finally the young woman stepped back.

"It's open," she said.

"By thunder! You're incomparable. I believe you'll be very useful."

"My brother too." Ethel King answered. "We've already done a lot of difficult things together."

"And we've often been up against the police," Charley answered in a significant tone.

"Maybe you can succeed in taking her revolver away from her," Jenny said to Ethel.

"I'm going to try, but you'll have to help me. If she's awake, I'll talk to her, and if she lowers her revolver, one of you come quickly and take it from her. However, I won't do that except on one condition."

"What's that?"

"You must promise me not to maltreat the prisoner."

"Oh! Oh! Why's that?"

"Well, I don't like that. Besides, I promise to make her tell who she is."

"In that case, we won't need to beat her," Jenny growled.

"Good. Two of you pick up the lanterns. When I open the door, raise them so that the light shines into the cell."

"Agreed."

"We must be able to see immediately whether she's asleep or if she's awake, and so that we may be ready for anything. It's possible that she'll receive us with revolver shots."

Ethel King put her hand on the latch. The two women holding the lanterns had placed themselves behind her, trying to be sheltered in case the prisoner should open fire.

The detective brusquely pulled the door open wide.

The prisoner was not asleep. Pale, but resolute, she was standing in the middle of the cellar, holding her revolver pointed at the gang.

"Don't come any closer!" she shouted. "The first one who moves, I'll blow her head off."

"Stay calm, Miss," Ethel King answered. "Do you care so much about staying in this cell where you'll finally die of hunger?"

The young girl trembled.

"You won't do that! A human being can't be capable of such cruelty."

"We'll give you your freedom immediately if you tell us who you are," Jenny Burde shouted.

"At no price. I suspect that you're hatching some plot against my father and I won't do anything to help you carry it out. I won't answer."

"It's not at all a matter of a plot. We just want to get a ransom to give you your freedom," Jenny insisted.

"I don't believe you. I know that you are capable of anything and you wouldn't hesitate to commit murder."

"You're right," Jenny Burde sneered.

"You can tell your name, Miss," Ethel King said. "I promise you nothing will happen to your father."

The tone of her voice seemed to calm the young girl's fears, because she lowered her revolver and answered:

"If only that were true!"

"You can believe me."

"If I trust you…"

The young girl didn't finish her sentence. Jenny had jumped on her like a tigress and snatched the revolver from her. The old woman brandished the weapon with a gesture of triumph. Her three accomplices rushed toward the unfortunate girl and dragged her brutally into the other cellar.

The young girl was elegantly dressed. She wore a white plume boa and an expensive hat, which in the scuffle fell with her loosened hair onto her neck. Ethel King vigorously pushed back the shrews, who were trying to beat the prisoner.

"What did you promise me? Don't touch her any more. I'm going to talk to her and she'll tell me who she is."

The poor girl had fallen down on a bench. She had clasped both hands to her nervous breast and was looking around her in terror. If she was capricious, inclined to extravagant behavior, nothing more of that now appeared. She was only a weak, defenseless woman. All her arrogance, all her pride had vanished. The unfortunate seemed to still have some confidence in Ethel King. She was looking toward her. But Jenny shouted:

"We're not asking you for your opinion, Mary. That stubborn girl will be severely thrashed if she refuses any longer to tell us her name and anyone who wants to take her away from us will have their brains blown out."

While she was talking, she was waving around her revolver, but her astonishment was great when Ethel King suddenly grabbed the weapon on the fly.

"If such are your intentions, it would be better for you not to have the revolver," the detective said.

The venom of anger rose to Jenny's face.

"Give me back that weapon, immediately!"

"That's not my intention."

"Be careful! You won't leave here alive if you refuse to obey me!"

"I will keep this revolver and I'll leave here alive. Do you imagine that I'm afraid of your threats?"

The other women intervened.

"Let Mary alone," they exclaimed. "You can see she's very clever and that she can help us. Don't quarrel with her right off."

"She has to give me back the revolver."

"I'm keeping it," Ethel King replied coldly.

"Then keep it. But you won't keep us from punishing our prisoner if she persists in not telling us her name."

The young girl, pale and trembling, had witnessed that scene.

"Give me my freedom," she said. "I promise to have $1000 in cash sent to you."

"A thousand dollars," Jenny exclaimed. "You believe we are stupider than we are. No, my dove, we require $40,000, $10,000 for each of us."

"Scoundrels!" the young girl cried out, trembling.

"This is the last time that I'll ask you. Who are you?" Jenny Burde screeched.

187

There was a moment of silence; then the prisoner answered in a firm voice:

"And I tell you for the last time. You will never know my name."

"Think about it! It means your liberty, your life."

"Nevertheless, I'm determined not to answer you."

Ethel King was standing beside Charley. She signaled to him furtively and the young man took advantage of a moment of inattention of the four old women to slip out.

"Listen to me," Jenny Burde continued. "You're not the first one whose stubbornness we have overcome. If you haven't answered me in one minute, you'll die."

"Murder me then, if you dare!"

Jenny's eyes flashed with cruelty.

"Don't take it so lightly. Do you really think it's pleasant to die?"

"I'm not afraid."

Then Jenny took out a long knife and the three others followed her example. The harpy then went to a corner of the cellar and stamped her foot on a tile.

"Do you know who is buried here? A young girl like you who at first refused to tell us her name. When she finally did, she didn't want to write to her parents to ask them for the ransom. We killed her. We took out our knives as we are doing now and we plunged them into her breast."

The prisoner, frozen with fear, looked around with haggard eyes at her tormentors.

"Who are you? What's your name? What's your father's address?" Jenny repeated.

"I won't tell you. My poor father must not become your victim."

Jenny Burde then turned to her accomplices.

"We can't hesitate any longer. Kill her."

The furious women raised their knives. Jenny was the first to rush forward to strike the livid prisoner. But she suddenly stopped, as did her accomplices, and looked with stupor at Mary, her new recruit.

"Get back, you scoundrels!" the detective shouted. "Get back! Surrender! I've come to put an end to your atrocities. Surrender! It's Ethel King speaking to you."

The effect of these words was extraordinary. The name of Ethel King obviously inspired great terror in the gang. The criminals stood petrified, unable to say a word.

"Don't move," the detective continued. "Here, Maud Sutter, take this revolver and be careful. If one of these rascals makes a suspicious movement, don't hesitate to blow her brains out!"

"You know who I am!" exclaimed the young girl. "Oh! Miss King, how can I ever thank you?"

She took the revolver and stood up resolutely. She was no longer afraid.

"Get over into that corner!" Ethel King ordered the harpies.

Jenny Burde didn't move, but the three others obeyed, trembling.

"You too, Jenny Burde!"

At that the criminal cried out in rage and made a movement as if to throw herself on Ethel King, but she had already fired. Jenny, wounded in the right hand, dropped her knife and fell back, moaning. On another order by the detective, she joined her accomplices in the corner, but it could easily be seen that she was in a fierce rage.

A few minutes later, Charley Lux reappeared, bringing policemen who proceeded to arrest the four women and put them in handcuffs. Jenny cursed and insulted Ethel King and the police agents. Ethel King had Inspector Golding called, and, with him and the policemen, she proceeded to investigate the cellar. In the spot Jenny had pointed out, they found a cadaver under the tiles. Research established that the victim was a young English woman that the gang had stabbed after having tried in vain to get a ransom from her.

Mrs. O'Beering visited the cellar and recognized the place where she had spent such horrible hours. As for Maud Sutter, she was metamorphosed. The terrible day she had passed among the human beasts put an end to her outrageous behavior. Tom Kensing, or rather Sam Workman, to use his real name, was the accomplice of the four harpies. He was the one who had clubbed the O'Beering chauffeur and taken his place at the steering wheel while Jenny Burde was hidden inside the car.

Jenny Burde was condemned to death and executed as leader of the gang. The three other women were given 20 years of hard labor. This was not the first time Sam Workman had been condemned and he also had to renounce liberty for many long years.

No. 52 Chaque fascicule contient un récit complet. 10 Cts.

ETHEL KING

LE NICK CARTER FÉMININ

Vengeance d'Étudiant.

«Regardez, Miss King.... là...» C'est la tête de miss Allen!»

9. TRAGIC RIVALRY

The End of an Artist

"Mrs. Howard! Mrs. Howard!"

A beardless young man with a likeable appearance and a pleasant face surrounded by beautiful brown curly hair had shouted that name. It was the great violinist, John Eryson, the renter of the widow Howard, an affable old lady who took a great deal of interest in the artistic career of her lodger. He occupied a corner room of the little house situated at No. 56 Seneca Street in Philadelphia.

Evening was coming on, twilight was darkening the outside when the artist came down the stairs into the vestibule. The door to the living room opened and Mrs. Howard appeared on the threshold.

"What is it, Mr. Eryson," the lady asked.

The young man came into the room and held out a letter.

"Look! I've been offered the position of Director of the Harrisburg Conservatory. I am to assume the position as of April 1st."

Mrs. Howard's face lit up.

"I wholeheartedly congratulate you, Mr. Eryson. You're already famous at the age of 32 and I must say you deserve your rapid advancement."

"I'm very happy," the violinist declared. "To tell the truth I didn't hope to get that position when I posed my candidacy. When I was told I was in the running, I still couldn't believe that I would succeed, because I was competing with older candidates."

"Yes, but nevertheless the choice has fallen on you. Most certainly it will be painful for me to lose a lodger who has become almost a son to me, but I hope we'll see each other from time to time, Mr. Eryson."

"That goes without saying. I'll come to Philadelphia often and I'm also counting on you to visit me sometime in Harrisburg."

The artist was beaming with joy. He sent the maid to get some bottles of good wine to toast his nomination with his landlady and a young friend who had come to congratulate him.

After supper he picked up his violin and played some concert pieces with virtuosity and incomparable charm. His mood influenced his playing. He was overflowing with enthusiasm; he could never have played a sad note.

Until that time, John Eryson had earned his living appearing as the soloist in major concerts. He always received large fees and each time brought away a triumph. Nevertheless, the young man had finally thought about getting a permanent situation. Concerts were becoming rarer and, then, Eryson intended to marry and start a family. He had therefore placed his candidature to the Harrisburg Conservatory and had beaten his competitors.

The party remained in the living room until midnight. The modest virtuoso then accompanied his friend to the door, before going upstairs to his bedroom. Mrs. Howard went to her bedroom, which was on the first floor. The windows at the back opened onto the garden. The night was pleasant and the widow opened the casement window to get a breath of air. Upstairs John Eryson had also opened a window. The beauty of the night was not without making an impression on the young man. He again picked up his violin and began to make the instrument sing. At such moments, John Eryson would have drawn tears of admiration from the most insensitive. It seemed his whole soul vibrated with the cords.

Mrs. Howard, leaning on her window sill, listened, plunged in a gentle reverie. She could imagine nothing more marvelous than to contemplate the starry heaven while divine music reached her ears. She trembled momentarily. The enchanting melody had been interrupted by a loud discordant screeching. A moan sounded in the night; the sound of a fall suddenly resounded. The old woman remained petrified with terror. She was agonized by the impression that something awful had happened.

"My God! What's happened," she stammered.

She remained motionless for a long time listening for noises, but she didn't hear anything else. She leaned out the window in order to see outside. The casement window in the corner was still open. The oil lamp, still burning, threw clear reflections on the tree leaves.

"Could I be mistaken? Could Mr. Eryson have simply stopped playing because he'd had enough of holding the bow? That isn't his habit."

She called out several times in a loud voice:

"Mr. Eryson! Mr. Eryson!"

She got no answer. If the young man had been in his room, he surely would have heard his landlady's call. Something unusual had happened. Perhaps the violinist had gone out. Mrs. Howard went to her door to call out the name of the artist in the stairway. But she didn't receive an answer any more than she did the first time. She felt more and more worried. She went up to the third floor to awaken the manservant and the maid. The sound of her voice betrayed so much anxiety that the two servants hardly took the time to dress.

"In the name of heaven, Mrs. Howard, what's happened to you?" the manservant asked.

"Mr. Eryson must have had an accident," the old lady replied. "Let's go up quickly."

A minute later, Mrs. Howard knocked on the violinist's door and called out, still with no answer. She lifted the latch, but couldn't open it; the door was locked or bolted on the inside.

"Go get the pólice!" Mrs. Howard instructed. "We have to force the lock. But come back immediately. I'm dying of fright."

"I'll be back in ten minutes at the most," the servant said. "The Commissioner's office isn't far from here."

He ran down the stairs. The widow and her maid stayed in front of the bedroom door. Mrs. Howard listened, hoping in vain that Eryson would finally give some sign of life.

It was two minutes after the manservant had left that the maid cried out:

"I hear some noise! It sounds like footsteps. Yes, someone is walking about," she said.

She knocked again and called out:

"Mr. Eryson! Mr. Eryson! Answer us, please. You're making us mortally worried."

At that moment someone opened the lock from inside the room. They pushed the door open so hard that Mrs. Howard was knocked over by the force and she began to cry out in fear. The maid herself let out a terrified cry and dropped the lamp she was holding in her hand. The light went out; the stairway was plunged into darkness.

A very tall man had come out of Eryson's bedroom. He was dressed in a long black cloak. A wide-brimmed hat was pulled down over his forehead. His features were hidden by a piece of black cloth wrapped around his face.

He rushed past the women and went down the stairs four at a time. Mrs. Howard had fallen behind the door and had not seen the stranger. She got up trembling.

"But, My God! What's happened?" she moaned. "Mr. Eryson, why did you open the door so hard? Elise, why have you dropped the lamp?"

The maid was stretched out unconscious beside the broken lamp. The door to the house opened suddenly; then it slammed noisily.

The widow felt around her automatically, pushed open the door to the bedroom, and stumbled over the body of the maid. She was shaken by trembling; a groan came from her lips. She had no matches on her.

"Light...I need some light!" she whispered.

She groped her way downstairs to look for a lamp and some matches. Terror was paralyzing her. A terrible foreboding distracted her. She never knew how she had made it downstairs. She went into the first room she came to and found a lamp. It took her some time to light it because, in her anxiety, she still could not locate any matches. When she finally got back to the landing, the lamp in her hand, the male servant had returned bringing policemen. She let out a sign of relief on hearing the men's voices, and called out;

"Come quickly! Come up, gentlemen. I fear that my house has been the scene of an awful misfortune."

The servant showed the policemen the way, and Mrs. Howard came behind with her lamp. At the threshold of the bedroom door, the little troop found the maid unconscious among the debris of the lamp in a big pool of oil. When the manservant pushed open the door, he saw there was no light in the bedroom. When the rays from Mrs. Howard's lamp fell into the room, the old lady and the policemen heard a cry of horror. The manservant still had the presence of mind to take the lamp from his mistress. Without that, she would surely have dropped it. A policeman caught Mrs. Howard in his arms and placed her in an armchair, where she remained prostrate, unconscious. The spectacle the policemen saw was terrible.

The body of the young artist was stretched out under the window, his violin beside him, his bow in his clinched hand. He had received a well-placed stab from behind which had pierced his heart. A large pool of dark blood had formed underneath the unfortunate man. His eyes were wide open in his pale face. He must have rolled over in his last convulsions. His cheek was bathed in his own blood. His hair was in disarray. It appeared that nothing had been touched in the bedroom. Everything seemed to be in its usual place.

One of the policemen left immediately to report to the commissariat and to bring the coroner. The manservant lavished care on his mistress and succeeded in bringing her back to consciousness. The maid also came around and told what she knew about the mysterious man who had passed in front of her.

Mrs. Howard was overcome. She could not have shown more sorrow if she had just learned of the murder of her own son. Fortunately for her, a flood of tears brought some relief to her deep sorrow.

The coroner arrived, bringing Mr. Carras, the neighborhood Commissioner. He verified that the victim had been killed by a knife wound delivered with great violence. The criminal must have taken advantage of the fact that the victim was playing the violin to slip up behind him.

The crime wasn't motivated by theft, because neither the victim's gold watch nor his wallet had been taken.

Mrs. Howard brushed aside revenge as a motive. She affirmed that Mr. Eryson led a very quiet life and visited friends, who were above suspicion, infrequently. The young artist couldn't have had any enemies, because he was very modest and had a retiring character; he had never had a quarrel.

But then, who could this mysterious character be who had so violently opened the door and fled? The murderer, surely. The information the maid gave about him, however, was too vague to be used as a basis for any investigation.

Carras, confirming that it was a strange and very confused case, decided to be safe and get the assistance of a very experienced detective. At daybreak he took a cab and had himself taken to 77 Garden Street, to the home of the famous Ethel King. He wanted to interest the young woman in the case.

The detective, who was not overburdened with work, agreed immediately to the Commissioner's request. She was even more interested in that murder because she knew the young virtuoso personally and had heard him with delight several times in concerts. She felt the most ardent desire to arrest the scoundrel who was so hardened as to cut short the days of such an artist.

It was 7 a.m. when, with Carras, she got on the way to the house of the widow Howard. Newspaper hawkers were already selling special editions in which they announced to the citizens of Philadelphia the tragic end of the famous violinist, John Eryson.

Mrs. Howard was somewhat in control of herself. She greeted the great detective whom she knew by reputation, and exchanged a cordial handshake with her.

Ah! Miss King," she exclaimed. "You'll find this scoundrel, won't you? Poor Eryson, so cowardly assassinated, must be avenged."

"Most certainly," replied the detective. "I'm determined to do it. I have often heard, with enthusiasm, John Eryson's admirable playing. It was a genius that we have just lost. The villain who had the heart to murder such a man while he was playing the violin must be a brute, inaccessible to any human feeling."

She had the events of the night told to her once more and interrogated the maid with particular care.

"So, the only thing you noticed was that the stranger was wearing a black overcoat, a black hat, and had wrapped a piece of black cloth over his face?"

"Yes, I didn't see the rest but for a second," the maid answered. "Then I dropped the lamp. I heard the unknown man's footsteps again on the stairs, and I fainted."

"How tall was the stranger? Was he tall or stocky?"

"He seemed to me to be very tall; he was at least a head taller than I am."

Ethel King could get nothing more out of the young girl. She went up to the victim's bedroom to go ahead with the investigation. The body was no longer there. The coroner had had it picked up and transported to the morgue in the cemetery. She first examined the floor, then turned all her attention to the furniture. She finally remarked, addressing the Commissioner:

"This is unusual. Despite what Mrs. Howard said, everything seems to prove that it was a matter of revenge."

"I agree with you," Carras stated. "Also, the crime may have been committed out of spite or envy."

"You mean to say that someone was jealous of John Eryson's talent?"

"Yes, but there's more. Yesterday the violinist received the news that he had been named Director of the Harrisburg Conservatory. The young man was delighted, Mrs. Howard told me."

The widow confirmed that statement.

"We stayed very late at the table yesterday evening. We had supper with a friend of Mr. Eryson. A sad feeling was mingled with my joy. The thought of being soon separated from my lodger, that I loved like a son, was painful to me."

"Who was that friend you dined with?"

"A young pianist, Mr. Holm Berger."

"Ah! I'm acquainted with him. He has a good reputation. He's surely not the guilty person."

"No, certainly not. His joy was sincere when he learned about John's appointment," the widow said.

"We're definitely faced with an enigma!" Carras said with vexation. "I don't at all see how we can pick up the trail of the criminal. Besides, duty calls me back to my office. Are you staying here, Miss King?"

"Yes, I haven't finished my investigation."

"Good. I wish you good luck. I have no great hope that we'll succeed in catching the murderer."

Ethel King shrugged.

"I can't yet confirm anything either, naturally, but this affair isn't any more obscure than a great number of others turned over to me and that I solved."

The Commissioner left. Ethel King was alone with Mrs. Howard in the violinist's bedroom. She sat down at the secretary and opened the long drawer. It contained musical notebooks thrown in pell-mell. The detective gave Mrs. Howard a questioning look.

"Was there always such disorder in this drawer?" she asked.

The old lady shook her head.

"I couldn't tell you. It's been months since I looked in it. Mr. Eryson usually kept it locked. But I can't imagine that he conserved his manuscripts and compositions with so little care. My lodger was very orderly. Why would he have given up his habits in this way?"

Ethel thoughtfully considered the sheets covered with musical notations.

"It looks as if someone rummaged around hastily in these papers," she said.

She began to examine the contents of the drawer and finally noticed a notebook bearing the inscription: *LIST OF MY COMPOSITIONS*. She opened it and found inside the titles of John Eryson's musical compositions. A great number of the pieces had already been published and very well received by the public. But the last titles were those of works still unpublished.

"Had Mr. Eryson composed lately?"

"Yes, he told me yesterday that he had finished two new pieces, a serenade in E Flat Major and a Spanish dance that he called Normida."

"Did he play that dance for you?"

"No, nor the serenade in E Flat. He wanted to give these two pieces in a concert next week, and I was to hear them then for the first time. He took a certain pride in having me hear his works in a concert, in front of the public that was to judge them."

"I understand. You see, moreover, that the titles of his pieces are set down here."

Ethel King pointed to the page in the notebook, the next to last line and the one preceding it. Written there was: *Normida, Spanish dance* and *Serenade in E Flat Major*. The last composition was a ballad in B Flat Major.

Ethel King was thinking, her gaze lost in the distance. A thought suddenly came to mind. She leafed through the notebooks spread out in the drawer. A strange fact! She found all the compositions listed in the notebook except the last ones. After having rummaged through all the corners of the secretary, she let out a soft whistle. Mrs. Howard, intrigued, approached and asked:

"Have you found something?"

"Perhaps," Ethel King replied. "I can't yet talk about this subject, but I've made an interesting discovery. You told me that Mr. Eryson was named Director of the Conservatory in Harrisburg?"

"Yes."

"Good. I now suspect the true motives for this abominable murder. If my conjectures are right, the murderer won't enjoy his liberty much longer, I guarantee you, Mrs. Howard."

Ethel King put the notebook in her pocket, closed the drawer, and kept the key.

"My investigation is complete, for the moment at least," she said. "I'll leave you, Mrs. Howard, asking you not to reveal, until you've been told otherwise, that I am in charge of this case."

"That's understood. I'll be discreet."

On leaving the villa, Ethel King went first to a photographer with whom she had a long interview. At the end of that conversation, he accompanied her to the cemetery morgue. The unfortunate violinist was

198

lying in a coffin. They had closed his eyelids, but they had come open again and showed his glassy pupils. The photographer took some shots of the livid and bleeding head. Leaving him, Ethel King said:

"Don't forget what I told. I want the photographs shot so that they can be enlarged with an electronic projector."

"You'll be satisfied, Miss King. I'll even try to get the color of the face, and most of all the blood stains."

"Perfect. If that succeeds, it couldn't be better!"

The photographer looked at the detective with curiosity.

"This photograph must undoubtedly be used to unmask the murderer?" he questioned.

"Perhaps. Most of all, don't forget that you've promised me secrecy."

"That goes without saying! No one will hear about it. But when the scoundrel is caught, will you allow me to talk?"

Ethel King smiled. "As much as you like. Then you can tell everybody that you participated in capturing a criminal."

The young woman went back home where she brought her aide, Charley Lux, up to date on the situation, and told him about her suspicions. The same day she left with the young man for Harrisburg, where they arrived in the morning.

She had spoken about her trip to no one. Commissioner Carras, himself, had not been told. Thus, when he went the next morning to Mrs. Howard's and learned that Ethel King had not reappeared since her visit of the night before, he supposed that the detective herself judged the case unsolvable and was not taking any trouble to pick up the murderer's trail.

James Rinehart

On arriving in Harrisburg, Ethel King and her aide registered in a hotel, where they spent the night. The next morning she went to the music conservatory. A sad feeling crept into Ethel King's heart as she stood in front of the majestic edifice from which so many artists had already graduated. She was thinking of poor John Eryson. The violinist had dreamed of becoming Director of that establishment. He could have exercised his talents and his capabilities in a worthy manner there, but he had been snatched violently from life.

"No, I won't stop until I lay my hands on the author of this hideous crime," the young woman murmured.

She asked her cousin to wait outside and she passed through the main door.

"May I help you?" the concierge asked.

"Yes. Who is the temporary Director of the Conservatory?"

"That's Mr. Edgins, until the new Director arrives."

"Did you know that Mr. John Eryson, who was named to this high position, has just been murdered in Philadelphia?"

"Yes, Miss. We have already been informed by the newspapers. The news has even produced considerable excitement here."

"And this Mr. Edgins is probably the eventual successor?"

"Mr. Edgins is already old. He had intended to retire as soon as the new Director took up his duties."

"Is Mr. Edgins here at the moment?"

"Yes. In the Director's office."

"Please tell him that a lady has an urgent need to speak to him."

"What name should I…"

"I'll tell Mr. Edgins who I am myself."

The concierge went to do as he was asked, and came back several minutes later to take Ethel King to the Director's office. The detective saw herself in the presence of a venerable man who rose, very intrigued, to greet her.

"To whom do I have the honor…," he asked politely.

"I'm Ethel King from Philadelphia."

"Ah! Very interesting! The famous detective."

"I do, in fact, exercise the profession of detective."

"You've come, no doubt, about the murder of poor John Eryson?"

"You're right."

"What a horrible thing! I hope with all my heart that you succeed in bringing the author of this abominable crime to justice."

"I'll do my best."

"Unfortunately, I can't furnish you with the least clue. I didn't know Mr. Eryson very well, although I had occasion several times to admire his talent. He would have been an ideal Director for me, because he was not only a great artist, but also an energetic man with excellent intentions. I supported his candidacy very warmly. What a loss for humanity!"

Ethel King was seated facing the old man.

"I would like to talk to you precisely about the committee meeting in which Eryson was named Director of the Conservatory."

"I must hasten to tell you that our committee meeting should remain secret. No one needs to be informed about it."

"I will keep silent. Don't worry. Don't tell anyone that Ethel King is in Harrisburg."

"It will be as you wish."

"Something tells me I'll find John Eryson's murderer here."

"That would be amazing. My God! Who could it be? Nothing proves that it isn't someone we know very well."

"Indeed. That's not impossible. But let's get to the question," Ethel King said. "When the position of Director was vacant, a great number of artists must have applied?"

"Oh, yes! There were some 30 candidates."

"And how many of the candidates did you consider?"

"My word, we took only two into consideration."

"Which ones?" Ethel King asked.

"Those of John Eryson and James Rinehart."

"Who is James Rinehart?"

"A music professor, rich and rather well known, who has a villa on the outskirts of Harrisburg."

"Why wasn't he chosen?"

"His talent can't be compared with that of John Eryson. He's a good musician, intelligent, who has a great deal of accomplishment, but who is not a virtuoso, a genius like the other man. That's why we elected John Eryson. We told ourselves that such a name, already famous in the United States, would contribute enormously to the reputation of our institution."

"You did the right thing. Can you tell me a little more about Mr. Rinehart?" Ethel King asked.

Edgins looked at her with astonishment.

"Why? What reason makes you take so much interest in this Rinehart?"

The young woman smiled.

"Inform me, Mr. Edgins. I may be in a position to explain to you the motives of my conduct tomorrow."

Edgins showed a certain nervousness.

"Rinehart teaches in our establishment," he stated. "If he were under suspicion…that would be terrible!"

"You don't yet have any reason to be worried on this point. How old is Mr. Rinehart?"

"He's about 40 years old."

"Is he attractive?"

"He's a man much above the usual in height, with black curly hair, and he wears a full beard."

"You say he's rich?"

"Yes, very rich. He lives in a villa very near here. He gives evening gatherings from time to time. For example, he has sent out invitations for tomorrow. I'll be at the party because we've been promised something interesting."

"May I ask what it's about?"

"But of course! Rinehart has tried several times to become known as a composer, but he's never achieved any serious success. Now, he's promised to play some new works that merit, he claims, the attention of connoisseurs. This is the first time he's shown himself so satisfied with his productions."

The detective had listened with the greatest attention.

"Has Rinehart told you the titles of his new compositions?"

"No, he hasn't as yet spoken about them."

"What sort of reputation does Mr. Rinehart have in Harrisburg?"

"It isn't bad. He's considered a competent teacher and he has a lot of students," Edgins answered. "What's more, he leads a quiet existence and passes for an eccentric. It's claimed that he goes away secretly to other villas and participates in expensive orgies, but that gossip is without foundation."

"Mr. Rinehart isn't married?"

"No."

"He probably has a large number of servants?"

"To my knowledge, a manservant, a housekeeper, a maid, a cook and a gardener."

"Can you tell me exactly where his house is located?"

"You have only to follow the main road to the west; you'll soon reach his villa. It's situated very near a kind of chalky cliff and it's surrounded by a magnificent park. It's a very pretty property."

"I'll go see Mr. Rinehart."

"Whenever you like. But Miss King, I would really like to know why you're so interested in him. You don't have any suspicions about him, do you?"

"I can't tell you anything about that subject, Mr. Edgins. Don't forget that you must not speak to anyone about my visit here. You'll probably meet me again tomorrow at Mr. Rinehart's party. I'll be introduced to you under another name as a student of the professor. Don't let it appear at that time that you know me. I'm a stranger to you."

"All right, all right, it's understood; you'll be satisfied, Miss King. I'm truly curious to know where you're going with this. I have a feeling something sensational is going to happen, although, in my opinion, Rinehart has nothing to do with it."

"That's possible. One more question: Who will now be appointed Director of the Conservatory?"

"Well, Mr. Rinehart, naturally."

"Consequently, Rinehart, who saw his way barred by the unfortunate Eryson, can't be sorry for the young violinist's death?"

"My God! Rinehart doesn't have such a hard heart. I don't consider him to be a wicked man."

"Have you spoken with him since Eryson's nomination was made public?"

"No."

"Has he said anything before this about this nomination?"

"My God! Yes. He once declared to me in a rather excited tone that it would be a great injustice if they preferred Eryson, 'that young greenhorn.' Yes, he said verbatim 'that young greenhorn.' "

"And what did you answer him?"

"I told him in so many words that he probably should resign himself to that preference, and that, besides, Mr. Eryson was a totally remarkable artist, a pre-eminent man to whom the name 'young greenhorn' couldn't be applied."

Ethel King rose.

"I thank you for your information, Mr. Edgins. Until tomorrow evening, and most of all, be discreet."

"Very good, Miss King. I will be as silent as the tomb."

First Assessment

When Ethel King was back in the street, she motioned to her cousin to join her and they walked a while down the street.

"I have a job for you, Charley. Go back to Philadelphia immediately. Go to the photographer I told to take the photographs of John Eryson. Place the negatives under glass and buy yourself a good projector, then come back here to our hotel."

The young man took the road to the railroad station. An hour later he was sitting in an express train that was carrying him toward Philadelphia. As for Ethel King, she left Philadelphia by the western route and arrived in front of James Rinehart's property at the end of a brief walk.

A beautiful villa, in the modern style, rose above some terraces in the middle of a large park. The gardens opposite the road were flanked by a high cliff that, at one point, came very close to the house.

The rock was chalky. Seeing it, Ethel King murmured:

"Well, well, that's something that will fit perfectly with carrying out my plan."

As the afternoon was far advanced, she put off her visit until the next morning and returned to spend the day at her hotel. The next day, she again picked up the road to the villa and rang at the wrought iron gate.

The manservant came to open the gate for her and asked her what she wanted.

"May I speak to Mr. Rinehart?" Ethel King asked.

The manservant took the calling card she handed him and read Elly Walthour engraved on it.

"What does Elly Walthour want to see Mr. Rinehart about?"

"It's for lessons."

"All right, I'll announce you, Miss."

Ethel King waited a minute in the luxurious entry hall; then the servant told her Mr. Rinehart was waiting for her. The young woman was ushered into a superb drawing room where James Rinehart greeted her. The musician was what is usually called a handsome man. He had a very black beard and hair. He had pale, regular features and a curious facial expression.

Rinehart was seated nonchalantly at a superb ebony piano.

"You are welcome, Miss Walthour," he said, with all the marks of extreme politeness. "How may I help you?"

"I've come to ask you to accept me as a pupil," Ethel King answered.

"Do you have talent?"

"Not a great deal, but I have the most ardent desire to acquire some. I don't want to become an artist as a career; I just want to perfect my technique so as to be able to execute the works of the great masters."

"Have you already studied the principles of the piano?"

"Yes, but I'm still only a very mediocre player."

Rinehart looked intently at his visitor.

"I don't recall ever having seen you. Are you from Harrisburg?"

"No, from Baltimore. I was living with my father, who died several months ago. I haven't been able to resist my desire to study music."

"I don't see anything to prevent your becoming my pupil. I must, however, point out to you that I usually ask rather large honorariums."

"That doesn't bother me. One more thing. Could you recommend a good boarding house for me?"

"A good boarding house? What do you expect to pay?"

"That makes absolutely no difference to me. Thanks to God, I'm rich and I don't have to be concerned about the price."

"In that case, you can be a boarder in my own house."

"Really! I would be delighted to do so."

Rinehart looked at his new pupil out of the corner of his eye.

"Complete boarding facilities, including instruction, will cost you $3000, approximately," he said in a hesitating tone. Clearly, he himself found his terms too high. He didn't notice the mocking smile that played over Ethel King's lips, and which seemed to say: "I was right in thinking that you were extremely avaricious."

To the great satisfaction of the professor, the detective said aloud:

"That's fine, we're in agreement. How long do you think my studies should last?"

"That depends on your aptitude. But you should count on three years at least."

"Good. May I move into your house here this afternoon?"

"But, of course!"

The professor took Ethel King up to the second floor and had her visit two luxurious rooms which would be used as her apartment.

"We will have a piano installed here," he stated. "And you'll be able to study without being disturbed, Miss Walthour."

"Oh! How happy I am!" Ethel King exclaimed enthusiastically.

When she had returned with him to the drawing room, Rinehart said to her:

"I'm giving a little musical party here today. I heartily invite you to attend."

"Oh! Better and better! I'll come down then, it goes without saying. I hope to have the pleasure of hearing the master."

"I'll play a few of my last compositions," Rinehart replied, hiding his vanity under apparent indifference.

"I can't wait to hear them. Can you tell the titles of these works?"

"You're too curious," he said jokingly. "Wait until this evening."

The young woman moved as if to leave, but she stopped.

"I was forgetting, Master. Should I congratulate you?"

"For what?"

"Haven't you been named Director of the Harrisburg Conservatory?"

"Not yet. But how do you know about that?"

"I heard it talked about on the train. Some gentlemen were saying that John Eryson of Philadelphia had been murdered and that you would probably be named to take his place."

James Rinehart straightened up proudly.

"You are well informed. I'll be Directory of the Conservatory; no one is better qualified than I to fill those high functions."

"I don't doubt that," Ethel King replied.

"That young man, that Eryson of Philadelphia, was perhaps an excellent violinist, but he was not made to direct a school of this importance."

Rinehart was speaking in a tone of profound conviction.

"I've come to the right place," Ethel King said. "Student of the Director of the Harrisburg Conservatory!"

She took leave of the professor.

"I'll send for my bags this afternoon. Then I'll move in. Will you give me my first lesson tomorrow?"

"But of course. We'll start immediately."

Ethel King was having lunch at the hotel when Charley Lux returned from Philadelphia. The young man brought the photographs under glass and an excellent projector. Ethel King began to give him his instructions.

"This evening, when James Rinehart is beginning his evening's entertainment, you will slip secretly into the park and you'll stay hidden there. At the right moment, I'll alert you with a soft whistle. You will then get settled with the projector in a darkened room of the house."

In the afternoon the detective had a big trunk that, on her orders, Charley had brought from Philadelphia, transported to Rinehart's villa. She herself arrived somewhat late at the home of the professor, who received her in a very friendly way. He insisted that she take a cup of tea and showed himself a charming host.

However, Ethel King felt that his affable and correct attitude in every situation did not fit the man's true character. As calm and cool as Rinehart wanted to appear, his inner agitation showed itself in certain signs. A gleam of worry sometimes manifest itself in his look. A nervous tremor shook him and, when the vestibule door opened, he listened to hear who was there.

"That poor John Eryson," Ethel King said in the course of the conversation. "What infamous wretch had the heart to kill a man so very gifted? It had to be a ferocious beast devoid of any sensitivity."

James Rinehart nodded his head in approval, but protested:

"Please, let's not talk about that. When I think about the tragic fate of my colleague, I am overwhelmed. It seems to me then that a similar menace is suspended over my head."

"You could well be right!" Ethel King thought, but she said aloud:

"I won't mention that subject again, since it's painful to you, Master. I understand very well that the horrible end of your famous colleague has affected you.

She went upstairs to her bedroom and put on, for the evening party, a red outfit, simple but elegant.

A Terrifying Vision

The big music room of Rinehart's villa and the other rooms on the ground floor were resplendent with light. The people brought together there belonged to the best society of Harrisburg. All the conservatory professors, without exception, had come. Mr. Edgins, venerable with his white beard, was there also. The musicians present were all impatient to hear Rinehart's new compositions, that the professor himself had said were so good. But Edgins was doubly interested in the gathering. On his arrival, he had cast a questioning glance around him.

Truly, that woman in the red outfit was Ethel King! So she was present at the soirée! James Rinehart introduced her later to the old master.

"Miss Elly Walthour, my student. Mr. Edgins."

The young woman and the old man acknowledged the introduction as if they had never before seen each other. Ethel King could be pleased with Edgins. But he was worried. It wasn't a simple premonition that he had; he was certain that a drama was going to play out that evening, and he saw the coming events with terror. As Rinehart tried to start a conversation with him, he scarcely answered, and then with monosyllables. Finally, the professor, astonished, asked him:

"Mr. Edgins, what's wrong with you? You seem preoccupied."

"I have an intolerable migraine. If the desire to hear your new compositions hadn't compelled me, I would have excused myself and you wouldn't have seen me this evening."

"Well! Let's hope that my music will chase away your migraine," Rinehart declared.

He busied himself with other guests.

Ethel King found the opportunity to leave the drawing room one time. She went up to the second floor and went through the rooms facing the cliff. She found one bedroom which looked out over a wide terrace encircled by a stone balustrade. You could go out from the drawing room onto that terrace by a wide glass bay window. The doors to it were still closed.

Ethel King, satisfied with her inspection, opened a window and looked outside.

"That will work marvelously from here," she murmured.

She went downstairs quickly and slipped into the garden through a concealed door. A soft whistle called Charley Lux, who until then had kept himself hidden in the bushes. The young man carried his projection lantern, which he had fitted with an oil lamp with an incandescent spout.

"It will soon be time to start," Ethel King whispered. "Get to your post. Go to the bedroom upstairs that is just above the terrace. Stay ready at the open window. Put down the projector. As a precaution, you can lock the door from the inside, but I don't think you'll be disturbed."

"And when should I project the photograph, Ethel?"

"Pay close attention to what happens on the terrace. As soon as you see me come out with Rinehart, listen to what I'm telling him. You'll pick the right moment for yourself."

The detective went back through the hidden door and made sure there was no one in the entry hall. Then she motioned to Charley, who went up silently to the second floor.

Ethel King returned to the music room, where a young pianist had just played a brilliant piece. The young woman entered among the applause. It was now the turn of Rinehart, with his new compositions. Those were written for violin and piano. The violin's part was played by a conservatory student with whom Rinehart had practiced the evening before. The author himself was seated at the piano.

A religious silence fell over the room. The young violinist tuned his instrument. Rinehart bowed and said:

"We are beginning with a serenade in E Flat Major."

When she heard that announcement, Ethel King felt as if stabbed in the heart. She was seated in a corner and was watching Rinehart without being seen.

The first notes were played. People held their breath to listen, and, at the end of some minutes, all the connoisseurs had the impression that a genius had just been revealed. The conservatory professors exchanged astonished looks. They hadn't expected such a delight. Rinehart filled his listeners with astonishment. They had to admit that they, until then, had misjudged their colleague.

When the last notes stopped resonating, applause broke out. Everyone came forward to congratulate the radiant composer and shake his hand. With a smile of superiority, Rinehart accepted the flattering words heaped on him. There were only two persons who abstained from congratulating him and taking part in the general enthusiasm. Those were Ethel King, who remained pensive and quiet in her corner, and Edgins.

The old man was standing by a window. An insupportable agony was clutching him. He couldn't chase away his fatal premonitions. It seemed to him impossible that James Rinehart was the author of that serenade in E Sharp Major.

The composer was asked to play another of his works and everyone went back to their seats.

Rinehart proudly looked at the audience and said:

"Thank you, ladies and gentlemen, for your warm applause. I see that by perseverance I have reached the summit of the art. I hope later to astonish the world by other considerable works. We're going to play for you now a ballad in B Flat Major."

Ethel King nodded her head slightly; she had already whispered the title before Rinehart pronounced it.

Edgins, who was watching the young woman from a distance, felt more and more troubled.

The musicians started the first measure and again plunged the listeners into rapture.

When the piece was finished, silence reigned for several seconds, then the composer was applauded. Some of Rinehart's colleagues came to beg his forgiveness for having misjudged him until then. They assured him that from that time on, they would count him among the number of great masters and that his name would soon be as famous in the new world as well as in the old.

Finally, people were going to sit down again, and James Rinehart bowed to make a new announcement. At that moment, Ethel King rose from her chair and said in a firm and loud voice:

"You're now going to play for us a Spanish dance entitled, 'Normida,' aren't you, Mr. Rinehart?"

The professor trembled and turned pale. He stared at Ethel King suspiciously and asked, after an uncomfortable look:

"How did you know that, Miss Walthour?"

"I have it from a reliable source."

"But...I, I had my notebooks locked in the armoire! You weren't able to..."

"No, Mr. Rinehart. I wasn't able to look into the armoire," the young woman answered.

The professor had to hold onto the piano. He was livid. All those present were anxious. They thought something terrible was about to happen. They looked with astonishment at the young woman who was standing up very straight and whose features seemed cut from marble. Ethel King walked obliquely across the drawing room to the door to the terrace. She opened it and turned back to Rinehart.

"Go outside with me for a moment, Mr. Rinehart. I'll tell you how I know."

The professor hesitated. His forehead had big drops of sweat like pearls and his hands were trembling. However, he followed the detective. He crossed the waxed drawing room floor unsteadily, in the midst of a devastating silence.

Ethel King was waiting for Rinehart on the terrace. She had left the door open so that everyone present could hear. She said in a loud voice:

"You wonder how I know the title of the piece that you're going to play, Mr. Rinehart?"

He didn't answer; he leaned heavily on the balustrade.

"I'm going to tell you," she said. "These compositions aren't by you, but by someone else, from whose secretary you stole them."

The professor moaned deeply, then he tried to protest.

"That's a lie," he exclaimed in a strangled voice. "How...how can you say such a thing?"

"I say it because it's the truth. You have stolen his works and you falsely claim to be the author of them."

Murmurs, whispers, began to circulate among the spectators of that scene.

"That's not true," Rinehart stammered.

"Do you want to see the man you stole them from…that you struck in the heart with a homicidal knife? Look there, in front of you."

She pointed to the rock face. At the same instant, a gigantic ghostly apparition was projected onto the cliff. The glassy eyes of the bleeding head seemed to be fixed on Rinehart. He cried out in fear and stepped back, shaking.

"Do you recognize that head?" Ethel King asked, measuring her words. "The admission of your crime can be read on your face. The murderer of this poor man, was you!"

James Rinehart then covered his face with his hands. Mad with terror, he cried out:

"Yes, I confess…I killed John Eryson!"

And he fell down, unconscious.

The terrified guests pressed toward the terrace door. Charley Lux, in his turn, appeared and handcuffed the scoundrel. Then the police were quickly telephoned, while the guests left the so tragically interrupted soirée.

Old Edgins had revealed to his friends the identity of the woman who had unmasked the guilty man.

An hour later, Rinehart was in a cell of the Harrisburg prison. He had lost all his strength. The next morning he made a complete confession. He had hated John Eryson for a long time. He held his indisputable superiority against him. His fortune had been considerably compromised by the life of debauchery he led in secret. There remained only one hope of getting himself afloat again; that was of obtaining the well remunerated functions of the directorship of the conservatory.

Since John Eryson had defeated him in both talent and reward, he went to Philadelphia, and hid in the violinist's bedroom while Eryson was having supper with Mrs. Howard. He then murdered the poor man, who back in his bedroom, was sitting in front of his window playing his violin. Before fleeing, Rinehart had grabbed the three compositions which were to betray him.

The scoundrel did not go to trial. He created his own justice. One morning they found him hanging in his cell.

ETHEL KING

LE NICK CARTER FÉMININ

Triomphé trop tôt.

«Vous teniez à me parler en particulier, Miss King Profitez de l'occasion: il vous reste cinq minutes à vivre.»

10. RUBY, THE BLACK MILLER

The Pond of the Suicides

"Again? This is unheard of! There's a veritable epidemic of suicides in Wilmington."

Mr. Haring, the police inspector in the industrial city of Wilmington, in Delaware, walked excitedly up and down in his office. The policeman who had come to give him his report was waiting at the threshold of the door. The inspector stopped in front of his desk and rummaged through some papers. He picked up a list covered with notes. Looked at it a moment in silence, and then observed:

"That's the 11th suicide that's taken place in that pond in six weeks. And you say that this time it's a well-dressed young woman?"

"Yes, Mr. Haring. A letter was found on her which stated that she died by her own hand. She also stated her address; she was a certain Miss Ella Spring, a native of New Castle, where her parents lived. I telegraphed there immediately."

Haring put his list back on his desk.

"I find that story extremely suspicious. The pond seems to exercise a deadly fascination. And that has come on suddenly. During the seven years I've occupied my post at Wilmington, no one ever had the idea of drowning in that pool and now it's become the rendezvous of all the people who are disgusted with existence."

"The general public has expressed doubts. Certain people claim that it's not a matter of suicide," the policeman said respectfully.

Haring looked at him in astonishment.

"Is that true? I myself have had that thought several times. However it is, all this is very bizarre. It's absolutely necessary to go ahead with an inquest. I want to get to the end of the situation. Unless....wait, I have an idea."

The administrator sat down at his desk and wrote several lines on a sheet of paper that he handed to the policeman.

"Here, take this. Send this telegram immediately. I believe I've found the best way to get to the bottom of this."

The policeman glanced at the telegram and read the address: "Miss Ethel King, 77 Garden Street, Philadelphia."

He smiled. His superior's idea had his approval.

"Hurry. By taking the first train, Miss King can be here in two hours."

The policeman left, while the inspector, very thoughtful, began walking up and down in the room again. Haring finally went back to work. Some hours passed, then there was a knock at the door and a policeman announced Miss Ethel King of Philadelphia.

The inspector, very happy, rose to his feet.

"Have that lady come in!"

The famous detective entered, greeted Haring and exchanged a cordial handshake with him. She was already acquainted with the inspector, since in the past she had taken charge of a sensational case in Wilmington that she had brilliantly solved.

"I'm very happy that you have answered my call so quickly, Miss King," the inspector said, while asking the visitor to be seated. I'll get immediately to the question I telegraphed you about, asking you to come."

"I'm eager to hear you, Mr. Haring."

The inspector settled himself in an armchair and began.

"When you leave Wilmington, toward the south, you go across a wood extending about a quarter of a league. In the middle of that wood, about 100 steps from the road there's a little pond that's called the Green Pool because of the color of its water. The bank is somewhat encumbered with bushes. Legend claims that the pond is very deep. Until now I have never visited the pond, since to get to it you have to cut out a path across the brambles, and that's not very pleasant. During the seven years that I've been in Wilmington, nothing extraordinary has taken place in that part of the woods, but during the last six weeks the Green Pool has acquired a sinister reputation."

"Ah! You're doubtless alluding to the number of suicides that have taken place there lately."

"Yes! You've already heard about it?"

"I've been informed by the newspaper," Ethel King replied.

"Well, that situation is becoming completely strange, because today the 11th cadaver has been fished out of the pond."

"Who was it this time?"

"A young girl from New Castle. Her name was Ella Spring. They found on her, as they did on the other suicides, a letter in which she stated that she had died by her own hand."

Ethel King shook her head.

"Have you put together the similar letters from the other cadavers?"

"Right!"

"And the dead hadn't been robbed of the valuable objects they were carrying on them?"

"No, they all had their wallet, their rings, or their watch. At different times the relatives have claimed that the victims should have had a great deal more than was recovered, but they haven't been able to prove their allegations."

"If it was a matter of crimes, their author went about it with extreme cleverness. He didn't take everything from the victims in order not to arouse suspicions. But don't you find it surprising that the suicides always had on them a letter to explain their intentions?"

"Oh, yes I do. It was shown each time that the letters were certainly in the desperate person's handwriting. The relatives testified to that, in most of the cases. Handwriting experts established the authenticity of the documents."

"That complicates the matter," Ethel King observed. "If the unfortunate persons had been murdered, it would have been necessary to force them to write those letters before throwing them into the water."

"That's almost inadmissible!" exclaimed the inspector.

"Why? That wouldn't have been the first time that similar atrocities have been committed. Have all the dead been identified?"

"All, except two. Eight were well-known people from Wilmington. Two were buried in an unmarked grave. The 11th, that they pulled out today, is Miss Ella Spring of New Castle."

"Do you have some of those letters here?" Ethel King asked.

"I have all of them, except the one from today."

Haring opened a drawer from which he took out a packet of letters. Those letters, hardly as big as a hand, were in a pitiful state, torn and yellowed. It could be seen that they had spent some time in the water.

The detective carefully examined each of the letters.

"The names aren't always indicated," she said. "In only a few cases did the unfortunate people, before dying, put their signature under the lines of goodbye that they addressed to their relatives and their friends."

There was a moment of silence. Ethel King was continuing her examination. She suddenly lifted her head, looked at the inspector and said in a serious and firm voice:

"Yes, Mr. Haring , there's no more doubt. Not a single one of the victims of the Green Pool died voluntarily. They were all murdered."

The inspector was startled.

"How can you affirm that in such a categorical manner?" he asked.

"I do affirm it."

"But how did you arrive at that conclusion? How will you prove what you're putting forward?"

"Look at these letters," she calmly continued. "They are all written on heavy, yellowish paper such as is found at a cheap price for businesses. Do you think, therefore, that each of the victims chose by chance this same paper on which to write down their last thoughts? Such an hypothesis is unacceptable. If the resemblance was found on only two or three of the letters, you still might let it pass; but on all of them, no. The criminals committed a gigantic stupidity in always using the same paper."

Haring tapped his forehead.

"God in Heaven! That's true, Miss King. Why didn't I notice that! You're perfectly right. Oh! This is disheartening. Some scoundrel has just committed a series of atrocious crimes and nothing has been done to find him."

"No," Ethel King answered, "but I'll do everything that's in my power to see that Ella Spring is the last victim of the Green Pool."

The young woman rose and went into the adjoining room where she found a telephone. She got in touch with her villa in Philadelphia and asked her cousin Charley Lux to come to Wilmington immediately. She put down the receiver and went into Haring's office just as a policeman was saying:

"Mr. Edward Spring of New Castle is here and asks to speak to Mr. Haring. He's the father of the young girl who was taken out of the Green Pool this morning."

"Have him come in!"

The policeman left and Ethel King observed:

"Mr. Spring is probably going to tell you that the hypothesis of suicide can't be substantiated."

She wasn't mistaken. Edward Spring, an old gentleman with a dignified bearing, on whose face suffering had left its ravages, came in, said hello, and exclaimed:

"Mr. Haring, I must tell you that my daughter, whose corpse was recovered this morning in the Green Pool, certainly did not commit suicide. No! a thousand times, no! It was an abominable crime."

"That's our opinion, Mr. Spring," the inspector replied gravely. "I present Miss Ethel King to you, the famous Philadelphia detective, who arrived a half-hour ago. We were just discussing that affair, as well as the similar misfortunes that preceded it. We have concluded that neither your daughter nor the ten other so-called suicides voluntarily killed themselves."

Edward King had turned pale.

"My God!" he exclaimed. "How can anyone commit such crimes! Are there really men capable of such abominations?"

"Get hold of yourself, Mr. Spring," Ethel King said gently. "A great misfortune has struck you, but I won't stop until I have discovered, and delivered to justice, the author of these murders. Have you seen your daughter?"

"Yes, I've been to the morgue."

"Did you see if anything was stolen from Miss Spring?"

"She still had her wallet with a small sum of money as well as a small gold bracelet, but the big diamond ornamenting that bracelet had disappeared. However, it's possible that the stone had come loose by itself and that my daughter had lost it without noticing it."

"How valuable was that diamond?"

"Oh! It was a remarkable gem. The bracelet was left to my daughter by a colossally rich aunt. The diamond must have cost more than $3000. It was very big and very clear."

"The murderer took it; you can be sure of that," Ethel King said. "What you have just told me proves how clever the scoundrel is. They left the wallet and the gold bracelet, but they took the diamond. No one would at first think the unfortunate girl was murdered by a thief."

"That's true," Inspector Haring agreed. "Did you also see the letter that your daughter had in her pocket, Mr. Spring?"

"Yes, here it is."

The gentleman took the paper out of his wallet and handed it to Ethel King.

"Is that really your daughter's handwriting?" the young girl asked.

"Yes, there's no doubt about that."

"You see Mr. Haring, it's still the same paper. The murderer probably has a supply of it. I'll go to the Green Pool today."

"Alone?"

"Yes. I want first of all to visit the place with my assistant. We may find some clues on the bank of the pond. Wait patiently for the result of my investigation, Mr. Haring. Don't undertake anything until you hear from me about this case and be absolutely discreet. The criminal must not suspect our intentions. I will ask you also, Mr. Spring, to keep this secret. It's only on that one condition that we have a chance of success."

The two gentlemen promised not to say anything to anyone, and Ethel King went directly to the train station and wait there for Charley Lux.

At the Edge of the Pond

Charley Lux arrived in Wilmington by the first train. While going with him across the city, his cousin brought him up to date about the case. The further along that Ethel King got in her story, the more indignation showed on the young man's face.

The detectives left the city by the southern route and after a 30 minute walk came to the Green Pool woods. They left the road and made their way across the bushes and small trees. They soon came to the edge of the pond. The water, turned green by the algae and the water lilies, was stagnant under the thick shade of the trees. The banks were overcrowded with thick bushes cut in places by narrow paths which allowed descent to the edge of the water.

"The murderer could only have dragged his victims to the pond by one of these openings," Ethel King noted. "First we're going to examine the paths."

The detectives began to examine meticulously all the places where the undergrowth had an opening and left the soil open to examination. They found numerous footprints left from the people who had taken up the drowned persons. Ethel King stopped a very long time to the south of the pond at a point where the soil had no undergrowth for a greater extent than elsewhere. She knelt down and even used a magnifying glass.

"I presume that the murderer came through here with his victims," she finally said. "If I can judge by the traces he left, the scoundrel dragged his prisoners here, pushed them into the water, and kept their head under the surface until they had stopped struggling. It's also possible that he had bound his victims and didn't untie them until after they had been killed.

"The murderer was barefooted and to judge by the size of the prints he must be much above middle height. Let's carry our investigations further! You go investigate the eastern part of the woods; I'll take the western side. If you make an interesting discovery, let me know by using your whistle; I'll do the same. If neither of us finds anything, we'll meet again on the road, to the north of the woods, a little before sunset."

"All right, Ethel."

"But be very careful. It's not impossible that the murderer is lurking in the vicinity. If he sees us searching the woods, he would suspect something and look for a way to get rid of us."

"If he got that idea, so much the better," Charley answered. "Even if there were several of them, they'd find out who they're dealing with."

The detectives separated. They didn't suspect then that Ethel King's prediction was soon to be realized. Ethel King made her way into the undergrowth to the west, while Charley took the opposite direction. The young detective advanced step by step, examining the ground and the roots of the trees. He wasn't long in discovering a white handkerchief embroidered with the initials E. S.

"Ah! It was Miss Spring who lost that!" he murmured. "It has to be concluded that the criminal passed by here with his victim. I may find something else by continuing in the same direction as far as the edge of the woods."

Charley Lux hadn't yet thought of calling his cousin. He was eager to distinguish himself by still more important discoveries. He was cheered by the thought of being able to tell Ethel King, when he rejoined her, that he had obtained decisive results. Therefore he again started to follow the path, still examining the ground. Shortly before sunset, he came to the edge of the woods and picked up traces of footprints similar to those Ethel King had noticed at the edge of the pond. The footprints had been left by a very large bare foot. They were clearly stamped in the soft earth, but they were lost several steps from the trees.

Charley Lux found himself at the foot of a gently sloping hill, the side covered by meadows. At the top of the hill there was a windmill with its wings turning. The young man could distinctly hear the sound of the millstones. He decided to climb to the top to view the surroundings before rejoining Ethel King. He had no trouble climbing to the top of the hill. He stopped in front of the windmill and viewed the surrounding countryside. He saw mainly wheat fields, most of which were already harvested and covered with stubble. In the distance, the detective noticed

•

a farm with several buildings; it would require at least an hour of walking to get there.

Charley was still busy observing the countryside with his binoculars when a husky laugh made him turn his head. He saw a black man looking at him through a small window of the mill. When Charley looked up, the man greeted him with a nod and said, while laughing:

"Ah! Massa…beautiful country! Superb panorama and doesn't cost a cent!"

Charley laughed and answered:

"That's true. Would you like to have a dollar for all those who come to admire the view from here?"

The man smiled broadly, and nodded affirmatively and showed his white teeth.

"Massa right. Tom Ruby, poor black man have lot of trouble to earn few cents. Business not good; farmers around here don't want their wheat ground at Tom Ruby's mill. Tom Ruby a black man, and the farmers no want a black miller."

The detective's assistant had no trouble believing the man speaking to him. He knew that most Americans professed the most profound contempt for black people. There was nothing astonishing in the fact that the country people of the area preferred to travel several miles to carry their wheat to white millers, rather than give it to a black person.

"Have you owned this mill for a long time?" the boy asked.

"Oh! No. Tom Ruby here only two months, but no want stay here; die of hunger if he stay in this country. Oh! Massa, how hard it is to live!"

"What you're telling me doesn't astonish me. Why don't you go to the town? You'll find a job there that will bring you in a lot more than your mill."

"Yes, me will leave soon as find someone buy my mill. Massa no want my mill?"

"No, no, Mr. Ruby," Charley answered, laughing. "What would I do with it? I wouldn't even know how to make it work."

"Oh! It's very simple. Massa want to see the inside?"

"Why not? I've never yet visited a mill. That will interest me."

"Good. Me come down. Climb up stairs and come in!"

Charley Lux went around the mill and found a narrow wooden stairway. He climbed the steps and went through a little door. The detective's assistant had never been inside a windmill. Interested, he went forward slowly in order to examine the gears which caused the wings to move. At that moment he heard muffled footsteps. He tried to turn around, but he didn't have time. From behind, he received a terrible blow to the head which made him lose consciousness.

Laughing, Tom Ruby observed the man he had just hit; he was holding a board with which he had delivered the blow.

"Ah! Business not bad as Massa thinks," he murmured. "Me already make much money and nobody knows...nobody. A lot more pass here still...be made to give me what they have in pockets."

The man, who was built like Hercules, bent down and picked up his unconscious victim. He carried Charley into a small room where he tied his feet and hands and then sat down in a rocking chair in front of a table. On the table there was ink, a pen, some paper and some pencils. He cut out a leaf about the size of a hand and placed it in front of his unconscious victim with a pencil, then he started to empty the young man's pockets. He was satisfied with taking the wallet and the coin purse and leaving Charley the weapons. He appropriated half the bank notes the wallet contained and took out several pieces of gold from the coin purse. After that, he put the objects back in the young man's pockets and sat down on a sack of flour to wait until he returned to consciousness.

At the end of half an hour, Charley regained consciousness, opened his eyes, and looked around him with astonishment. He immediately understood what had happened. He saw the man in a dark corner wearing only trousers and a colored shirt.

"The bare feet!" he thought.

Yes, it really was the big bare feet that had left their prints at the edge of the pond. Hatred for whites and his own avarice had pushed this man to odious crimes. Charley Lux didn't for a moment doubt that he had before him the scoundrel 11 times a murderer whose victims had been pulled out of the Green Pool. The criminal was preparing a 12th horrible crime.

The young man didn't have the least fear, however. He was, on the contrary, delighted with what had happened. Ethel King was at her post; she would intervene at the decisive moment, even if she didn't as yet suspect the critical situation of her assistant.

"What does this mean?" Charley Lux shouted. "How dare you treat me this way?

Ruby didn't answer immediately. The diabolical expression of triumph which could be read on his face inspired Charley with real horror.

After a long silence, the scoundrel finally spoke.

"Didn't I tell Massa that business bad? Me had to find a way to add to my revenues. That's why me have put my hand a little in the coin purse and wallet of Massa."

"Rascal!" the detective shouted. "If that's what you wanted, you can turn me loose now. Take everything but let me leave!"

The man laughed.

"No, no, Tom Ruby not so stupid! If me let Massa leave, Massa turn me in to police; then poor Tom go to prison and to the scaffold. Tom no want that!"

"But if I promise not to say anything?"

"Me believe not. No, no, me not let leave Massa. The others also beg Tom Ruby."

"What others?"

"Well…those who sat in that chair before Massa. Massa share fate of the others."

Charley put on a worried look. He wanted his captor to believe that he was afraid.

"What fate?" he asked.

"Massa die suicide."

"Me, a suicide? I don't have the least desire to do that."

"Oh, yes, Massa finish suicide, drown in Green Pool."

Charley cried out in horror.

"Did I hear right? So it was you, you scoundrel, who has on his conscience the death of all those poor people!"

"Oh! Those only be whites," the man replied with a sardonic laugh.

"Scoundrel!" shouted the detective. "If I were free I'd shoot you down like a mad dog."

"Tom willing believe it," the man answered. "But let's finish it. Me untie your right hand and you write on that sheet what I dictate."

"I won't write anything at all!"

"Let Massa think about it. Him at my mercy. Me can make him."

"Nothing can make me decide to do what I don't want to. Once and for all, I refuse. I won't write a line."

"Even so, Massa have to agree."

Tom Ruby went into a corner of the hideout and called out:

"Pluto! Fox!"

Furious barking answered him. He opened a little door and two huge bull terriers bounded into the room. They began immediately to run angrily around Charley Lux's chair. They snarled, showing their fearful fangs and stared at the prisoner with their bloodshot eyes.

"Well, how Massa like the little beasts?" the man asked. "My good dogs have beautiful teeth; if I tell them to, they jump on Massa and tear him to pieces."

Charley couldn't hold back a feeling of terror. To die devoured by these animals must be an atrocious end.

"Massa want write? If Massa no agree. Pluto and Fox tear him in pieces. Nobody hear him cry out. Country deserted. Massa want to write?"

"No."

"Pluto…Fox…Jump!"

The beasts stood up on both sides of the chair and placed their front paws on Charley's shoulders. Their terrible muzzles, which exhaled a warm and moist breath, opened menacingly in front of the young man's face. He understood how the man had forced all his victims to write what he required them to. There was no human being capable of submitting voluntarily to such torture.

"Massa want to write?" the man asked again, placing his two hands on the table and staring at the pale and impassive expression of the detective.

"Yes," said Charley.

"Pluto! Fox! Go to bed."

The dogs dropped down. Tom Ruby pushed the piece of rough paper he had prepared in front of Charley. Then he untied the detective's right hand.

"Good. Massa write now."

The young man really wanted to reach into his pocket to take out a revolver, but Ruby was at his post. He was watching every movement of his prisoner and the two dogs were only waiting for a signal to jump on the unfortunate man.

Charley picked up the pencil and asked:

"What must I write?"

"This: 'I'm dying by my own hand. I have wasted my fortune in gambling. I can no longer endure living. May everyone forgive me!' "

The young man obeyed.

"It's done," he said. "Is that all?"

"Yes. If Massa wants to sign, it's up to him."

Charley dispensed with that last formality and put down his pencil. Then Tom Ruby tied up his hand again. But the prisoner was able to place his arm in such a way that it would be possible for him to get out of his bonds. His captor didn't notice that trick. He tightened the knots and put the letter in the detective's right-hand pocket.

"Everything ready now," he said. "We go to the Green Pool."

It had been night a long time. The man had lit a little smoky lamp which he did not extinguish before leaving the mill with his victim. He shut the dogs up in the kennel and stayed several minutes looking out the window. During this time Charley was trying to untie his hands, but it wasn't as easy to do as he had imagined.

He hadn't yet succeeded when Tom Ruby turned around.

"Nobody near here," he declared. "Massa soon swim in Green Pool."

While talking, he hoisted Charley over his shoulder. He quickly descended the outside staircase with his living burden and went across the prairie to the edge of the woods. Charley's hands were hidden from view and the boy continued his efforts to loosen his bonds.

A Desperate Combat

They arrived at the edge of the pond just as Charley Lux finally managed to untie his hands. Ruby had stopped at the place where Ethel King had found the footprints in the afternoon. The night was clear; the Moon spread its silver light over the pond and under the trees. Toby Ruby first deposited the body of the detective's assistant on the bank. He hadn't noticed that his victim had his hands free.

"The time for suicide come," he said. "Since you might be afraid of death, me help by holding head under water."

He picked up the boy and threw him into the water, while pressing on his neck; but Charley was already prepared to act. He had taken out his knife. He extended his arm and plunged the blade into his adversary's leg. Tom Ruby jumped backward, letting out a howl of pain and rage. He had turned loose of his victim, who immediately disappeared under the surface.

Charley first dove deeply and cut the bonds holding his feet. He then reached the center of the pond with some vigorous arm strokes and came back to the surface. At the same moment he saw his adversary's head very near to him. Without hesitating, Tom Ruby had dived into the water to seize Charley, since he didn't want to let the one who could inform on him escape at any price.

The young detective's assistant hadn't counted on that. Therefore his adversary had time to grab him by the throat and squeeze so hard that Charley lost his breath. He nevertheless kept his presence of mind and grabbed the man's hand and delivered a violent kick. He got what he wanted. The man momentarily let go of his victim and Charley reached the bank with several rapid arm strokes. He lifted his head above the water to search for his enemy, but the surface of the water was mirrored by the Moon and Ruby's head was nowhere in sight.

Charley hoisted himself cautiously to the bank and hid in the bushes. He remained on alert, still watching the pond, but he couldn't see his adversary. Either the scoundrel had drowned, or he had reached the bank before the detective. Charley took out his two revolvers and verified that the water had not made them useless. He stayed at his post for 30 minutes and then decided to return to the mill. He could no longer count on Ethel King's being at the rendezvous agree on. His cousin must be worried and had undoubtedly started to search for the young man.

Charley was very tempted to use the whistle to warn Ethel, but fearing to draw the criminal's attention, he refrained from doing so. He decided that if the scoundrel had returned to the mill, he would slip up to him and arrest him, kill him if necessary. Ethel had perhaps picked up the trail that had led him to the mill. If so, she should have been drawn by their shouts made during the fight.

The intrepid Charley, a revolver in each hand, went cautiously back to the edge of the woods. He reached it without having noticed anything suspicious. He first watched for some time the grassy slopes that the Moon fully lit. He didn't want to climb up this way because if Tom Ruby had returned to the mill he could be watching the area around it. He went along the edge of the woods, staying prudently in the shadows, to go around the base of the hill. He finally noticed a small brush-covered ravine which led to the summit. He slipped in there. Charley was doubly cautious. He walked stealthily three quarters of the way through the underbrush. Everything was quiet in the mill; the wings no longer turned. The lamp was still burning in the hideout where the miller had forced his prisoner to write the letter. The young detective hoisted himself to the edge of the ravine, and he was going to stand up, when he heard a noise in the bushes behind him. Tom Ruby rushed at the surprised young man and knocked him over. Some blows of his heavy fist knocked his victim unconscious, and he triumphantly carried to the mill the one he had made prisoner for the second time.

When Charley Lux regained consciousness, he found himself in a strange situation. He was tied to one of the wings of the windmill and, this time, so firmly that he couldn't budge. The wind was blowing like a storm from the east. His captor was looking out the window.

"Well, how go Massa?" the scoundrel asked when he saw his prisoner open his eyes. "We hope cold bath no hurt Massa. Massa very brave but no match against Tom Ruby."

"Don't gloat too soon!" Charley answered. "Punishment's waiting for you, and you won't have time to put your dastardly project into action."

Ruby shook his fist under his prisoner's nose and shouted:

"If Massa want bet, Massa sure to lose…but me be good to him…Tom has soft heart; he reserve a pleasure for Massa. Massa make a little trip in the air."

"That's very kind of you," replied Charley, who suspected what he meant. "But that kind of distraction doesn't please me at all."

"Tom Ruby no ask Massa opinion. Pay attention, Massa! We going begin. Yes, Tom keep a nice pleasure for Massa."

The man's head disappeared from the window. Charley began to shout for help at the top of his voice, in hopes of attracting his cousin, but he received no answer. The mill turned slowly on its pivot. Tom Ruby oriented the wings in the wind's direction. Still several seconds went by; then the wings began to move. Since the wind was blowing like a tempest and the machine was set to full speed, the unfortunate detective began to spin rapidly.

Charley had given up calling out. He had closed his eyes, but vertigo overtook him even so. His temples beat violently. The young man tore at his bonds with all his strength. He would rather have fallen to the ground than endure any longer that horrible torture; but this time Tom Ruby had tied the ropes tight; he remembered his prisoner's first escape. The eastern sky turned pale and the wings still turned. Charley had lost consciousness at the end of the first hour.

As daylight approached, the wind calmed, the mill's movement slowed down, and Charley regained consciousness. Nevertheless, the young man was incapable of thinking. His head was dancing; he had the impression that he had had a terrible nightmare, from which he was vain-ly trying to wake. However, the man, leaning out the window, watched him, laughing and heaping sarcasms on his adversary.

Finally Rescued

What had become of Ethel King?

When she separated from Charley Lux in the woods, she had continued her investigations toward the west, as her assistant had done in the opposite direction. She examined the ground minutely for the slightest tracks. But her search was in vain. She discovered nothing that could put her on the murderer's track.

She naturally thought that Charley hadn't discovered anything either, because, if the contrary were true, the young man would have whistled to tell her so. Therefore she continued her vain search until nightfall. Then she went back to the road. The Sun had just set and the Moon was rising. Ethel King was hoping that her aide had preceded her to the rendezvous point at the north edge of the woods, but she didn't find him there. She waited for him for an hour and then she began to be very worried.

Had something happened to the young man? Had the criminal surprised him? Maybe Charley now lay dead in some ditch.

The young woman, in prey to great anxiety, went back down the road to the pool without noticing anything unusual. She advanced in an easterly direction, her flashlight in her hand. The flashlight threw a rather bright light on the ground, but did not, however, allow the detective to make out the footprints as clearly as during the day. She finally came to the edge of the woods and discovered the signs of the bare feet. Several minutes later, she climbed up to the mill.

At the same moment, Tom Ruby was entering the woods by another path with Charley Lux thrown over his shoulders and was carrying the young man to the edge of the Green Pool, where the fight we've just described was to take place.

Ethel King came to the top of the hill and without hesitation climbed up the stairs to the mill. Her intention was simply to question the miller and ask him if he had noticed, during the afternoon, a young man at the edge of the woods.

The millstone room was deserted. A door opening onto another room was ajar. Noticing a light, she approached it and knocked. Getting no answer, she pushed open the door. She stopped at the threshold, and, exclaiming in surprise, she immediately guessed what had happened. Her assistant's soft felt hat lay in a corner of the room. There was paper, a pen, some pencils and ink on the table. And the paper immediately struck Ethel King; she recognized it: it was that on which the supposed suicides had written their letters.

From that instant she knew that the owner of the mill was the murderer. This was where the scoundrel forced his victims to write their lying letters. When the young woman heard the ferocious barking of the dogs in their kennel, she also suspected the way in which the scoundrel terrorized his victims.

She examined the paper. There was no possible doubt; it was what Haring had showed her. The prudent detective thought first of getting rid of the dogs. If the miller came back unexpectedly, the dogs could be a great help to him. The young woman approached the slatted door to their kennel. There were four shots and the dogs' barking stopped. The beasts, both shot in the head, were dead.

Ethel King, after that execution, proceeded to an investigation of the mill. It was possible that the miller was locked in a hideout with his victim. Ethel found no one in the house. However, she made another discovery which furnished irrefutable proof of the miller's guilt. She noticed a small cupboard, so cleverly hidden in the wall that only an eye as experienced as hers could have been aware of its existence. The keyhole was miniscule and she had to choose the smallest of her lock picks to open it. The door gave way after long effort. The cupboard contained stacks of bank notes, piles of gold pieces. The detective picked up a bright object which was shining in a corner and found that it was a large diamond.

"This is extraordinary," she murmured. "I would never have thought that chance would have put me this way on the trail of the murderer. This diamond certainly came from Miss Ella Spring's bracelet. The scoundrel would try to deny it in vain."

But what had become of the miller and Charley Lux? Had the criminal killed the young detective and had he carried his body away to make it disappear? That wasn't impossible, but the criminal could also have taken Charley for a simple inoffensive tourist. And in that case, he would surely have dragged his victim to the Green Pool.

Ethel King went again to the table to examine the pieces of paper. Charley Lux, when writing with the pencil, had borne down hard by design so that the words had been imprinted on the sheet of paper placed below that on which he had written them. Ethel King recognized the writing immediately as that of her assistant. She placed the paper under the light to decipher the words.

"give...death...wasted...fortune...gambling..." And then: "existence... everybody pardon me!"

She deduced the sense of the whole from these bits and pieces. So the murderer had forced Charley Lux also to make his death seem a suicide. The scoundrel must have taken a large sum from his prisoner, naturally without taking everything from him; then he had carried his victim to the Green Pool.

The detective had trouble controlling her emotion. The murderer must have reached the pond some time before with Charley. Then everything was over. Charley was no longer in this world! And, nevertheless, it might still be possible to save the young man!

Holding her revolver, the detective hurriedly descended the mill's stairs and ran to the edge of the woods. Less than half an hour later, she was at the edge of the Green Pool. Bad luck was decidedly following her. At the moment she entered the woods, Charley Lux had again fallen into the hands of his enemy, behind the mill, at the top of the hill.

Tom Ruby had rightfully told himself that his adversary, whose boldness he had experienced, would not run away, but try to take revenge. He had therefore hidden at the edge of the woods and was not long in seeing his young captive. He had slipped behind Charley so expertly that despite Charley's practiced good hearing, he hadn't heard anything. Besides, Tom Ruby always stayed a certain distance from his enemy. He had only gotten closer when he judged the opportunity favorable, and then he had jumped on the unsuspecting person from behind. And this was how the murderer had snatched his new victim, for the second time.

When she came to the edge of the pond, Ethel King turned on her electric flashlight to see the surface of the water. Nothing showed her the presence of her assistant. That didn't prove that the young man hadn't been thrown into the water, because the drowned man might very well not yet have risen to the surface.

Intense sorrow clutched at Ethel King's heart. Charley Lux's death would be a terrible blow to her! The young man was a beloved, devoted cousin, an intelligent, resolute assistant. The young woman made a tour of the pond and finally came to the spot where Tom Ruby had thrown Charley into the water. She found the obvious traces of the fight. She understood what had happened as if she had been there. She recognized that the two adversaries had fallen into the water, and she told herself that they had probably drowned each other.

Deeply upset, her eyes full of tears, she stared fixedly at the water where the Moon's silver disk was reflected as if she expected to see the face of her cousin, turned pale by death, surge up. She finally got control of herself, carried her whistle to her lips, and blew some strident sounds in the feeble hope of getting a response. Then she went through the woods once again to search for clues. After all, it was not impossible that the murderer had carried his victim somewhere else.

But she discovered nothing. She spent the time until morning in this way, walking aimlessly around the edge of the pond. She finally decided to return to the mill. If the criminal hadn't been killed in the fight, he surely was up there, and the young woman might catch him. If not, she would take the contents of the cupboard and go to Wilmington to tell the police what had happened.

Daylight was turning the horizon red when Ethel King again found herself at the edge of the woods and raised her eyes toward the mill. Surprise nailed her to the spot. Great gods! Could she believe her eyes? Wasn't that a man attached to a wing of the mill? She took out her binoculars, raised them to her eyes. She soon knew who was the victim of this new torture. It was Charley Lux, her assistant!

Is he still alive? Ethel King worried anxiously. She watched the unfortunate man for a long time. She finally saw his face, the space of one second. The young man had his eyes open; his lips were moving.

Ethel King quickly recovered all her calm, all her self-control. There was not a minute to lose; Charley had to be saved at any price. Then the young woman saw the wings of the mill stop. Then a man, a black man, put his head through the window and watched Charley Lux.

His face seemed contorted with rage and he was brandishing a knife. Ethel King took to her heels and raced across the edge of the woods, climbing the hill as fast as her legs would carry her.

Tom Ruby had spent almost the whole night watching his victim attached to one wing of the mill. When the wind died down and the movement of the windmill slowed down, he was greatly exasperated.

The man told himself that his prisoner might be seen by some passerby. He therefore stopped the wings of his mill and he was going to come back to the window, when he thought about his two dogs and was surprised by their silence the past night. The miller went to the kennel, opened the door and raised his lamp in order to see better. He let out a cry of fury when he saw that his two dogs were dead.

"That rogue killed them!" he screamed.

In his blind rage it did not occur to him that his prisoner couldn't have been the author of that assassination. He took a big knife from a drawer and ran to the window. The wings of the mill had stopped. He looked down below him at the detective, who was placed head downward.

"Rogue," he bellowed. "What you do? You pay dear for this!"

"What do you claim I've done?" Charley answered in a feeble voice.

He was hearing the words as if in a dream. He had not completely recovered his lucidity.

"Rascal! You shoot my two dogs with revolver!"

"Your two dogs?" Charley stammered.

"Don't lie; it was you! And now you going die!"

Charley was becoming, little by little, capable of thought. The news of the death of the two dogs reached him. A feeling of triumph crept into his soul, because he immediately realized that only Edith King could have killed the dogs. The young woman was, then, in the vicinity! She was perhaps already about to arrest the murderer. And that thought gave the young man back all his calm, all his presence of mind. He burst out laughing and shouted:

"The beasts are dead? God be praised! You'll soon share their fate, with this difference: your death will be on the gallows and not with bullets."

"You think so?" the man asked, gritting his teeth. "Oh! You, you very mistaken! You killed my two faithful friends, my good dogs. Me leave this country carrying fortune. Nobody see me again."

"I tell you again, in a short time, you'll be swinging at the end of a rope. You're lost without any recourse."

"You become crazy!" Tom Ruby shouted. "No power in the world get you out of my hands. Even if 100 people tried storm mill, there be no time to stop me plunging knife into your heart.

Charley gave another disdainful laugh.

"So, then try!" he said, taunting his enemy. "Your life will be over the same moment that you lift your knife to strike me!"

Tom Ruby couldn't be any more enraged.

"All right! We going right now see if you right or wrong. Watch out! Me pierce your heart!"

A tremor shook Charley Lux. Where was his cousin? If she didn't come, the young man was lost. The blade glittered under the rays of the rising Sun. Ruby brandished his weapon. At that critical moment, a shot rang out and the man bellowed in pain. Ethel King had entered the mill and had arrived just in time to see the murderer threaten Charley. Without hesitating, she had lifted her revolver and fired. The bullet hit the man in the hand and made him drop his weapon. If she had missed her shot, the blade would have been driven right up to the handle in Charley Lux's chest.

Ruby turned around and saw Ethel King, who was still covering him with her revolver. He charged like an infuriated bull toward his adversary.

"Stop!" Ethel King shouted at him. "Stop, you scoundrel, or I'll kill you!"

"Ah! A woman tries to order me; me kill you, scoundrel!

He tried to grab her, but she pressed the trigger and he fell down, hit by a bullet in the stomach. The man rolled onto the floor shouting threats and curses, trying in vain to get his enemy between his powerful hands. Strength soon left him, however: he lost consciousness. The detective hurried to put handcuffs on him and to tie his feet. Then she leaned out the window and got Charley Lux out of his horrible situation. She had to call on all her strength to lift the young man and drag him into the mill. Charley's arms and legs were stiff; he could hardly move.

As soon as he was inside, he admitted, very contritely, that he was wrong not to immediately call his cousin when he found Ethel Spring's handkerchief and picked up the miller's trail. He tightened the murderer's bonds and stayed, a revolver in his hand, at the mill to watch the prisoner while Ethel King went back to Wilmington to report to Inspector Haring, who was overjoyed when he learned of Ethel King's rapid success. With the detective and some policemen, he started to the mill. They put Tom Ruby on a stretcher, and two hours later the scoundrel was in the prison infirmary.

The miller's wound was serious, but not mortal, and Ruby was soon well again. The money found on him, the diamond from Miss Spring's bracelet, and his treatment of Charley Lux were conclusive proofs against him. Faced with such charges, the murderer didn't try to deny anything but made cynical confessions. He had lured passersby into his mill, making them prisoners and forcing them to write the letters, after which he took part of their valuables and then transported them to the Green Pool, where he drowned them. He had made 11 victims in this way. The scoundrel paid for his crimes on the scaffold.

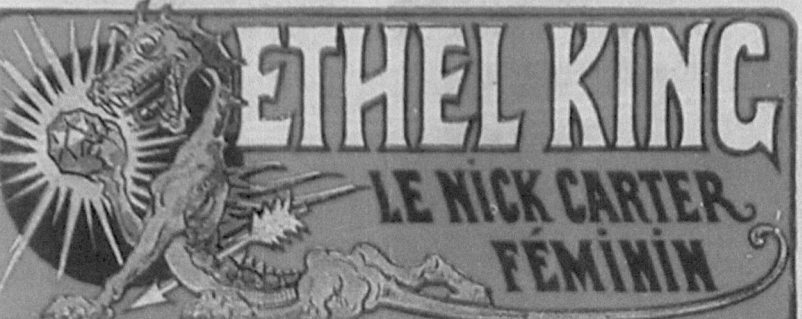

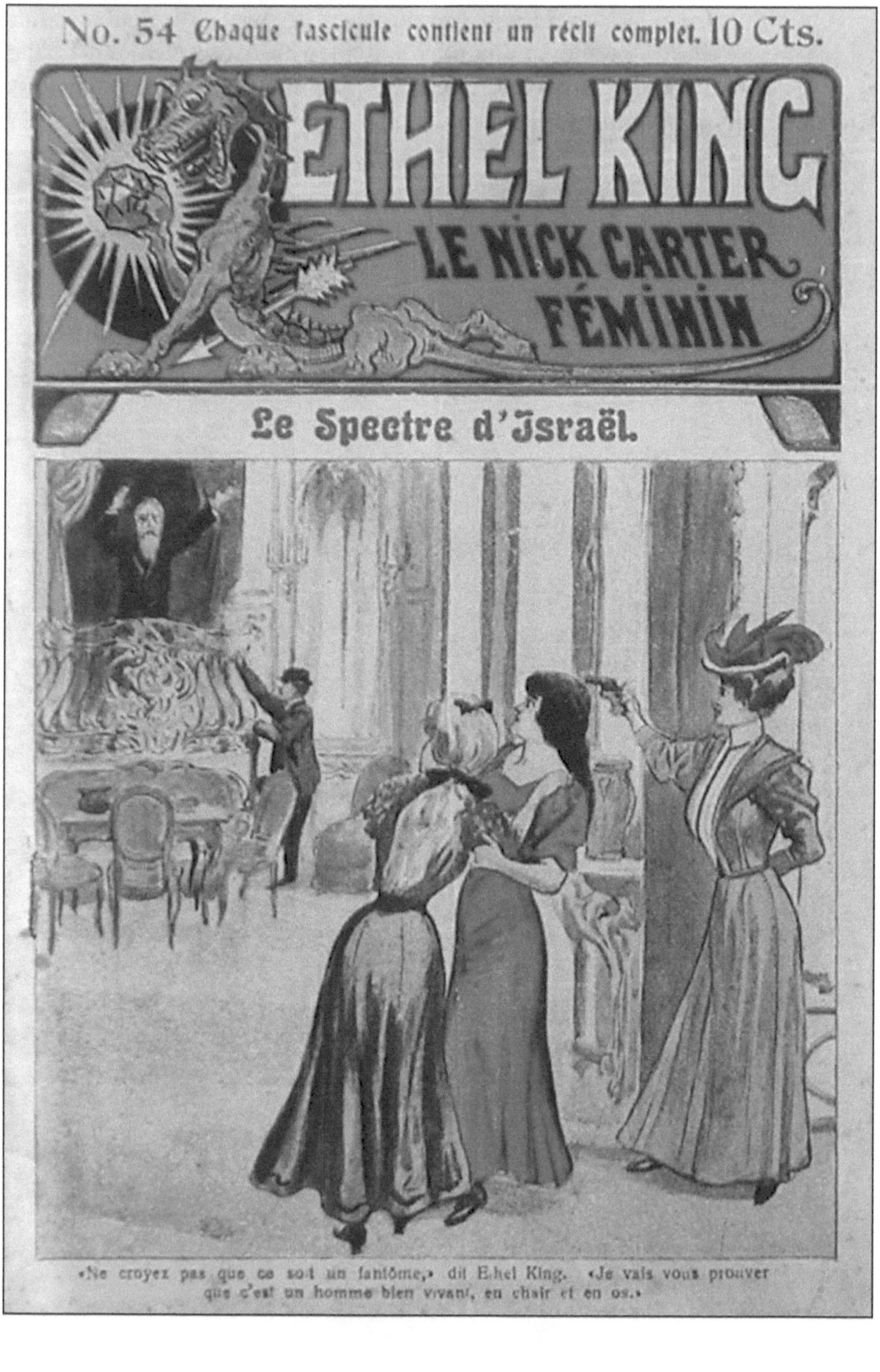
No. 54 Chaque fascicule contient un récit complet. 10 Cts.
ETHEL KING
LE NICK CARTER FÉMININ
Le Spectre d'Israël.
«Ne croyez pas que ce soit un fantôme,» dit Ethel King. «Je vais vous prouver que c'est un homme bien vivant, en chair et en os.»

MYSTERIES & THRILLERS

M. Allain & P. Souvestre. *The Daughter of Fantômas*

A. Anicet-Bourgeois, Lucien Dabril. *Rocambole*

A. Bernède. *Belphegor*; *Judex* (w/Louis Feuillade); *The Return of Judex* (w/Louis Feuillade); *The Shadow of Judex*

A. Bisson & G. Livet. *Nick Carter vs. Fantômas*

André Caroff. *The Terror of Madame Atomos; Miss Atomos; The Return of Madame Atomos; The Mistake of Madame Atomos; The Monsters of Madame Atomos; The Revenge of Madame Atomos; The Resurrection of Madame Atomos; The Mark of Madame Atomos*

V. Darlay & H. de Gorsse. *Arsène Lupin vs. Sherlock Holmes: The Stage Play*

Séamas Duffy. *Sherlock Holmes in Paris*

Paul Féval. *Gentlemen of the Night; John Devil; The Black Coats ('Salem Street; The Invisible Weapon; The Parisian Jungle; The Companions of the Treasure; Heart of Steel; The Cadet Gang; The Sword-Swallower)*

Emile Gaboriau. *Monsieur Lecoq*

Goron & Emile Gautier. *Spawn of the Penitentiary*

Rick Lai. *Shadows of the Opera: Retribution in Blood; Sisters of the Shadows: The Curse of Cagliostro*

Steve Leadley. *Sherlock Holmes: The Circle of Blood*

Maurice Leblanc. *Arsène Lupin vs. Countess Cagliostro; Arsène Lupin vs. Sherlock Holmes (The Blonde Phantom; The Hollow Needle); The Many Faces of Arsène Lupin*

Gaston Leroux. *Chéri-Bibi; The Phantom of the Opera; Rouletabille & the Mystery of the Yellow Room; Rouletabille at Krupp's*

Richard Marsh. *The Complete Adventures of Judith Lee*

William Patrick Maynard. *The Terror of Fu Manchu; The Destiny of Fu Manchu*

Frank J. Morlock. *Sherlock Holmes: The Grand Horizontals; Sherlock Holmes vs Jack the Ripper*

Jean Petithuguenin. *The Adventures of Ethel King*

Antonin Reschal. *The Adventures of Miss Boston*

P. de Wattyne & Y. Walter. *Sherlock Holmes vs. Fantômas*

David White. *Fantômas in America*

Pierre Yrondy. *The Adventures of Thérèse Arnaud*